Praise for Vicki Grant and
36 Questions That Changed My Mind About You:

"Realistic, lively and hilarious, the ongoing discussions make this book easily accessible. The gradual revelations of the events of their lives provide depth that will resonate with most readers of contemporary YA fiction. An intriguing premise and quirky, oddly endearing characters make this book a joy to read."
—*Atlantic Books Today*

"[A] meet-cute story that offers lots of laughs and a message about looking past appearances to make a connection."
—*Publishers Weekly*

"A good concept with smart characterization."
—*Kirkus Reviews*

"Full of heart, humor, and the occasional flying fish, *36 Questions That Changed My Mind About You* is an absolute delight. I dare you not to fall in love with this book!"
—Rachel Bateman,
author of *Someone Else's Summer*

"What do I love most about Vicki Grant's new novel? The brilliant setup? The witty banter? The heart-pounding, swoon-worthy, sweep-you-off-your-feet romance? Yes, yes, and 36 times yes!"

—Sara Mlynowski,
New York Times bestselling author of
I See London, I See France

"I'm completely obsessed! Filled with some of the wittiest, most authentic dialogue between two strangers I've ever read, this book is one part true romance, one part grit and compassion, and one part sass. If there is a more modern, more relevant YA story than this one out there, I've yet to see it!"

—Jill MacKenzie,
author of *Spin the Sky*

"A fun, fast-paced read with real heart. I was laughing on page one and had fallen head over heels for Hildy and Paul by the end of the first chapter. There's only one question: when should I read this phenomenal book? And there's one answer: right now."

—Stephanie Kate Strohm,
author of *It's Not Me, It's You*

36 Questions That Changed My Mind About You

36 QUESTIONS THAT CHANGED MY MIND ABOUT YOU

VICKI GRANT

RP | TEENS
PHILADELPHIA

Running Press Teens
Hachette Book Group
1290 Avenue of the Americas, New York, NY 10104
www.runningpress.com/rpkids
@RP_Kids

Printed in the United States

Originally published in hardcover and ebook by Running Press Teens in October 2017
First Paperback Edition: September 2020

Published by Running Press Teens, an imprint of Perseus Books, LLC, a subsidiary of Hachette Book Group, Inc. The Running Press Teens name and logo is a trademark of the Hachette Book Group.

The Hachette Speakers Bureau provides a wide range of authors for speaking events. To find out more, go to www.hachettespeakersbureau.com or call (866) 376-6591.

The publisher is not responsible for websites (or their content) that are not owned by the publisher.

The author and publisher wishes to thank Arthur Aron, PhD, for permission to use copyright material: "The Experimental Generation of Interpersonal Closeness: A procedure and some preliminary findings," published by Personality & Social Psychology Bulletin, Sage Publication, 04/01/1997. Licensed Content Authors – Arthur Aron, Edward Melinat, Elaine N. Aron, Robert Darrin Vallone, Renee J. Bator

Print book cover and interior design by Frances J. Soo Ping Chow
Stock photo: p 102 copyright © Gettyimages/ Soulfultography

Library of Congress Control Number: 2019953814

ISBNs: 978-0-7624-9849-9 (paperback), 978-0-7624-6318-3 (hardcover), 978-1-4789-9242-4 (audio book), 978-0-7624-6319-0 (ebook)

LSC-C

10 9 8 7 6 5 4 3 2 1

For @cheese_gypsy, @call_me_edwina, @thevirlbox

with <3

36 Questions
That Changed My Mind
About You

CHAPTER

1

There were three rapid knocks, then the door opened and a girl stumbled in, out of breath.

"Sorry. Sorry I'm late. I had to talk to my English teacher about my term paper and he wasn't in his office and . . ."

Jeff jiggled his head like *no problem.*

". . . by the time he got there I'd missed my bus and I had to go downtown for—"

"It's fine. Don't worry about it. You filled out the form?"

"Oh, yes. Sorry." She looked around the room for a place to put the live tropical fish she was carrying in a small bag full of water.

"Here." He patted the corner of his desk.

"Thanks." She put it down. "Yikes. Wet. Apologies." She picked up the bag, wiped it on the sleeve of her big gray vintage overcoat, then put it back down. "This stupid fish. Only one place to get it and my brother—Gabe. He's twelve. He has a . . . sorry. You don't want to know. You want the form." She began rifling through the large leather book bag slung across her chest. A battered copy of *Brideshead Revisited* fell onto the floor.

"Why don't you sit down?" He pointed at a plastic chair in front of his desk. "Might be easier."

She sat, retrieved her book, and began rifling again. "I'm not usually this disorganized. Really. It's just. What a day. I mean, *week.*"

"It's blue," he said. "Eight and a half by eleven . . . There it is. Next to the, uh, change purse."

"Oh. Right." She rolled her eyes at herself and handed him the form. "I also brought my résumé."

"No need." He smoothed the paper she'd given him and did a quick scan.

"Are you sure? Because I added a short paragraph about possibly pursuing psychology as a minor, especially as it relates to—"

"Really. No qualifications necessary."

While he read her form, she looked around his office. "You like toys," she said.

He didn't look up. "Action figures," he corrected her. They were arranged on his bookshelves according to genre, rarity, age, and a hard-to-quantify X factor: the little buzz he got from the really cool ones. These were not toys.

He made some notes, then said, "So . . . Hilda Sangster . . . Citadel High—"

She groaned.

Now he looked up. "Is there a problem?"

"Sorry. The Hilda thing. I should have explained."

He checked the form.

"I know I wrote Hilda but that's because it said 'First Name, Last Name,' not 'Name Used,' and I figured you needed it for official purposes so I just, well, *did as instructed* despite the fact that I can't stand the name. It's so, like, Teutonic or something. Nobody ever calls me Hilda."

"So what should I call you then?"

"Hildy."

"Hil-dee, not Hil-da."

"Doesn't sound like much but, honestly? To me? Huge. I'll change it someday—I mean, legally and everything—but my grandmother's still alive and, well, feelings to consider, family legacy, etc., etc."

She must have realized she was talking too much. She gave an awkward smile and sat up straight.

"Hildy it is then. I see here you're a senior. You're single?"

She laughed in a way that could only mean yes.

"And you're . . . what? Eighteen? Good. Because you'll need to sign a consent form."

"Sure. No problem but . . . Um. Maybe I should find out what this is about first? I mean, there is a limit to what I'll do in the name of science." She laughed again, but she wasn't fooling either of them.

"Absolutely. Okay. My name's Jeff. I'm a PhD student here at the university. I recently got a grant to look at—well, the easiest way to describe it is 'relationship building.' Basically, I'm interested in finding out if we can influence subjects such as yourself to develop a close interpersonal bond with another participant, which might then develop into—"

"Sorry. Um. Am I understanding this right?" She put her arms around her book bag as if it were a toddler in need of comfort. "You're trying to find out if you can make people like each other?"

One side of his mouth smiled. "Not *make*." He'd be a billionaire if he could do that. "We're not interested in brainwashing anyone. We're just looking to see if it's possible to—let's say—*facilitate* a personal closeness, which could result in a relationship."

"You mean, like a friendship?"

"Yes. Or, more significantly, a romantic relationship. I'm looking at how people initiate intimate bonds and if that process can be nudged forward in some way."

Hildy went, "Love?" like it was an accusation. "That's what

you're talking about?"

He made a note. "Yes, potentially love although—"

"Did Max give you my name?" She sounded annoyed.

"Max? No. Max who?"

"Xiu?"

"What? I don't even know what that is."

"Xiu Fraser?"

"No. No one gave me your name. *You* contacted me. Remember? This is just a psychological study to see if love—"

"Love!" she said again, and jumped up.

He didn't know how she managed to knock his bookshelf off the wall—she wasn't that tall—but suddenly Disney-themed action figures were torpedoing down around them as if there'd been an explosion in an animated film.

She went, "Oh. God. No. Sorry," and turned around to see what she'd done. Her book bag swung behind her and hit a lamp, which slammed against another shelf and sent supervillains flying, too.

She put her hand over her mouth and made the type of whining noise dogs make when they need to go outside.

She crouched down and began picking up action figures and piling them by the handful onto his desk.

"I'm sorry," she said. "I shouldn't have come. I shouldn't have left my room. Seriously. This is what happens when I—"

"It's just an accident."

"No. No, no, no, no." She waved her hand around at the room. "All these little bodies everywhere? All the mess? Perfect metaphor for my life. This is. Exactly. What I do."

She had a 1930s Prince Charming by the feet and was batting the air with it for emphasis. It was one of Jeff's favorites. He worried the head was going to come off.

"That's okay." He tried to sound relaxed. "No big deal. I can put them away. Really. There's a system. Please. Stop."

He had to say it a few times before she nodded, apologized again, and stood up, or at least tried. She stepped on the bottom of her coat and slammed her forehead into the edge of his desk. It must have hurt, but by now she'd regained a weird sort of calm. She took a loud breath in through her nose, lifted the hem of her coat like it was Cinderella's ball gown, and got to her feet.

"Um. Sorry for that little outburst . . . And for the mess . . . And, like, wasting your time and everything, too. I didn't understand what the study was about. I shouldn't have signed up." She arranged her mouth into something like a smile and walked out the door.

Jeff looked at the action figures scattered over the floor. He was too busy to put them back in the correct order. He scooped them all up and put them in a box under his desk where he wouldn't be able to hear their tiny screams.

He thought about Hildy.

What the hell was that all about? Fight or flight? Conflict avoidance? Some weird religious thing?

He sat down at his desk and checked his notes. Had he foreseen this at all? Had he inadvertently triggered something?

As part of the study, he had a little side bet going with himself. He wasn't 100 percent sure how ethical it was, but it kept things interesting. He took notes on participants, gave them each a numerical score, and then tried to predict whether sparks would fly when he put them in a room together.

In the course of their conversation, he'd scribbled some notations next to Hildy's name. He'd done it quickly—he always did—because he figured if participants had to rely on first impressions, he should, too.

WG-PP
HIQ/HM
DG
FIT

By which he meant:

White Girl—Professional Parents
High IQ/High Maintenance
Drama Geek
French Language Tattoo

He pictured an obscure quote from some eighteenth-century philosopher or postwar film director, written in cursive on the arch of her foot.

(In that, at least, he was wrong. An obscure quote might have appealed to her, but Hildy would never get a tattoo. She was afraid of needles and, more importantly, permanence. She liked to think she was still at the pupa stage of existence.)

Coming up with a number was the part Jeff always had the most qualms about. It was, of course, out of ten and it was, of course, based on physical attractiveness. But it wasn't sexist. He rated the male participants and the transgender ones, too.

He was also, he told himself, only being realistic. Looks counted, although he honestly didn't know which ones or why. He'd have thought smoldering eyes and impressive breasts or shoulders would win every time but that didn't seem to be the case. There were a lot of wild cards in the human sexuality deck.

He struggled with a score. Hildy was no beauty—eyes too small, mouth too big—but he knew for a subset of guys that wouldn't matter. She'd get extra points for *interesting*. The giant winter coat she was wearing meant he couldn't tell much about her build. Average, he would guess. Maybe small to average.

Top marks for hair, though. Hers was long and shiny and must have been blond when she was little. Most straight guys are suckers for hair, especially those wispy bits that fall out of braids and make throaty suggestions about *having just crawled out of bed*.

He gave her a 7.5. Too bad, he thought, she wouldn't be in the study. She'd have made an interesting addition.

There was a knock at his door. He checked the time. A little early for the next participant.

"Yes," he said.

Hildy stepped in. She was holding Prince Charming.

"I took this by mistake." She grimaced apologetically and put it on his desk. "I didn't realize I had it until I was downstairs."

"You took Prince Charming by mistake." Jeff raised his eyebrows. "Wonder what Dr. Freud would've had to say about that."

He meant it as a joke, but Hildy said, "I know. That's why I came back. I mean, I had to return the action figure and I forgot the fish, too, so it wasn't the *only* reason but—" She stopped herself. "Look. I'm not superstitious or anything, but I had a moment to think down there and, um, it just seems like when the universe goes to that much trouble to give you a sign, you should probably take it." She sat down. "So I'm going to do the study after all. I mean, if that's okay with you."

"You're sure?" he said.

"Yes. Well, as much as I'm ever sure about anything." She smiled and he scribbled *CC* for Camp Counselor. He could picture her talking to little kids about trying their hardest and always being good sports.

"So. Mind telling me about the experiment again? I promise not to flip out this time."

He forced himself not to glance at the undisturbed shelves on the other side of the room. "Great. Well. We're basing our work on a study called 'The Experimental Generation of Interpersonal Closeness.' It was developed in the nineties by a psychologist named Dr. Arthur Aron. His results weren't conclusive at the time, but this is a different world. We're wondering how the digital age may—or may not—have changed the way intimacy is experienced. Basically, we want to see how young people who've grown up with twelve hundred online 'friends' might respond to intense face-to-face emotional sharing. Sound like something you might be interested in?"

"What do I have to do?" That wasn't quite a yes.

"Not much. We pair you with a random stranger—male or female depending on your sexual orientation—and give you thirty-six questions to ask each other. There's no right or wrong answer, no good or bad. Our only request is that you respond as honestly as possible."

"Um. 'Random'?"

"What?"

"Did you say 'random stranger'?"

"Yes."

"So it could be anyone?"

He was worried about another outburst. "Well, *could be*, I guess, but realistically it's more likely to be another student than, say, Drake or one of the Olsen twins . . ."

"Or a serial killer?" Sort of a joke but not really.

"Highly improbable. And anyway, the study is conducted here at the university. We'll have all the pertinent data about participants but you won't know each other's real names or contact information."

"Well. I guess that should be okay."

Should be okay.

He let that go and looked at her form again.

"You self-identified as hetero. So you'll be paired with a male more or less your age. To each other, you'll just be Bob and Betty. Those are the names we ask male and female participants to use. We've taken every precaution to ensure your privacy and physical safety."

She nodded but her eyes had gone too blinky to ignore.

"You're not convinced," he said.

"No, I am. Well. At least about *physical* safety."

"But not about? . . ."

Fluttery hands. Shrug. Sigh. "This probably sounds stupid."

He waited.

". . . but what about, like, *emotional* safety?"

"Meaning?"

She let out a puff of air. "I don't know. Anything! Rejection. Disappointment. Crushing heartache. Haha. You know. The usual."

"I'd say that's just life." And one of the reasons he'd always preferred action figures.

"Fine. I know but. I mean, I could get in there with a total stranger and do the thirty-six questions and next thing you know I'm hopelessly smitten with some kind of, like, troll or something."

"To the best of my knowledge, no trolls have applied."

"Dumb question."

He hadn't said that. She fiddled with the buttons on her overcoat, then sort of laughed.

"Who am I kidding? The *real* problem would be if the troll didn't love me back. But, again, as you say, that's just life. Or at least *my* life." She shook it out of her head. "Sorry. Babbling. I get this way when I'm stressed. Just a lot of stuff happening in my life right now. My own fault, of course. Big mouth. Tunnel vision. Faulty social radar. That kind of thing. My friends are always telling me I should—Oops. See? Babbling again. Sorry. Ignore me."

"No pressure," he said, and left it at that.

She pulled down her sleeves and scrunched the cuffs into her fists. She stared at Prince Charming for a few seconds, then looked back at Jeff. "Okay. I'll do it. I should do it."

"There's no 'should' here. Really. I don't want you participating just because the universe said you had to."

That made her laugh for real. "Don't worry. I won't let some mean old universe push me around. I want to do it. Seriously.

At some very deep level I think I actually do. 'Nothing ventured, nothing gained,' right?"

"Awesome." He took one final look at her registration. "Everything's in order here, so unless you have any more questions I'll just get you to sign the consent form."

He gave her a moment to look it over. She ran her finger along every line as she read, then scribbled her name at the bottom.

"Okay. My heart's in your hands!" Hildy smiled and her eyes disappeared into thick tangles of lashes. Her teeth were large and straight and white. Her skin was perfect.

He amended her score to 7.75 and took her form.

"All right then. I'll get you to go to room 417, just down the hall to the left. Help yourself to coffee. On the table, there'll be a deck of index cards with the questions, but please don't turn them over until the session begins. We'll have a subject partner for you shortly. I'll do my best to weed out the trolls."

She pulled the collar of her coat over her mouth and laughed again. She might even be an 8.

"And don't forget your fish. He's going to start to take it personally."

CHAPTER

▶────────◀

2

The guy walked in without knocking.

Jeff looked up from his laptop. "And you are?"

"Paul Bergin." No smile. Little eye contact. Voice not much more than mumble.

"You're here about the interpersonal closeness study?"

"I'm here about the study that pays forty bucks. That the one?"

"Could be. That's what we pay."

"Then that's the one I'm here for." He took a neatly folded square of pale blue paper out of his jacket pocket and handed it to Jeff. His hands were red with cold. "How long's this going to take?"

Jeff motioned for him to sit down but he already had. "Depends. Probably an hour or two, but we don't impose any time limits, so it could take a bit longer. Up to you."

"If it takes longer, is there overtime?" Paul flashed a smile now, maybe figuring a little charm might pay off in extra cash.

"Sorry. Flat rate. Still interested?"

Paul looked around as if he was sizing up the street value of the various action figures lining the metal bookshelves on the far side of the room. "May as well. When do I start?"

"I'll just give you some background information on the study and then we can get going."

"What do I need background info for?" He rolled a small gray raisin of Juicy Fruit between his front teeth.

"Thought you might be interested."

"Not really. Ad said I just had to answer some questions."

"Yes. Well, you and your partner have to ask each other thirty-six questions."

"I don't have a partner."

"We choose a partner for you."

"I have to make up the questions?"

"No, they're already written. You'll each get a set of cards with the questions written on them. You just have to do your best to answer them."

"That's all I have to do?"

"Sign a consent form now and fill out a short report when you're done." Jeff checked Paul's registration form. "You a student?"

"I have to be?"

"No."

"Then I'm unemployed."

"You're eighteen?"

"Almost nineteen."

"Hetero?"

"What?"

"Straight."

"Yeah. I put that down."

"Single?"

"As much as possible."

"Okay. Then sign this and go to"—he checked his notes—"room 417. Your subject partner should be there."

Paul didn't bother reading the form. He wrote his name neatly at the bottom, stood up, and was gone.

Jeff waited until the door shut, then he wrote B.R.O. But he meant "bro" as in "dude" (as in "asshole"). Then he wrote:

BC (for "blue collar")

COS (for "chip on shoulder," by which he also meant "asshole")

SS (for "street-smart," although it pained him to admit Paul may be smart at all. Nothing he hated more than a guy with a swagger.)

Then Jeff wrote *9*.

Which was childish. If he knew anything about heterosexual females, he knew that Paul would be a solid 9.5 if not a full 10 for most of them, despite the fact his nose had obviously been broken at some point. Or maybe because of the fact. Nothing like a little DANGER: KEEP OUT sign to get some girls scaling the walls.

Paul also had a tiny teardrop tattoo just below his right eye. In Jeff's opinion, that was a little bad boy overkill, although, obviously, it wasn't his opinion that counted.

It was Hildy's.

That almost made Jeff laugh.

Hildy and Paul.

This should be interesting.

QUESTION 1

PAUL: Hey.

PAUL: Hello.

PAUL: Hel-lo?

HILDY: Oh. Um.

PAUL: You okay?

HILDY: Ah, yeah. Yeah. Sorry.

PAUL: You look like you saw a ghost or something.

HILDY: No, no. I, um, was just reading and lost track of time and you sort of surprised me that's all. So, like, ah, hi.

PAUL: Yeah. Hi. I'm Paul.

HILDY: You mean Bob.

PAUL: No. I mean Paul.

HILDY: (Laughs) I didn't hear that.

PAUL: I said Paul.

HILDY: Um. We're not supposed to know each other's names.

PAUL: No one told me that.

HILDY: Really? I was told we're supposed to call each other Bob and Betty. You know for, like, privacy and everything.

PAUL: Fine. So who gets to be Betty?

HILDY: Ha! Good point. How very, like, *cisgendered* of them to—

PAUL: What the hell's the matter with this chair?

HILDY: Want to switch? I don't mind. I'll—

PAUL: And have you land on your ass instead? No. I'll take my chances.

HILDY: Sure? I bet we could get a—

PAUL: You planning on staying or what?

HILDY: Ah. Yes. Why?

PAUL: You gotta be hot in that thing.

HILDY: Oh. Right. My coat. One of my little weirdnesses. I like being really warm. Drives my friends crazy. They always say they get sweaty just looking at me. Not going to bother you, is it? Because I could—

PAUL: Just don't go passing out on me.

HILDY: Don't worry. I'll do my best not to, you know, *swoon* . . .

PAUL: Thanks. Great. Can we get started?

HILDY: Sure. How should we do this? Maybe one of us reads the question out loud and the other answers?

PAUL: Fine.

HILDY: Then we could alternate?

PAUL: Fine.

HILDY: You start or me?

PAUL: Whatever.

HILDY: Or, hey. Why don't we flip a coin?

PAUL: I don't really care that much. You go first.

HILDY: Sure?

PAUL: Yeah. Look. Can we just get started?

HILDY: Right. Sorry. I'm nervous. Are you nervous?

PAUL: Why would I be nervous?

HILDY: (Laughs) Things like this make me anxious, although Jeff did say there are—

PAUL: Jeff?

HILDY: The psychologist. He said—What are you laughing at?

PAUL: *Psychologist.* The guy's, like, some dweeb college student with his little forms and his joking-but-not-really hard-on for Happy Meal toys.

HILDY: He's a PhD student.

PAUL: Yeah. That's what I said.

HILDY: Well, not quite . . .

PAUL: Close enough.

HILDY: In any event . . . He says there are no right or wrong answers but still. A lot riding on this. Which is why, I guess, I'm a tad, you know, *wound up.*

PAUL: Really? Hadn't noticed. How about you pour yourself a couple of Jäger shots when you get home? In the meantime, I'll start. Question 1: *Given the choice of anyone in the world, whom would you want as a dinner guest?*

HILDY: Only one? That's all I get to pick?

PAUL: Yeah.

HILDY: It says that?

PAUL: It says "Whom—Christ, I can't believe it—*whom* would you want as *a* dinner guest." That means one.

HILDY: Hmm. That's hard. I want to say someone like Jane Austen or D. H. Lawrence or Barack Obama but honestly? I'd be so awed in the presence of all that brilliance I probably wouldn't enjoy it. Then again, I don't want to waste my one and only invitation on some, like, joe-on-the-street . . .

PAUL: So who's it going to be then?

PAUL: It's just dinner.

PAUL: We're not talking about sleeping with anyone here.

HILDY: Sorry. Am I taking too long?

PAUL: Gee. What makes you think that?

HILDY: Oh. Hey. I know. (Laughs) Taylor Swift!

PAUL: Done. Taylor Swift.

HILDY: No! I'm joking. Sort of. She's my guilty pleasure and I honestly don't think she gets the credit she deserves but if I can only ask one person, I'm not sure she'd be the person I'd pick . . . You better go first. I need some time to think about this one.

PAUL: Fine. I'd ask someone who could cook.

HILDY: (Laughs)

PAUL: Question 2.

HILDY: No. Seriously. Who would you ask?

PAUL: Someone who could cook. If they're coming for dinner at my place, they better be able to cook because I sure as hell can't.

HILDY: That's actually not a bad answer. I didn't even think of going for—

PAUL: Question 2. *Would you—*

HILDY: Hold on. I haven't answered Question 1.

PAUL: Well, mind answering it then? There are thirty-five more questions. Not worth the money at this rate.

HILDY: What money?

PAUL: The forty bucks.

HILDY: What forty bucks?

PAUL: The forty bucks you get for doing the study.

HILDY: We get paid?

PAUL: Yeah. Why else would you be doing it?

HILDY: I don't know. I like psychology and the thought of being part of an experiment interested me and . . .

PAUL: (Laughs) Talk about starved for entertainment.

HILDY: You know, I hate to bring this up but there's a tone you're using that I don't appreciate.

PAUL: Sorry, Ma.

HILDY: Gee. And there it is again.

PAUL: Can we just get on with this?

HILDY: Yes. If you change your tone.

PAUL: You're kidding.

PAUL: You're not serious.

PAUL: Fine . . . How's this? Better?

HILDY: And your facial expression.

PAUL: Who made you boss?

HILDY: Nobody. But I am your equal and I don't feel obliged to participate with someone who refuses to show me the respect I deserve.

PAUL: Unbelievable.

HILDY: Not really. When you think about it, totally reasonable. Respect is the hallmark of a civilized society. I'd appreciate it if you watch the swearing, too.

PAUL: I didn't swear.

HILDY: Out loud.

PAUL: What? You read lips now, too?

HILDY: Right. Like I have to be a trained lip-reader to figure out what you just said.

PAUL: You never heard it before or something?

HILDY: I've heard it plenty. I just don't think I should have it, like, flung at me.

PAUL: Can we just get back to the stupid question?

HILDY: Yes. Sure. If you answer respectfully.

PAUL: Okay. Here's my voice . . . Here's my face.

HILDY: Beautiful. Thank you. And given that you're concerned about time, I'll hurry things along and just say that I'd invite my grandfather for dinner. I never had the opportunity to meet him and I think if I had, I'd better understand the man my own father is today. Hopefully, that would help us resolve some of our current, you know, issues.

QUESTION 2

PAUL: I'm going to keep asking the questions.

HILDY: Probably not a bad idea. I tend to go off on tangents. Time management, as you probably guessed, is not one of my strong points.

PAUL: And it's not the answer to any of the questions, either.

HILDY: There's that tone thing again.

PAUL: Nothing the matter with my tone.

HILDY: Sorry. You're right. It was the actual content of what you said this time.

PAUL: Oh, you got a problem with the truth now?

HILDY: Popular misconception. So-called honesty is not always the best policy, especially if you're just using it as an excuse to be nasty. There's no reason to voice your—

PAUL: And that's not an answer to any question, either! So, Question 2: *Would you like to be famous? If so, in what way?*

HILDY: I'm only responding because I signed up to do the study so I feel, I guess, honor bound to do so.

PAUL: And I'm only *responding* for the money. Whatever. Just answer the question.

HILDY: I want to do something important with my life, and since fame can be a useful soapbox, yes, I would like to be famous. In fact, this might sound crazy and wildly ambitious and everything, but I'd love to someday be remembered as the next—I don't know—Nelson Mandela or . . . What's so funny?

PAUL: You're a five-foot-two white chick carrying your books around in a six-hundred-dollar Coach satchel. You're not going to be remembered as the next Nelson Mandela.

HILDY: I'm five foot four and the "satchel" was a birthday present.

PAUL: What? From your cellmate?

HILDY: No, my parents.

PAUL: My point exactly. You are not going to be the next Nelson Mandela. And you're still white. Like *really* white. Or am I wrong about that, too? You got that Michael Jackson thing or something? And P.S. You're not five foot four.

HILDY: Yes, I am. And please stop clicking your gum.

PAUL: In those boots maybe. Barefoot, no way you even come up to my armpit.

HILDY: Yeah, but what are you? Six foot two?

PAUL: Whoa. What are you on?

HILDY: What does that mean?

PAUL: I'm six foot if I'm trying to impress someone. Five eleven if I'm being honest.

HILDY: Guess I don't have to ask which it is today. And, to get back to the topic at hand, the question is not "Are you going to be famous?" It's "Would you *like* to be famous and in what way?" and guess what? That's how I choose to answer the question. Your turn.

PAUL: Okay. A) Yes and B) Extremely.

HILDY: You're not taking the questions seriously.

PAUL: I wasn't asked to take them seriously. I was asked to answer them. So, yes, I would like to be famous. And in what way? Extremely, because that's where the money is. Those are my answers. You're not the boss of me.

HILDY: So childish.

PAUL: Whoa. Who's got the tone issue now? And also, just so's you know, people who walk around with a fish in a bag trying to look all rom-com cute have no business calling anyone childish.

HILDY: You know nothing about this fish or why I have it or why it's important to me.

PAUL: And, strangely, nor do I give a shit.

HILDY: I just wish you'd be half as honest answering your questions as you are in your comments to me.

PAUL: Who was it who once said, "Guess what? That's how I choose to answer the question"?

HILDY: Fair enough. You do it your way. I'll do it mine. So much for "relationship building."

PAUL: What?

HILDY: Nothing.

PAUL: Next question.

QUESTION 3

PAUL: *Before making a telephone call, do you ever rehearse what you are going to say? If so, why?*

HILDY: Of course.

PAUL: Of *course?* Seriously? "Whazzup? . . . Yeah . . . Okay . . . Bye." What's there to rehearse?

HILDY: Believe it or not, some people use the phone to do more than order pizza or arrange drug deals. Some people have actual conversations.

PAUL: For which they practice. Is it just me or is that pathetic?

PAUL: Oh. So you're not talking to me now.

PAUL: So much for being "honor bound" to respond.

PAUL: Fine. I'll just do the remaining thirty-three questions on my own, get my forty bucks, and catch the next bus out of here.

HILDY: So you're telling me that you *never* rehearsed before you called a girl to ask her out on a date.

PAUL: Yeah. That's what I'm saying.

HILDY: Never?

PAUL: Okay. Maybe not never.

HILDY: I knew it.

PAUL: Maybe when I was twelve I did.

HILDY: You started asking girls out when you were twelve.

PAUL: Yeah.

HILDY: Twelve?

PAUL: Okay. Eleven then. . . . What? . . . Like, when did *you* start dating?

HILDY: Is that one of the questions?

PAUL: Oooh. Too-shay.

HILDY: Can we just get this stupid thing over with?

PAUL: Thank you, Jay-sus! Thought you'd never ask.

QUESTION 4

PAUL: *What would constitute a "perfect" day for you?*

HILDY: Well. Hmm . . . I'd be in the country somewhere, I know that. An old inn or a cottage . . . something with a sense of history. Ideally, by the ocean . . . Nice if it had a window seat. I'd get all bundled up in a blanket with a good book and a large latte. Oh, and since we're talking perfect, the latte would be in a bowl, like they do in France, not in a cup, which I suppose would technically make it a café au lait but whatever. I'd maybe have some imported chocolate bickies on a plate nearby in case I'm feeling like something sweet. Then I guess I'd read for most of the day, go for a walk along the beach, maybe get myself a green tea smoothie or, if I'm feeling decadent, a . . . You're not listening. You don't have to like what I'm saying but you can at least stop drawing and, like, *pretend* to listen.

PAUL: ". . . go for a walk, maybe get myself a green tea smoothie or, if I'm feeling decadent . . ." I don't have to look at you to listen. So go on. Anything else you'd like to add? A hot yoga class? Some journaling? Maybe a mani-pedi with a few of your BFFs?

HILDY: I knew you were going to make fun of me but I promised Jeff that I was going to answer the questions honestly so that doesn't bother me. And, yes, I probably would do some hot yoga, just as I will when I finally get out of here. It's an excellent way to relieve tension. I don't, however, "journal," primarily because that's not a verb. Neither is "BFF" part of my vocab, which, I'd have thought, would be pretty obvious by this point. Now let's hear about your perfect day, shall we? Or are you living it?

PAUL: (Laughs) Good one. Okay. I'd get up late. I'd have three Egg McMuffins and an extra-large Dunkin' Donuts coffee, double creamer. I'd play the drums for a while. Eat again. Sleep again. Repeat as necessary.

HILDY: That it?

PAUL: There'd probably be a girl at some point, too.

HILDY: Just any girl?

PAUL: Oh, nice. Like I'm an animal. I have my standards.

HILDY: But not a particular girl?

PAUL: Depends on the day but, at the moment, no.

HILDY: So not the one whose hand you're drawing then.

PAUL: I'm not drawing.

HILDY: Then what are you doing?

PAUL: I dunno. Doodling.

HILDY: Pretty good for a doodle.

PAUL: Yeah, well, "pretty good" is in the eye of the beholder I guess.

HILDY: Come on. Can you at least be honest about this?

PAUL: No idea what you're talking about.

HILDY: Oh, right. "This old thing?" Like I'm too stupid to get what's going on.

PAUL: Still not computing.

HILDY: Well, then let me spell it out for you. That's not a doodle. It's a drawing. And it's really good. And you know that.

PAUL: I do, do I?

HILDY: Yes, you do.

PAUL: Thanks for telling me.

HILDY: No one has ever told you that before?

PAUL: Didn't say that.

HILDY: Did they mention how fast you are, too?

PAUL: Speed doesn't count. This ain't Pictionary.

HILDY: You draw a lot?

PAUL: Doodle. Yeah. Better than biting my nails.

HILDY: So it's a nervous habit.

PAUL: It's a habit. I've got worse ones.

HILDY: Oh, do tell!

PAUL: (Laughs)

HILDY: Or don't.

PAUL: That's a better idea. Trust me.

HILDY: Okay. Well. Fine. We won't go there. But I'm serious. That's some "doodle." It's so realistic. Something about the bend in the fingers. It's almost like the hand's alive.

HILDY: That was a compliment.

PAUL: I get that.

HILDY: What's with the look then?

PAUL: Nothing.

HILDY: Wow. I'd hate to see you if something was actually bothering you.

PAUL: Yeah, well, I'd hate to see you if something was actually worth getting excited about. It's a *doodle*.

HILDY: So you keep saying, but hands are super hard.

PAUL: What? You draw?

HILDY: No. Not really. I tried. I took lessons for a while but—

PAUL: Lessons? You don't need lessons. You just need to pick up a pencil and keep drawing until you get it. That's the problem with you South End kids, you—

HILDY: You don't know I'm from the South End.

PAUL: Are you?

PAUL: I knew it. (Laughs) You've got nannies and playdates written all over you.

HILDY: Tone.

PAUL: What? I changed my tone.

HILDY: Yes. From belligerent to smug. Big improvement.

PAUL: But sarcasm is apparently okay.

HILDY: You know, for a few itty-bitty shining moments there, I thought we were going to manage to have a conversation, but now I'm not so sure that's ever going to happen. I can't even give you a compliment without kicking off another argument. You know what? This is a waste of time. I'm going home. I've got stuff to do and, frankly, I don't need the abuse.

PAUL: Here. I offer my hand in a gesture of peace.

HILDY: (Laughs) Very funny.

PAUL: No. Take it. It's yours.

HILDY: Gee. Thanks . . . You shouldn't have torn it like that. I would have liked the whole thing.

PAUL: Girls. Give 'em an inch and they want your whole body.

PAUL: You're blushing.

HILDY: I am not.

PAUL: Yeah, right. You're just naturally fuchsia.

PAUL: What now? Where're you going?

HILDY: I told you. Home.

PAUL: Relax. Sit down. Boy, you complain how I react when you give me a compliment. Least I don't storm out like a—

HILDY: Saying I'm fuchsia is a compliment?

PAUL: It is. Pink's your color.

HILDY: Right. Really smooth. This is ridiculous. I've got enough problems to deal with at the moment. I don't need your constant little jabs and—

PAUL: Sit down, would you.

HILDY: I don't take orders from you.

PAUL: C'mon. "Honor bound." "Doing the right thing." Blah. Blah. Blah. Nelson Mandela wouldn't just give up after a little spat.

HILDY: You're unbelievable.

PAUL: Why, thank you! So sit.

HILDY: No. Why? You've been doing everything you can to infuriate me; now suddenly you want me to stay? How come?

PAUL: 'Cause we're almost there! Only thirty-two questions to go . . .

PAUL: . . . which you solemnly promised Jeff you'd answer . . .

PAUL: . . . in the interest of science . . .

PAUL: Attagirl.

HILDY: Shut up and read the next question.

QUESTION 5

PAUL: *When did you last sing to yourself? And to someone else?*

PAUL: Wow. Mood swing. What are you smiling about all of a sudden?

HILDY: Funny question.

PAUL: That's funny?

HILDY: Well. Only because I do it a lot. I don't even mean to. When I was little, my grandmother—like my father's mother; she's dead now. Anyway, she used to sing this song about how the war—as in World War Two—was going to end someday, and when that happened, everything was going to be perfect. Love. Laughter. Peace ever after. The whole, like, shebang. Whenever I feel worried, that song just kind of pops into my head and then just kind of pops out my mouth. I'm almost not even aware of singing it. I guess it's some sort of a self-soothing technique. I probably sang it this morning, or at least hummed it or something.

PAUL: What have *you* got to worry about?

HILDY: What does that mean?

PAUL: You got a leather satchel and drawing lessons and coffee in, like, bowls and—

HILDY: Forgive me if this sounds rude, but you have an incredibly shallow understanding of the human psyche.

PAUL: You mean, unlike Jeff? The, you know, *psychologist?*

HILDY: Unlike anybody. I mean, I get it. I'm lucky. Way luckier than most people. But seriously. You really think having enough money to occasionally buy a good-quality handbag is enough to solve all life's problems?

PAUL: Sure would love to have the opportunity to find out one of these days. But to answer the actual question, no. I don't sing to myself.

HILDY: Never?

PAUL: Never. Question 6: *If you were—*

HILDY: Wait. You're skipping. There's a part two. It says, "When did you last sing to yourself? *And to someone else?*"

PAUL: This is starting to piss me off. The guy specifically said there were thirty-six questions. That's what I signed up for. But then it turns out, no, actually there are thirty-six questions plus a shitload of subquestions which I also have to come up with subanswers for. That's misleading advertising.

HILDY: That's splitting hairs. And if you just answered truthfully instead of having to "come up" with something, you wouldn't find it quite so draining. But that's an aside. I'm just going to answer the question myself. When did I last sing to someone? Hmm. Do dogs count as someone? . . . Why am I asking you? You don't care . . . So I'll make a ruling myself and say no, in which case Friday evening would be the last time. There's this little girl I babysit. Hazel. Adorable. I always sing her to sleep. Sometime I sing her a real lullaby. Sometimes, I just take some song I like, slow it down, and then just keep singing it over and over again until she passes out. Okay, you.

PAUL: A while ago.

HILDY: Can you be more specific?

PAUL: Can I or will I?

HILDY: I can't force you, obviously, so will you?

PAUL: No.

HILDY: Okay, then to whom?

PAUL: It doesn't ask to *whom*.

HILDY: Was it a female perchance?

PAUL: Yes, for your information, it was.

HILDY: Why are you saying it like that?

PAUL: Like what?

HILDY: "Yes. It was," emphasis on the "was."

HILDY: Oh, I get it. Was a girl—now a boy? Did your girlfriend transition or something?

PAUL: Goddamn.

HILDY: What? That's not that crazy. You're not homophobic are you?

PAUL: No.

HILDY: Then what's with the *you're-an-idiot* look? Or is that just your resting face?

PAUL: It's not my *you're-an-idiot* face. It's my *you're-wrong* face with my *you're-really-starting-to-bug-me* eyebrows. Can we just move on to the next question? Please.

HILDY: Gee. You smiled.

PAUL: Yeah, well, I was desperate.

HILDY: You should be desperate more often.

PAUL: So help me if the next thing you say has anything to do with "turning that frown upside down," I'm out of here.

HILDY: What are you drawing now? It's hard to tell from this angle ... Oh my! That's not some type of erotic doodle, is it?

PAUL: You are so wrong.

HILDY: Those are definitely women's legs.

PAUL: No, they aren't.

HILDY: They so are.

PAUL: No, they aren't. They're ...

PAUL: ... antlers, see?

HILDY: Yeah, well, now they are. Very clever.

HILDY: Oh my god! That's The Great Prince from *Bambi*! I love that book!

PAUL: Bambi's not a book. It's a cartoon.

HILDY: But it was originally a book.

PAUL: Which nobody but you knows.

HILDY: Untrue. Millions—no, maybe even billions—of children have read the—

PAUL: Well, I don't read. Oh. I forgot to mention that part of my perfect day. Absolutely no reading. Or bickies, whatever the Christ they are.

HILDY: That's what the Brits call cookies. My grandmother grew up in the UK and orders them for Christmas and I just love—

PAUL: Oh, sorry. You misunderstood me. I wasn't asking.

HILDY: You know, I think you're nowhere near as bad as you like to make out. There was this little flicker of real emotion in your eyes when you had to admit you sang to someone, and your smile—I mean, your smile when you're not being totally obnoxious to me and inexplicably pissed off at the world—is pretty, like, you know, lovely.

HILDY: Hey, you did it again!

PAUL: Yeah. Well, don't get used to it. And the fact that I'm pissed off is not inexplicable. Trust me.

HILDY: How so?

PAUL: None of your business. Question 6:

QUESTION 6

PAUL: *If you were able to live to the age of ninety and retain either the mind or body of a thirty-year-old for the last sixty years of your life, which would you want?*

HILDY: My mind. Obviously. You?

PAUL: Depends on whose body I get to retain. Can I retain the body of a thirty-year-old female? Every ninety-year-old man's fantasy.

HILDY: (Laughs) I'm not sure that's what "retain" means.

PAUL: Yeah, well, does to me. And whom would I like to retain? The redhead in that sci-fi movie. *Impossible* Something or Other.

HILDY: *Impossible Forever*? That's not sci-fi. That's speculative fiction. Two entirely different things. Sci-fi is—

PAUL: Yeah, well. I'm speculating she must be about thirty. I wouldn't mind retaining her. Not against her will, of course. I'm talking about a consensual relationship.

HILDY: A thirty-year-old movie star and a ninety-year-old you. Consensually? Good luck with that.

PAUL: Thanks. And good luck with retaining your mind.

HILDY: (Laughs) Good point.

QUESTION 7

HILDY: Why don't I ask the questions now? Don't want to get in the way of your artistic pursuits—especially since you're waaay more docile when you're drawing. . . . Who is that, anyway?

PAUL: You at ninety.

HILDY: It is not. If anything, that looks more like me now.

PAUL: Yeah, well, plastic surgery is getting better all the time.

HILDY: I don't believe in plastic surgery.

PAUL: Maybe *now* you don't.

HILDY: Ever. Beauty isn't just about being young. It's about—

PAUL: Yeah. Talk to me when your pretty face starts looking like that cowhide satchel of yours.

HILDY: I get the feeling that in your world looks and money are all that matters.

PAUL: In *my* world. While in *your* world it's the—let me guess— *spiritual* values that really count.

HILDY: Amongst others.

PAUL: Well, lucky you. Frankly, I don't have time for that shit. Speaking of which, if you're going to ask the questions, do it now or I will.

HILDY: I don't feel it's fair letting you have the last word on that particular issue. You're making it sound like I'm some pampered kid who's never had to—

PAUL: Okay. I'm asking the questions.

HILDY: No. I am.

PAUL: Then do it.

HILDY: (Sigh)

PAUL: *Do you have a secret—*

HILDY: No. It's my turn. *Do you have a secret hunch about how you will die?*

PAUL: Yes. Before I get the chance to retain that thirty-year-old's body.

HILDY: This is getting tiresome.

PAUL: I'm serious. Old ain't my thing. I'm dying young.

HILDY: Well, then, how about this? Same way you think I'll cave and get the plastic surgery, I think you're just saying that because you're young. Maybe if you knew what it was like to be old you'd think differently. Maybe it'll turn out you enjoy the wisdom that comes—

PAUL: Look. I answered the question. Drop it.

HILDY: Crabby or what.

HILDY: Fine . . . How I'm going to die . . . Gee. When you think about it, that's a terrible question. It could be very upsetting for some people. What if one of the participants knew they had cancer or a predisposition to a fatal illness? That might be—

PAUL: I don't. Do you?

HILDY: No.

PAUL: Okay. So enough with the ten-minute intro then. Answer the question.

HILDY: Alone.

PAUL: What?

HILDY: I think I'll die alone.

PAUL: Yeah. So? Everyone dies alone. That's what they say.

HILDY: No, I mean, like in an unheated basement apartment with a bunch of mangy cats crawling over my bloated body. That's the kind of alone I'm talking about.

PAUL: Right. You're more likely to be the next Nelson Mandela. And anyway, you got a bunch of mangy cats crawling over you, you're not alone.

HILDY: Very funny.

PAUL: See? Look how much they love you. They're not crawling over you. They're comforting you.

HILDY: (Laughing) Nice drawing. I like the cat with the peg leg.

PAUL: Yeah. Poor old Tripod. Sucks to be him. He also has a serious smack habit, which is why he has those cords tying off his good legs.

HILDY: That's terrible.

PAUL: Yeah, well, he'll be dead soon, too. Despite the love of a good woman who—side note—he still finds beautiful under all that baggy old skin, he just can't get his demons under control . . . I figure you're the type that takes in the hopeless cases.

HILDY: And yet, ironically, is still alone.

PAUL: Yeah . . . you . . . alone. I bet you're ten minutes late for dinner and your parents start calling the police, all frantic and everything.

HILDY: So? What if they do? I'm not talking about *now*. I'm talking about later. When I'm older. They'll probably be dead by then.

PAUL: Nice.

HILDY: I don't mean I want that to happen. I just mean it's true. They probably will be.

PAUL: So? There'll be somebody else to take their place.

HILDY: How do you know?

PAUL: Because. It's obvious. It doesn't take a genius. You'll be married to some lawyer or doctor by then.

HILDY: Like I need some rich guy to look after me.

PAUL: Okay. Fine. Some starving artist who's also your soul mate and a loving stay-at-home dad to your three perfect children. That better?

HILDY: Marriage is not in the cards for me.

PAUL: Yeah. Right.

HILDY: You have a totally distorted image of me. And anyway, marriage isn't everything it's made out to—

PAUL: Fine. No husband then. You'll still have all your friends from work, from book club, from yoga, from girls' night out, from crafting circle, from Save the Squirrels—

HILDY: Save the Squirrels? What are you talking about?

PAUL: From whatever. Doesn't matter. You're not going to be lonely. Crazy maybe, but not lonely.

HILDY: If I didn't know you were trying to insult me, I'd say you were just saying that to shut me up.

PAUL: You mean "in a vain attempt" to shut you up.

PAUL: Oh. Hey. I can't believe it worked.

HILDY: I've always been terrified of ending up alone.

PAUL: I can't keep up with your mood swings.

HILDY: And not just alone but having caused it. I guess that's my real fear.

PAUL: Caused it? What? You planning on going on some rampage and offing everyone you know or something?

HILDY: I'm serious.

PAUL: Okay. How then?

PAUL: Look. You were the one who brought it up, not me.

HILDY: Ending up alone because I alienated everyone who cares about me. Even my three perfect children, I mean, if I get that far, which I seriously doubt given the way things are going.

PAUL: Whoa. You really are afraid of it. I'm going to give one of the kitties here a box of Kleenex. See? Don't worry. They'll look after you.

PAUL: Please stop.

HILDY: I've stopped.

PAUL: Not really.

HILDY: No. There. See? No more tears.

PAUL: You know, you don't come across as the type of person who'd wipe their nose on their sleeve.

HILDY: Don't make me laugh or I'll just have to do it again.

PAUL: Oh. Gross! Quit it, would you?

HILDY: (Laughing)

PAUL: Tell me when I can open my eyes.

HILDY: Yeah, I'm done.

PAUL: Thank god.

HILDY: Well, that was embarrassing. I forgot to eat. I sometimes get a little, you know, fragile when I'm hungry and then I *can't* eat because I'm fragile. Vicious circle. But, gee. Sorry. Tears and everything. A new low. Kind of snuck up on me.

PAUL: Yeah, well, I'd cry, too, if I thought I was going to end up in an unheated basement apartment with a bunch of fleabag cats. Even then, though, I still wouldn't wipe my nose on my sleeve.

HILDY: See, but that's the thing. You don't know what you're going to do until you find yourself in the situation. And anyway, you're the one who made me cry. You shouldn't have mentioned the kitty dying.

PAUL: No kitty is gonna die. Here's my number. Call me the first sign one of your cats is looking poorly and I'll be right over.

HILDY: Promise?

PAUL: Promise.

HILDY: You're not worried I'll abuse this? I might end up calling you thirty times a day. That's the type of thing people who burst into tears around total strangers do.

PAUL: I'm not worried.

HILDY: This isn't your real number, is it?

PAUL: I underestimated you.

QUESTION 8

HILDY: *Name three things you and your partner appear to have in common.* Well, that's easy. A sunny disposition.

HILDY: That's number one! You laughed.

PAUL: I laughed at you, not with you.

HILDY: So? Still counts. Number two: We both have nice smiles, although I use mine more often. And brownish-greenish eyes. Okay, there's three.

PAUL: Hold on. How come you get to choose all three first?

HILDY: Because you weren't doing it.

PAUL: I didn't have a chance.

HILDY: You did so.

HILDY: Rolling your eyes is rude.

HILDY: So is sighing. Why do you even care?

PAUL: Don't like being pushed around, that's why.

PAUL: I thought you said sighing was rude.

HILDY: Just choose three, would you?

PAUL: Okay. One) We're both stubborn.

HILDY: But not equally stubborn.

PAUL: Agreed. You're worse.

HILDY: No. *You* are. No way I'm going to—

PAUL: See? Who's the stubbornest one now? Proves my point.

HILDY: Very clever.

PAUL: Which is my second answer. We're both clever.

HILDY: I'll accept that. You're not quite the knucklehead you pretend to be.

PAUL: And three) Facial hair.

HILDY: What?!

PAUL: (Laughing)

HILDY: Oh my god. That's like something a little kid would do. And I take that back. You are a knucklehead.

PAUL: I loved the way your hand, like, *flew* up to your chin. You got a hormone problem or something? Anything you want to tell me?

HILDY: Yes, as a matter of fact there is. That better be another mangy cat you're drawing and not a picture of me.

PAUL: I'm calling her Whiskers. You decide.

QUESTION 9

HILDY: *For what in your life do you feel most grateful?*

PAUL: I know what you're going to say.

HILDY: What?

PAUL: Tweezers.

HILDY: Haha. Wrong.

PAUL: What then?

HILDY: My family.

PAUL: Shoulda known.

HILDY: Like, I mean, my family I grew up with.

PAUL: Yeah. I got it. That's what "my family" usually means.

HILDY: I meant I'm grateful for, like, growing up when I did with my family at a time when my parents, uh . . . look. It's not important. It doesn't matter.

PAUL: Wow. You finally figured that out. It doesn't matter.

HILDY: Okay. Your answer.

PAUL: Sriracha sauce.

HILDY: Come on. At least try.

PAUL: When you can't cook, you become very grateful for sriracha sauce. It's a modern miracle drug. Makes everything almost edible.

HILDY: You know, it's way more interesting when you answer honestly. All this, like, "quipping" just makes me suspicious you've got something to hide.

PAUL: You're not the next Nelson Mandela. You're the next Dr. Phil.

HILDY: Seriously. Why don't you dispense with the punchlines? It's lazy and stupid and, at a very basic level, emotionally dishonest.

PAUL: Jesus Christ. I know what I'm *going* to be most grateful for. Getting this goddamn thing over with.

HILDY: You remind me of my older brother. You both affect this tough-guy thing. The slouch. The snarky laugh. The whole who-gives-a-shit attitude, but you're not like that.

PAUL: OMG. I'm shocked. I thought you said no swearing.

HILDY: I saw the look on your face when I lost it back there. You're not like that. You're actually quite empathetic.

PAUL: Yeah, well, one thing I learned early is that if you *pretend* to be concerned at the beginning, you can often avoid a bigger emotional outburst later.

HILDY: You hate admitting your softer side.

PAUL: Quick. Pass me the wastebasket. I'm going to puke.

HILDY: Good. Get it out. You'll feel better. Which is also true about whatever you're so frightened of. Just admit it.

PAUL: Christ. I can just imagine what your Facebook posts are like. Listen. I'm an open book. What do you want to know?

HILDY: Great. Then answer the question.

HILDY: Some open book.

PAUL: I'm thinking.

HILDY: Right. Thinking of how to get out of it.

PAUL: Thinking of the forty dollars I'll get to finish.

HILDY: Whatever it takes.

PAUL: Okay. Time.

HILDY: What? We're not done yet.

PAUL: No. I mean time. That's what I'm grateful for.

HILDY: Wow. That surprised me.

PAUL: Why?

HILDY: You don't have to be so hostile. I just mean it's a pretty big leap from sriracha sauce to "time" in the larger sense of the word which, reading your expression, is what I believe you were suggesting. It's so . . . kind of ethereal or something.

PAUL: *E-thee-re-al?*

HILDY: Yeah.

PAUL: What the hell does that mean?

HILDY: You don't know what that means?

PAUL: No. It's not a word any normal person uses.

HILDY: Well, I use it.

PAUL: My point.

HILDY: For your information, then, it means airy. Delicate. Subtle.

PAUL: Then, no. Wrong. There's nothing ethereal about being grateful for time. Nothing fucking subtle about it. I'm grateful for a specific historic moment in time.

HILDY: This better not be the discovery of sriracha sauce.

HILDY: That was a joke.

HILDY: Why are you looking at me like that?

PAUL: Twelve minutes on July third, two years ago. That's what I'm grateful for. Now I need to piss. If you don't mind, of course.

TEXT MESSAGE TO DAD: This is taking longer than I thought. Might be a little late for dinner. Sure you can't go to the movie with us tonight? Gabe was looking forward to some family time. x H

TEXT MESSAGE TO XIU FRASER: Major developments. Call when you're thru choir. You're not going to believe this

TEXT MESSAGE TO MAX BUDOVIC: I think I'm finally ready to move past spooning!!!!!

TEXT MESSAGE FROM MAX BUDOVIC: Wha?! Who?!

HILDY: Remember that psych study I signed up for?

MAX: Ur scaring me . . . someone probing the dirty part of ur brain with a metal stick or something?

HILDY: No

MAX: R u talking about an actual human being?

HILDY: Flesh & blood

MAX: Ooh baby mazel tov!!!!! Tell me more

HILDY: Last person in the world you'd imagine me with. Kind of surly. Zero in common & he makes me really mad

MAX: Not sure I like where this is going

HILDY: Me neither or maybe I do. I can't tell

MAX: Repeat: ur scaring me

HILDY: Scaring myself, too, but hey yolo

MAX: UR SCARING THE SHIT OUT OF ME

HILDY: GTG

MAX: Noooooooooo!!!!!!!!!

HILDY: Hey.

PAUL: Hey.

HILDY: Look. I'm sorry. I didn't mean to upset you.

PAUL: You didn't upset me. I needed a piss, okay? Next question. And I'm asking from here on.

PAUL: And P. fucking S. I can fucking swear if I fucking feel like it.

HILDY: O fucking K.

HILDY: Made you smile.

PAUL: Did not.

HILDY: Did so.

PAUL: Next question.

QUESTION 10

PAUL: *If you could change anything about the way you were raised, what would it be?*

HILDY: I wish I hadn't been kept in the dark so much.

PAUL: Explains why you're so pale.

HILDY: Thought you said I was fuchsia.

PAUL: Comes and goes. Right now, you're kind of white again.

HILDY: I'm going to ignore that. I want you to answer honestly so I'm going to answer honestly. What I mean is: I wish I'd been told what was going on. I know my parents were trying to protect me—

or maybe just protect themselves—but, of course, that backfired, big time. Now I have this constant worry that there are other bad things going on that I don't know about, either. I'm scared about setting off another landmine. Truth hurts way more when it's been festering underground for a while.

PAUL: Wouldn't know.

HILDY: Or care by the sounds of it. Fine. I'll just leave that heart-wrenching admission dangling there in the breeze and ask you: what would *you* change? And don't say your socks or underwear or anything stupid like that.

PAUL: You wanted more truth. Yeah, well, I guess I wanted less. Less truth, but better. That's what I would have changed.

HILDY: Wow.

PAUL: What?

HILDY: Just wow. Interesting thought.

PAUL: Don't sound so shocked. I have them occasionally.

HILDY: Can truth be better? If you make it better, is it still the truth? . . . Or do you mean better as in "better for you"?

PAUL: (Laughs) What do *you* think I mean?

HILDY: I don't know actually. You like to come across all hard-hearted and only out for yourself but I think that's just an act. I get the feeling something like the real meaning of truth would concern you.

PAUL: Because I'm so, like, empathetic and everything?

HILDY: Yeah. Amongst other things. So, come on. Tell me. What is truth?

PAUL: To find out, shut up and dial 1-800-ASK-BUDDHA. That's 1-800-ASK-BUDDHA.

HILDY: (Laughs) Rude but funny.

PAUL: Just let me finish this little "doodle" and I'll put it on a T-shirt for you.

HILDY: There's the hand again. Why do you keep drawing that? . . . Hey, don't! . . . Why'd you go scribble it out?

PAUL: You got enough truth out of me for one question.

QUESTION 11

PAUL: Oh. Shit. Please. No.

HILDY: What?

PAUL: (Sigh) *Take four minutes and tell your partner your life story in as much detail as possible.*

HILDY: So?

PAUL: Four minutes from you? That's like ten years to life for the rest of us. I'm clearly going to be doing some serious doodling. Give me some of your paper, would ya?

HILDY: You know this is what you do with little kids when you're babysitting, don't you? Find something for them to draw on so they don't get bored and break the furniture or scribble on the walls or something.

PAUL: Just give it to me. Why do you have all that junk in there, anyway? That why you got the satchel? To transport your recyclables? Tuesday's garbage day. You might want to lighten your load.

HILDY: What are you complaining about? You're the one who needs the paper. Here. Take this.

PAUL: Don't have anything unused in there?

HILDY: Picky, picky. Draw on the back. It's just a first draft. I've got the—

PAUL: Fine. So answer, would you?

PAUL: What's taking you?

HILDY: Sorry. I just needed to take a moment to mentally bludgeon you before I went on.

HILDY: Okay . . . Four minutes . . . I was born in Montreal but moved here when I was three. I've got two brothers, one older, one younger. Alec with a *c*—he's doing a semester in Dublin at the moment—and Gabe.

PAUL: I knew there'd be a Gabe.

HILDY: Pretty ordinary family. My father's principal at the fine arts high school I go to. My mother's an ER doctor. In fact, she's department head.

PAUL: Gee. Congratulations.

HILDY: That's not why I'm saying it. It's just she's the hospital's *first* female to run the ER so I like to mention it. People have to hear about women in positions of authority.

PAUL: Roger that. So can we speed this up a bit then? No way you're getting this all done in four minutes.

HILDY: So annoying . . . My father was the "primary caregiver." That's one thing that made us a little different. He had summers and holidays off while Mom always did shift work. What else? I had a lisp until I was ten, which is awful when your last name starts with *S*. I had to do a lot of speech therapy to fix it and even now when I get tired my speech can get pretty slushy . . . You know, Thylvethter the Cat—that kind of slushy. Okay. What else? Um. You were right. I took all the usual lessons—piano, ballet, Saturday morning art classes. This is boring.

PAUL: No, no. I'm on the edge of my fucking seat.

HILDY: I was in a car accident when I was twelve?

PAUL: Why are you asking me?

HILDY: I mean, that's sort of interesting. Mom hit black ice. We went flying. I still have nightmares about it.

PAUL: Someone die?

HILDY: No. Ick. Why would you even say that? My brother got a concussion, and Mom sprained her ankle or something. It was just she was so scared. That's what got me. Mom always knew what to do. I mean, she's a physician. Up until that point in my life, she was like this warrior goddess or something. Brave. Unflappable. But then she just totally freaked. I still have these dreams when I need her for something and she loses it. And it could be something totally random, too, like, "Have you seen my socks?" or "Can you pick me up after work?"—but she goes *kaboom*. Little pieces everywhere. And then I'm the one worrying about her, trying to put her back together. It's as if I got this one brief glimpse beneath the armor and now I can't forget she's, I guess, vulnerable, too.

PAUL: Yeah. That's the problem with parents. They keep turning out to be human.

HILDY: (Laughs) That's good. I might use it.

PAUL: What? In your novel?

PAUL: I *knew* you were writing a novel.

PAUL: Just don't go putting me in it.

HILDY: A) What difference would it make? You don't read, remember? And B) You honestly think after knowing me for less than an hour you've made enough of an impression to show up in my novel?

PAUL: Maybe. You strike me as impressionable, if that's even a word.

HILDY: It is, and you know it. You like to act like you're—

PAUL: Um. Excuse me? But I think we're still on *your* life story. Mine's next.

HILDY: Do you always get want you want?

PAUL: I'm sitting here on a broken chair in a windowless room with, like, ninety more questions to go and you have to ask?

HILDY: (Laughs) Fine . . . my life . . . I can't even remember what I was going to say now. You got me all flustered . . . Don't look at me like that. I mean it. I don't normally just, like, dissolve into tears around other people. I'm reasonably—

PAUL: Fuck sake. The question.

HILDY: Okay . . . I was the classic high school nerd.

62

PAUL: I knew you could do it.

HILDY: Did all the extracurricular activities. Everything from improv to fashion studio to Model UN, and not just because we got to go to the Hague that year . . . I've had the same group of friends forever, although I sense Iris and I are moving apart. Xiu's been my bosom buddy since Theater Tots. Max and I are as close as we've always been but it's different, of course, since he came out. He's still my best friend. Um . . . What else? . . . I have a sort of weird interest in anything to do with the 1950s. Don't know where that came from but I have this passionate desire to one day own a pink refrigerator. On the other hand, I'm really drawn to that totally pared-down European aesthetic so I also fantasize about an all-white kitchen—glazed concrete counter, smooth-faced cabinets, no handles, that sort of thing. It gives me such a sense of calm. I hate skiing, mostly because everybody, including my parents, makes it sound like you have to love it, whereas, in fact, it's cold and the boots hurt and it's just up and down, up and down the hill over and over again. It's boring. As is soccer. And homecoming week—which is *beyond* boring. "Enforced frivolity." Nothing worse . . . Um. I'm planning to major in English but will probably write my LSATs and go to law school like everyone else.

PAUL: Like everyone else.

HILDY: You know what I mean. Not everyone but . . .

PAUL: No, I don't know what you mean. In fact, I *usually* don't know what you mean. Shocking, I know, but when you say "ordinary families" I don't automatically picture mothers who run emergency departments and kids who have to be forced to go skiing.

HILDY: So? *Everyone's* idea of ordinary is different. We're individuals. Different circumstances. Different influences.

PAUL: No kidding.

HILDY: Okay. So what's ordinary for you?

PAUL: Not that.

HILDY: Give me your four minutes then.

PAUL: Sorry. Don't have that much material.

HILDY: Right. You've been alive what? Eighteen? Nineteen years? I'm sure you can squeeze out a four-minute highlight reel.

PAUL: Whoa. *That* was your highlight reel?

PAUL: What? Can't take a little repartee?

HILDY: I thought you said you don't read.

PAUL: So?

HILDY: You're lying. "Repartee"? That's a book word.

PAUL: That's a Bugs Bunny word.

HILDY: I don't remember Bugs Bunny ever saying "repartee."

PAUL: Oh, well, then I must be wrong because you obviously memorized every word.

HILDY: This is the type of argument you have with a six-year-old.

PAUL: It's not an argument. It's repartee. About repartee. I thought you'd appreciate the simple beauty in that, you being an English major someday and everything.

PAUL: You smiled.

HILDY: I did.

PAUL: Okay. Where were we? My life story. My parents aren't around. No siblings, at least that I know of. I play the drums. You know that. I draw. You know that, too. I almost graduated from an inner-city high school. I consider that one of my greatest achievements.

HILDY: Almost graduating?

PAUL: Yeah. Hard *not* to graduate there. Got a heartbeat and they put you on the honor roll.

HILDY: Well, congratulations. What else you got?

PAUL: I'm currently unemployed.

HILDY: That's it?

PAUL: Yeah. That's it. Story of my life.

HILDY: Wrong. You know what that was? That was a ten-second cover-up of a thirty-six-part docudrama. What you didn't say was way more interesting that what you actually said. For instance, what happened to—

PAUL: Don't ask me about my parents.

HILDY: What about friends?

PAUL: I've got a few.

HILDY: Yes? And?

PAUL: Not bad guys. They improve with alcohol.

HILDY: Girlfriend?

PAUL: Too messy. I prefer girls with an *s*.

HILDY: Bond. James Bond.

PAUL: Teacher! Betty's making fun of me again.

HILDY: I'm making fun of the image you try to project.

HILDY: Which I shouldn't do. Because I hate it when you do that to me.

HILDY: Sorry.

PAUL: My image doesn't care.

HILDY: Nor should it. That was an inappropriate thing for me to say.

PAUL: Again. Doesn't care.

HILDY: So. What do you want to do?

PAUL: When?

HILDY: When you, you know, "grow up"?

PAUL: Did that already.

HILDY: Okay. Fine. What do you want to do *in the future*?

PAUL: Get by. Haven't thought too much beyond that.

HILDY: Seriously?

PAUL: I think I've answered the question.

HILDY: Four minutes it says. You've got about three minutes and thirty-seven seconds to go.

PAUL: I'm going to fill it with a drum solo.

HILDY: Ouch. Doesn't that hurt your fingers?

PAUL: That's what tables are for.

HILDY: No, they're not and that's not an answer, either. So stop, would you?

HILDY: Thank you. I'll let you catch your breath and you can begin.

PAUL: I don't need to catch my breath.

HILDY: All right so begin then.

PAUL: I *doodle*. That's what I like to do. Maybe in an ideal world I'd draw for a living but this isn't an ideal world, is it? Or I guess I'm asking the wrong person. Miss High School Trip to Europe and— natch—proud possessor of a gay best friend.

HILDY: Why would the sexual orientation of my best friend deserve that type of response from you?

PAUL: I dunno. You seem to be trying really hard to be "an individual" but you do these totally predictable things. I bet I could name your favorite food, your favorite musician, your favorite book—if I read, that is—your favorite beverage, your favorite brand of . . .

HILDY: Look. Your four minutes are up. Ask the next question.

PAUL: Hit a nerve, did I?

HILDY: I'd like to hit you.

HILDY: And that's not funny. So quit laughing, would you?

QUESTION 12

PAUL: (Laughing) Sorry. Maybe it's being stuck in this room for hours—

HILDY: It hasn't been hours.

PAUL: I can't help it. Sorry. Nothing is funnier than seeing someone like you snap.

PAUL: If you want me to stop laughing, you're going to have to do something with your face.

PAUL: I mean it.

PAUL: And those little puffs of smoke coming out your ears.

PAUL: Oh. My. God. You are so not what you think you are. You did this big thing about claiming how you're so ordinary but then as soon as I agreed, you lost it. Which makes me think that you didn't really mean what—

HILDY: Just shut up and ask the question.

PAUL: And there you did it again. Who's crabby now?

PAUL: Okay, okay. Here goes: *If you could wake up tomorrow having gained any one quality or ability, what would it be?*

HILDY: Patience, especially now.

PAUL: Good one. Me too.

HILDY: Too late. I got there first. No copying. Come up with something different.

PAUL: I'd have the ability to turn you off entirely while still being able to collect my forty dollars.

HILDY: Hahaha. I'm choosing to laugh at that good-naturedly but I don't think that's the real answer. I want the real answer.

HILDY: You know, I've noticed that the touchier the question, the more compulsively you draw. It's obviously a defense mechanism for you.

HILDY: Well, look at that. *Les tables ont tournées.* Not so funny now, is it?

PAUL: If this is a defense mechanism, it's not working very well. You managed to bug me even in Spanish.

HILDY: French, and you know it.

PAUL: I knew you reminded me of someone. Jean-Claude Van Damme.

HILDY: I don't know who that is.

PAUL: He's an actor, and you know it.

HILDY: Are you done?

PAUL: Oh yeah. I was done ages ago.

HILDY: TATQ

PAUL: What?

HILDY: TATQ. As in "Then Answer The Question." It's exhausting having to spell it out all the time.

PAUL: *You're* exhausted?

HILDY: I think the real answer is in your drawings. You draw a version of the same thing over and over again. That hand. It must mean something.

PAUL: The answer to the question is in my drawings? How very mind reading of me. I didn't even know what the question was until I read it and yet somehow I was able to miraculously draw the answer.

HILDY: I don't mean the answer to that particular question. I mean the answer to who you are as a person.

PAUL: I'm going to hurl.

HILDY: If I'm so wrong then why are you crumpling it up?

PAUL: So I don't do something worse.

HILDY: Such as? Reveal yourself?

PAUL: Oh my god. You are unbelievable. Who do you think you are now? Oprah?

HILDY: I—

PAUL: Don't say you don't know who that is. You watch TV like everybody else. You don't think I actually believe your bullshit, do you? You're hiding as much as I am. So that's what I'd like.

HILDY: What?

PAUL: I'd like the ability to see what you're really like underneath all your posing and big words and old man's overcoat or army tent or whatever the hell it is you're wearing. You might say "ethereal" and know what's so goddamn good about kitchen cupboards without handles, but you're not fooling anyone. You just decided what part of the shitshow you want to make public. My guess is your family is as screwed up as the rest of us.

PAUL: Wow. That sure shut you up.

QUESTION 13

PAUL: Now you're mad.

HILDY: No, I'm not. There's just not much I can say to that. If you remember, I was the one insisting we all have problems. You were the one dismissing mine because I happen to own a Coach "satchel."

PAUL: Yay. We agree. So what's with the face?

HILDY: Just because something's true doesn't mean you have to like it.

PAUL: Wow. Two things we agree on.

HILDY: Now what are you drawing?

HILDY: It's me again, isn't it? . . . Thanks for the giant lips, by the way.

PAUL: What's wrong with giant lips? I like giant lips. And no. It's not you. It's Pandora. Updated version of the story. Instead of a box, all the world's woes are stuffed into her genuine Coach satchel.

HILDY: (Laughs) I thought you don't read.

PAUL: I don't.

HILDY: Then how do you know about Greek mythology?

PAUL: Comic books. Amazing what you can pick up just looking at the pictures.

HILDY: I like it. Despite your best efforts to appear shallow, you have once again revealed your depths. Can I have it?

PAUL: Take it. Nothing like someone explaining a joke to kill it . . . Here . . . Let me sign it for you.

HILDY: (Laughs) *To Betty. You're going to need a bigger satchel if you're collecting my problems, too. Bob* . . . Hey. No xoxo?

PAUL: Bob's kinda shy with the ladies.

HILDY: Unlike Paul, his alter ego. Or is it the other way around?

PAUL: You'll never know.

HILDY: I already do.

PAUL: Wow. What a coincidence. Question 13 is also about things beyond your comprehension.

HILDY: Smooth segue.

PAUL: Whatever that means. Okay, here goes. *If a crystal ball could tell you the truth about yourself, your life, the future, or anything else, what would you want to know?*

HILDY: I'd want to know if . . .

PAUL: Yeah?

HILDY: I don't know.

PAUL: Do so.

HILDY: I'd want to know if things will ever go back to the way they were.

PAUL: Christ. You need a crystal ball for that? The answer is no.

HILDY: I know but . . .

PAUL: No buts.

HILDY: You didn't listen to what I was going to say.

PAUL: There's nothing you can say. Can't go backward. Get over it. Move on. Seriously. Next question.

HILDY: I don't know what you're so mad about all of a sudden. I wasn't talking about you. I—

PAUL: Next question.

HILDY: We're not at the next question. It's your turn.

PAUL: I'm sick of this stupid thing.

HILDY: Too bad. We're not done yet. What would you want to know?

PAUL: Is there a God and, if so, what was he thinking?

HILDY: Oddly serious response.

PAUL: And you thought you'd gotten to the bottom of Bob's twisted psyche.

HILDY: What do you mean, "what was God thinking"?

HILDY: Go ahead. Doodle away. Act like you don't hear me.

HILDY: You're so childish.

HILDY: C'mon. Just tell me. What was God thinking—about what?

HILDY: You can't tease me with some big heavy response and then just stop talking.

PAUL: So I'm a tease now, am I?

HILDY: You're once again trying to deflect attention from the issue at hand. Tell me what you mean.

PAUL: Giraffes. See?

HILDY: This is normally where I'd sigh loudly.

PAUL: Seriously. What was—so-called—"God" thinking? I mean, no one would build something that looked like this on purpose.

HILDY: I don't believe you and I also hate it when you do that.

PAUL: What? Draw? Gee, Betty, I thought you liked my drawings.

HILDY: I hate it when you're going to say something real, then chicken out.

PAUL: No. Truth. Look at this thing. The neck. The scrawny legs. And what's with these pathetic horns? Go big or go home.

HILDY: Neither funny nor charming nor even particularly insightful.

PAUL: You're *so* mean. I'm going to retreat into the safety of my imaginary world for a while. You ask the questions now.

QUESTION 14

HILDY: *Is there something that you've dreamed of doing for a long time? Why haven't you done it?*

PAUL: Have we been here a long time?

HILDY: Why?

PAUL: Nothing.

HILDY: Why are you smiling like that?

PAUL: Nothing . . . Okay. Is there something I've wanted to do for a long time? Yes. Drive.

HILDY: You can't drive?

PAUL: What would I drive? I don't have a car, which—whaddya know—is also the answer to the goddamn supplementary question.

HILDY: Oh. Hey. How about you teach me to play the drums, and I teach you to drive?

PAUL: You. Play the drums?

HILDY: Yes.

PAUL: No.

HILDY: Why?

PAUL: Just no. Betty. Take a look at yourself. Think about your interests, who you are as a person, your upper arm strength—and now tell me you're actually going to play the drums.

HILDY: All right. Fine. Then teach me to draw.

PAUL: I told you how to draw. Pick up a pencil and start. That's basically how you play the drums, too. Pick up a stick and start hitting something.

HILDY: I can see why you wouldn't want to teach me drums. I'd pick up the stick and start hitting you.

PAUL: Exactly. Now you answer. Something you've always wanted to do.

PAUL: Is your face ever fuchsia.

HILDY: You're going to mock me.

PAUL: I thought you said you were okay with that. Honor bound. Doing the right thing. The Righteous Code of the Knights of Betty. Whatever.

HILDY: You're right. I did. Fine. Something I've dreamed of doing for a long time . . .

HILDY: Kissing Evan Keefe. What?

PAUL: Nothing.

HILDY: Quit laughing. It's not funny.

PAUL: It is.

HILDY: You don't even know him.

PAUL: I don't have to know him. You want to kiss him? So kiss him. Why haven't you?

HILDY: I don't have to tell you that.

PAUL: Yes, in fact, you do. Two-part question.

HILDY: Damn.

PAUL: Damn! Wow. You must be, like, hoppin' mad. C'mon. Spit it out.

HILDY: Okay. Well, no real reason. Just Evan Keefe and me? It would never happen.

PAUL: Why? He gay or something?

HILDY: No! Why would you say that? He's just, I don't know, out of my league. I mean, look at him.

PAUL: You have a picture of him on your phone. That's kind of creepy. You're not a stalker, are you?

HILDY: We just happened to be in a lot of things together.

PAUL: Just happened . . .

HILDY: Yes. Just happened. We're both interested in drama, music, writing—

PAUL: And he's not gay.

HILDY: That's called stereotyping.

PAUL: So why hasn't he kissed you?

HILDY: You mean why haven't I kissed him? The question is: what have *I* dreamed of doing.

PAUL: Oh my god. Nitpicking. You must drive people crazy. That's why he hasn't kissed you.

PAUL: What?

PAUL: What?

PAUL: Oh, for shit sake.

HILDY: Don't you for-shit-sake me!

PAUL: What are you? Someone's grandmother? Only eighty-year-olds say things like that.

HILDY: I don't care who says that! Your comments are hurtful. You've known me for, like, forty-five minutes and you feel you have the right to say I must drive people crazy? I'm apparently so irritating that mere contact with me is—

PAUL: Jesus. You're not crying again, are you? Christ. Sorry. Please. Stop doing that, would you.

HILDY: I am NOT crying. Female tear ducts are smaller than male tear ducts so there's, I don't know, a little spillage or something. I'm just. So. Angry.

PAUL: Whoa. Listen to yourself. I only asked why he hadn't kissed you. What's wrong with that? I figured any normal straight guy would have wanted to kiss you.

HILDY: Don't patronize me.

PAUL: I'm not. Swear to god. I just had no idea you were so sensitive.

HILDY: Don't say "sensitive."

PAUL: Christ. What's the matter with "sensitive"?

HILDY: You're not kidding anyone. That's a loaded word. The sugarcoating wore off years ago. You say "you're sensitive" and everyone knows you mean "you're irrational."

PAUL: No.

HILDY: Okay, "hysterical" then?

PAUL: I didn't say that—but frankly, I'm starting to think it.

HILDY: Oh, right. Just *now* starting to think it. How convenient. Like I put that idea in your head or something. Like I forced you to—

PAUL: What's your problem? You on your period or something?

PAUL: Oh my god! Did you just throw your fish at me?!

CHAPTER

3

"It was as if my arm was . . . I don't know." Hildy scanned the crowded café for the right word. "*Possessed* or something. I mean, me? Throw. I don't even know *how* to throw."

"Guy deserved it." Xiu was checking her reflection in the window and pretending not to. "Douchebag, if you ask me."

They were sitting at their usual table. It was too cold for Hildy, right by the door with people coming in and out all the time, but Xiu had to have it. It gave her the best view of the tall guy with the seventies hair busking on the corner. She'd pledged to sit there every Saturday until Sweet Baby James looked up from his guitar and noticed her. Hildy, if she wanted to talk, had no choice but to join her there. (Xiu was queen bee. She even had the tattoo to prove it.)

Max joined them with lattes and three almond croissants to share. Two for him. The girls split the other. Today was his turn to buy.

"You haven't missed anything." Xiu took her coffee from him without taking her eyes off SBJ strumming away across the street. "She's still talking about—sigh—Bob."

"Oh. God. Drop it, Hildy. *Please.*" Max squished his rangy

six-foot-four-inch self into the chair next to hers. "Every time you mention his name I picture that poor little King Kong puffer fish sailing through the air to its doom."

"Max. Enough already with the gay voice." Xiu picked the almond slivers off her part of the croissant. "You're starting to sound like you're waving a cigarette holder around."

"My life. My voice."

"Fine. If you're okay with turning into a caricature of yourself, but I—"

"Guys!" Hildy slapped the table. "Can you listen to me for a bit? I know I'm obsessing but, seriously, you're usually worse than me and, right now, I need you to listen."

Max pulled an invisible zipper across his lips. Xiu had just taken a nibble so she wouldn't be talking for a while. She never spoke with her mouth full.

"I just need to figure out how I managed to go so drastically off the rails, then I'll shut up. Promise."

Xiu swallowed, and said, "Well, that's easy. Overstimulation."

Hildy looked away. She shouldn't have asked.

"You were all worked up about the problems at home and nervous about the little blind date you'd just had sprung on you, then His Hotness walked in, pushed a few buttons and you lost it. There. Case closed. Back to me."

"It's not that simple."

"Is so. You've done it before."

"Have not."

Even Max laughed.

"Opening night, *Oklahoma!* National debate semifinals. The morning we left on our three-city tour of vintage clothing stores. I'm missing one. . . . oh-oh-oh-oh-oh!—your eighth birthday party."

Hildy smiled like *very funny*.

"Only *that* time, as I recall, it was the Dora the Explorer ice cream cake that tipped you over the edge. Remember your mother banishing you to your room?" Xiu closed her eyes, put one perfectly manicured hand over her mouth, and snorted. "I love Amy but, wow. She's like the banishing *queen*. The arched eyebrows. The long shaking finger. God. That time she caught us in her makeup? I doubt I'll ever fully recover."

"Please." Max adjusted his horn-rims. "She caught Hildy and me in *bed*."

"Shit. I forgot about that."

"I'm glad you two find this amusing." Hildy scooched toward the table so a man with a howling baby and several canvas bags full of vegetables could get by. "Go ahead. Laugh at me. I don't care."

"We're not laughing at you. We're just laughing. Know why?" Xiu threw her napkin over her plate so she wouldn't be tempted to eat any more. "One) Because we're young and alive and two) because it's not that big a deal. It's normal. I don't know what it is about surly guys but they make girls do crazy things. Especially so-called 'sensitive' girls. Witness Heathcliff."

"Yeah. But I blew up."

"Spontaneous human combustion. Also normal. Well-known phenomenon."

"This isn't a joke, Max."

"Not saying it is. Someone gave me a stick and hung a young Steve McQueen piñata full of Jujubes in front of me, I'd have combusted, too. Only so much a body can stand."

Hildy stared into her latte and pictured the baggie flying across the table. Heard the smack as it hit his face. Felt the water splash over her hand and up her sleeve. Saw herself scramble, honking and spastic, out of the room. "I should have gone with my first instinct and left as soon as I found out what the study was about. I knew I couldn't do the love thing."

Max clamped his hands on either side of his head and went, "Hildy. Por favor!"

Xiu said, "Don't be so stupid," and began declumping her eyelashes with her fingertips.

"I'm not being stupid. I'm taking an honest look at my life and drawing the obvious conclusions. This is what happens when you pretend to be something you're not. I'd somehow managed to convince myself that I'd get in there with my random stranger and it would be like improv. I'd be terrified but the adrenaline would kick in and I'd pull it off. And for a while I did. Had a little trouble with tears halfway through but I pretty much held my own—until one stupid comment and *bang!* The real me busted out again. Like she always does. So that's that. Doesn't matter. Lots of people are single their whole lives and are totally fine with it."

"Sure." Max took her croissant because she clearly wasn't eating it. "The pope, most guidance counselors—and who else?"

No one came to mind. Max raised one thick, well-groomed eyebrow. Hildy let it drop.

"You're making stuff up, Hildy." Xiu flicked some crumbs out of the floppy bow of her disco-era polyester blouse. "You've had a bit of a late start and a few setbacks but you've got to stop obsessing about it. Especially with regards to Douchebag here. I mean, good riddance. What kind of guy thinks he can get away with accusing you of being on your period?"

Max showed his teeth and nodded. "Yeah, Hil. Deal breaker. I mean, my *dad* knows that and he's a mechanical engineer from a former Soviet-bloc country."

Hildy resisted the urge to suck on the end of her braid. "Look. I know. Paul crossed the line and—"

Xiu raised her hand. "Stop. For starters, don't call him Paul."

"Why? That's his name."

"Too confusing. Pauls are potentially datable. Bobs are retired gym teachers and alcoholic great-uncles and, thus, are not. Stick to Bob. Or Douchebag. Your choice."

"Fine. Bob crossed the line and I'm not defending him . . ."

"Although you're no doubt about to." Xiu checked her nails.

". . . but who am I kidding? *I'm* the problem." Hildy moved the handle of her latte back and forth in a tick-tock motion. "It's precisely because I liked him and in some weird way I could see that he liked me too that it was doomed to failure. Again, that's just who I am."

Max turned to Xiu. "Do you think that by listening to this endless shit we may actually be enabling her in some way?"

"Okay. Look." Xiu shoved their dirty dishes aside like a general laying out a war map. "You're right. Complicated guy. The sketching. The drumming. The glimpses of humor. Even, within limits, the douchiness. All very attractive. But let's be realistic. You don't want a caveman."

"You're not listening to me. I don't want anyone."

"Wrong. But you certainly don't want a guy who doesn't *read*."

"He's not stupid." For some reason, it was important to Hildy they know that.

"He had to ask you the meaning of *ethereal* and—what was the other word?"

"*Segue*." Max said it with a pronounced French accent.

"Yes. *Segue*." Xiu shook her head in disbelief. "Words the average seven-year-old throws around like LEGO blocks."

She reached out and held Hildy's hand. "Forget Neanderbob. What about that Trevor guy in Modern World History? He sounds doable. I mean, once you fix his hair."

Hildy took her hand away. "I'm not interested in Bob *or* Trevor. I'm not interested in guys, period. I told you. I'm through."

"Ooh. So dramatic! And inaccurate too. How can you be through with something you haven't even started?"

"Thanks, Max. You, in particular, should know I'm not totally inexperienced."

Xiu raised a finger in the air and gave one point to Hildy.

"There were other guys, too." Hildy hated the way they both nodded. Just because they were suddenly sexperts didn't mean they could treat her like a child.

"William Foster," she said. "Junior high prom. I went to the washroom and came back to find him making out with Elianna Bulmer."

"You were fourteen. He was a jerk. Move on." Xiu was slightly uncomfortable because she'd made out with him, too.

"I did move on. Anton Friesen. And how did that work out?"

"What did you expect? You never tell someone you love them on the third date."

"Fine. Nate Schultz."

They both groaned. "You didn't even like him! I'm amazed he stuck around as long as he did," Max said. "And anyway, he wasn't cute enough for you."

Hildy had several more humiliating examples to add but instead looked right at Max and said, "You."

He dropped the jokey tone. "Hildy. You don't *actually* want to go down this road again."

She didn't. "Okay then. Evan Keefe."

Max flopped his neck over the back of his chair and stared dead-eyed at the ceiling for a few moments before answering. "He didn't ravage you when he had the chance. Know why? He's 98 percent plastic. He doesn't have the working parts."

"Not to mention, he's full of himself." Xiu was getting bored. "As is Bob by the sound of it. Can we change the subject?"

Yes, Hildy thought, but Max said, "I find his twelve-minutes-on-such-and-such-a-date comment oddly intriguing. What do you think that's all about?"

Xiu smiled sadly at Hildy, then began fishing in her purse for her makeup bag. "Obviously something sexual. Again, *so* not the guy for you."

Hildy thought of the look on Bob's face. She knew he wasn't talking about something sexual. This was something serious. But she wasn't going to tell them that.

"Normally, I'd find it semi-offensive that you think anything sexual would be so wrong for me, but luckily in this case it just proves my point. I'm done."

Xiu shrugged and put on the deep burgundy lipstick she'd recently started wearing. "You're done with *him*. Which is great. Now you don't have to explain the teardrop tattoo to your parents. Amy would not have been cool with that."

Max put his arm around the back of Hildy's chair and leaned in close. "You'll get over this. I was a mess with the first guy who made me feel that way, too."

"*You* were the first guy who made me feel that way, Max."

Xiu squawked. "Ooh. Burn!" She kissed the extra lipstick off onto her napkin. "If you hadn't wanted to experiment with heterosexuality, Hildy never would have . . . Oh my god. Sweet Baby James. On the move."

The busker had picked up his guitar case and was coming inside. Xiu snapped her earrings back on, air-kissed her friends, then beetled off to a strategic spot by the counter.

Max called out after her, "Don't forget: party tonight. Rendezvous at ten." She waved at him either like "Yeah, I know," or "I'm not interested." Sweet Baby James got in line behind her and started blowing on his fingers to warm up. She turned toward him and smiled.

Hildy watched Xiu move in on her prey and shuddered. "Even the thought of doing that again makes me feel slightly queasy."

Max's mouth was full with the remains of Xiu's croissant.

"That's like waking up with a hangover and swearing you're never going to drink again. Everybody says it. Nobody means it."

"I do. I wonder if I'm asexual."

Max gave a big phony bark of a laugh. "You aren't. I have proof."

"You mean, us? That doesn't count. We barely got past shirts-off."

"Not talking about us, although you were quite enthusiastic as I recall."

"More enthusiastic than you."

"Well, we know there was a reason for that now, don't we?"

"So what's your proof then?"

He fished his phone out of his pocket and read the text. "Quote: 'I think I'm finally ready to move past spooning' by which you clearly meant ready to advance to big-girl sex to which I replied, 'Mazel tov,' and I meant it."

"I wasn't thinking straight."

"This is not about thinking, Hildy. Once again, you have to try to aim a little lower."

"Can we get out of here?" she said, and got up. She hated having her words thrown back at her. For a while there, she'd been so sure she'd figured this out.

She had to go to the fish store, so Max tagged along. She could tell he had something on his mind.

"Okay, Hildy," he said, once they'd settled into a seat near the back of the bus. "Hit me." He turned his face toward her and smacked his cheek. "Right here. Best you got. C'mon."

"No." This wasn't what she'd expected. She didn't feel like joking around.

"I want you to hit me."

"No. Why?"

"'Cause I'm a prick."

"True. So what?" She looked out the window and thought about Bob. She clearly had a thing for pricks.

"I didn't realize until now how bad I'd made you feel about yourself."

"That's because you're a prick. See above."

"What can I say? Sixteen-year-old boys are assholes anyway and I was confused. You were so cute and fun and smart I thought you'd be able to banish all those fantasies of half-naked lacrosse players dancing in my head. I loved you. You know I did. You know I *do*." He nuzzled her neck but she pushed him away. "But I was using you, too. I get that now. Sorry I was such a douchewad."

She turned and looked at him. "And now you want me to punch you in the face so we can call it even."

"Yeah. Deal?"

"No." She remembered Bob making fun of her upper arm strength. "One punch from scrawny little me. You call that even? You deserve way worse than that."

"Yeah. I do."

"A lifetime of punishment, that's what you deserve. And I'm damn well going to make sure you get it."

"Pinky swear?"

"Yup."

"That's my girl."

He kissed her forehead. She leaned into the crook of his arm. They rode like that for a while and then Hildy said, "Ever feel like a complete screwup?"

"Yeah. Daily. But I also shit daily. In both cases, I flush, wash my hands, and blame the stink on the last guy."

Hildy didn't laugh.

Max took the elastic out of her hair and started rebraiding it. "Fine. What have you gone and screwed up now, or are we still on Bob?"

She sighed. She knew he wasn't going to like it but if she couldn't tell Max, who could she tell? "No. But I feel like I'm doing the same thing to everyone."

"Doing what to everyone?"

"Not throwing stuff at them maybe but chasing them away. Alienating them. You know. Messing up their lives."

"Is this part of your whole 'lifetime of punishment' thing? Just punch me in the face, would you? *Have mercy.*"

"I'm serious. I feel like I'm ruining things."

Max wrapped Hildy's braid around her neck and pretended to strangle her.

"I mean it," she said, and flicked it back over her shoulder.

"Okay. Who exactly have you chased away? I'm only asking to humor you, of course." He put the elastic in her hair and patted everything into place.

"Iris."

"Please. You're why she didn't show up today? She never shows up anymore. She's with the costume design people. She's got a new group of friends and I, for one, am okay with that. I've heard enough about whalebone corsets and French seams for one lifetime. And coming from me, that's saying something."

"She's moved on because I opened my big mouth and mentioned us going to the Thai restaurant while she was . . ."

"Aargh. She was away! We have to go into hibernation until she's available? Frankly, if she's not coming because of something you said, I owe you. Bus driver! Next ride's on me! Okay. Who else?"

"Evan."

"We did Evan already. He's a moron whose only possible appeal is that he rejected you. Why even worry about him? He's at college. Forget about him."

"Dad and Gabe—"

"Stop." Max turned to face her. His parka squeaked against the seat. "I mean it. Enough. You had nothing to do with that."

"I did."

"No. You didn't. You know what? In your own quiet way, you're kind of a megalomaniac. You think you control the world or something? This may come as a shock but you have no power over how your father reacts to your brother. Or anyone else for that matter. Get over it."

"But if I hadn't shown him that picture, they'd—"

"The picture. That was taken two months ago. And Gabe is what? Twelve? Twelve and a half? The problem started *at least* thirteen years ago. Not by you. By your mother. And maybe your father—but definitely not by you."

"I know that. I mean, I sort of know that, but what is it that compels me to, I don't know, blurt things out? . . . It's like I'm this, this, liaison to disaster or something."

"Liaison to Disaster. Isn't that a brand of skateboard apparel? Why, yes, I believe it is."

"I'm the common denominator. It's as if bad things happen merely because I'm there."

"You're a jinx. That's what you're saying. A megalomaniacal jinx."

"You make it sound like I'm just being superstitious and—"

"Jinx Sangster. Btdubs, excellent stripper name, should the occasion arise, but totally inaccurate."

Max pulled the cord for their stop and dragged her off the seat.

"Nothing *compels* you to blurt things out. It's not like you've got some particularly vicious form of Tourette Syndrome. A bubble came up on your computer. You read what was written therein. That's not leaking government secrets to ISIS. That's reading aloud—which I've always thought of as one of the Sangster family's quainter traditions."

They got off the bus.

"But why? Why would I do that?"

Max grabbed her shoulder and snarled at her. "Because any-one would. Difference is, other people would feel bad for a while in an *oops silly me* kind of way. You, on the other hand, soak up all the guilt in any given situation. I wish you'd stop. The slurping sound is positively deafening plus—I hate to say this, sweetheart—it's giving you a bit of a tummy. Such a pretty girl but positively bloated with guilt."

Hildy liked it when Max put his arm around her even when he was telling her off. He was tall and strong and smelled sort of cin-namony. He was also always the exact right temperature and she was always cold.

"Know what? You're not Jinx Sangster. You're Sponge Sang-ster which, btdubs part two, is a terrible stripper name. No one's going to pay to see someone called Sponge take off her clothes . . . Just thought I should mention that before you got any ideas."

Hildy laughed because it was funny and also because she was worn out. Max got a hot dog from a sidewalk vendor and they walked to the fish store.

H2Eau Aquarium Supplies was tucked between a new Ethio-pian restaurant and an old paint store. It was tiny and full of fish tanks and everything had a kind of eerie turquoise glow. They went inside. Max took a bunch of selfies with one eye pressed against an aquarium and various cartoony fish seeming to swim into it.

Hildy talked to Barry the owner. He made her slightly uncom-fortable. He was always a tad too happy to see her. When Gabe had still needed a babysitter, she'd been in the store all the time despite having absolutely no interest in fish. Gabe could never wait until their father finished work to go there.

Barry asked how Gabe liked his King Kong. Hildy avoided the question and told him she was here to buy another one.

"'Fraid you're out of luck there, missy. That was my last one. I'm having a pile of trouble getting them in these days." He hefted himself off his stool and squeezed around the counter. "Closest thing I've got is this little varmint."

He led her to a tank near the front. Hildy could see it wasn't the same thing. Even if she hadn't seen the difference, it wouldn't have mattered. Gabe wanted a King Kong puffer fish and nothing else. Her dad and Gabe had talked about getting one for years.

Her dad and Gabe had talked.

That used to seem so normal.

She shook her head and dredged up some kind of smile.

"I'll put you on the waiting list. Best I can do."

Max called her over to the other side of the store to see what he claimed were guppies in love. He read the look on her face immediately.

"Disappointed. I get it. But this is not your problem to fix— even if a hundred-and-twenty-dollar fish could do it, which it can't. It would have cheered Gabe up for a little while, but then what? He and your dad would be back to square one and none of your singing or dancing or flinging money around would be able to do anything about it."

Hildy couldn't even disagree because she knew none of her arguments made sense in the way people expect arguments to. She decided it was better to just keep her mouth shut and quietly nurse them to strength. She was going to get another King Kong for Gabe no matter what anyone said. It would make him happy in that pure way of his, and her father would see that and he'd succumb. He'd stop all this nonsense. He'd be the man he was supposed to be.

Hildy wanted to get out of H2Eau but Max coaxed her into sitting on the floor and watching the drama unfolding in the guppy tank.

Fish are actually pretty boring just doing fish things, but Max put on a *Planet Earth* voice and provided narration. It started off as a slightly warped nature documentary, then morphed into a kind of cross between *The Little Mermaid* and *Orphan Black*. Hildy allowed herself to become distracted until a plot twist involving a mysterious angelfish brought her back to Bob.

"I think I was drawn to him because we both have a secret."

"I think you were drawn to him because he's hot. Everyone has a secret. Not everyone is hot."

Max waited until Barry went into the back office before tapping the aquarium tank and agitating the fish.

"And I know that's hard to ignore, but here's the truth, Hildy. None of us guys is good enough for you—especially not Neanderbob. You deserve someone who's kind and creative and super hot."

"And straight."

"Yeah, that too. Now shut up for a while and watch. We could all learn something from tropical fish. They're utterly useless and yet content."

"Be still and find your inner guppy."

"Yeah. Basically."

Hildy shut up. After a while her ass hurt and Max had to pick up his skates at the sharpener's so they left. He took the long way to the rink so he could stay on the bus and badger her into going to some stupid party with him that night, but then her stop came up and Hildy had to get off and go home alone.

CHAPTER 4

Hildy's parents were in the kitchen talking when she got in. They were slim and blondish and almost the exact same height. People always said they were made for each other.

Her father was at the stove, his back to Hildy. Her mother was standing with her hands flipped out to the side as if she was acting out "WTF" in charades.

They stopped talking as soon as Hildy walked in the back door. They did that a lot these days.

"You're early." Her dad tried to make that sound like a good thing. His name was Greg but her friends always referred to him as Gregoire or occasionally Gregorinko. (He was their principal, and some of them had him for drama, too. They knew him well. He was simply not a Greg.)

"No. Didn't I say I'd be home by six? What are you making?"

"Vindaloo."

Hildy looked at her mother who turned and straightened the cookbook shelf. Gabe hated spicy food.

"Smells good," she said because to say otherwise would be to open a can of worms. "When will it be ready?"

"Forty-five minutes or so." Greg threw something into the

pot. "I started later than intended."

"How was your day, honey?" Amy glanced her way. She had the same small eyes as Hildy. When she smiled, even a little, they disappeared.

"Good." Hildy toed off her boots and put her coat on a hook. "I got some stuff done, went to the market, hung out. Nothing much."

Amy acted more interested than the non-answer deserved. Greg leaned his back against the counter. A long yellow booger of curry rolled down his black apron. He took a sip of wine. He usually went cold turkey between Christmas and Easter, just to prove that he could.

"Gabe around?"

Greg turned back to stirring the vindaloo.

"Haven't seen him," Amy said. "Owen got a drone for his birthday. My guess is they're doing something with that. Peering into people's windows. Scaring old ladies. That kind of stuff." She gave a little laugh. Greg started chopping the cilantro.

Gabe wasn't the type to scare old ladies but again Hildy didn't say anything. She didn't ask how her parents spent their day, either. She got herself a glass of water, looked in the pot, then moved some letters around on the magnetic scrabble board stuck to the fridge.

Awkward small talk followed with weirdly stiff body language and only fleeting eye contact. Hildy took the first opportunity to slip off to her room.

She thought she'd read a bit more *Brideshead Revisited* or perhaps practice calligraphy from the art deco book Xiu had lent her, but it dawned on her that these might be some of the stereotypical things Bob accused people like her of doing, so she didn't. She opened her laptop, put on her headphones, and mindlessly scrolled through her social media feed.

When Hildy went downstairs an hour later, the vindaloo was

simmering on the stove but her parents were out.

Hopefully together.

Hopefully talking.

Hopefully screaming at each other, if that's what it took.

There was a note on the table in her mother's handwriting saying Gabe was sleeping over at Owen's. Her father had added, "Help yourself to curry but be careful." He'd drawn three little fires beside it. Neither said when they'd be back.

Hildy took it off the stove and put it in the fridge. She couldn't eat. Maybe they'd get some food on the way to the party Max was making them go to.

CHAPTER

5

Max had neglected to mention that the party he'd badgered them into going to was a fund-raiser for the university drama department. Hildy wasn't keen on going back there so soon after the Bob fiasco, but she also wasn't keen on staying home.

The party was being held in one of the big old houses on the outskirts of campus that used to be mansions but were now slummishly cool frat houses. The walls were already pulsing by the time they arrived at eleven.

They stepped into the massive foyer and Max was immediately sucked into the adoring crowd.

"He spends every waking moment with us." Xiu shook her head. "How could he possibly know all these people?" Hildy shrugged. She was always impressed by how he'd managed to parlay his special brand of weirdness into instant popularity even among the hockey players and the nursing students and the millionaires-by-thirty crowd.

"How long before he takes his shirt off and/or starts juggling?" Xiu adjusted the massive shoulder pads on her silver jumpsuit. "I don't know why he insists we come out with him. It's not like he needs the emotional support."

They pushed their way through what must have once been the parlor and found a spot to sit on a windowsill. Xiu had a thing about always having to be near an exit. She believed she'd picked it up subconsciously during her time as a baby in a crowded Chinese orphanage. Hildy thought it more likely had something to do with wanting to make a quick getaway if things got boring.

They scanned the crowd for people they knew—a few nodding acquaintances, some kids who'd graduated a couple of years before them—then Xiu said, "Ooh. Fabulous. They're selling swamp juice at the bar. Want one?"

Hildy wasn't a big drinker of cocktails spiked with 100-proof medicinal alcohol, but a cup would at least give her something to do with her hands.

"Sure." She gave Xiu the purse. They only ever brought one purse when they went out, in case they felt like dancing. Less to keep track of.

Xiu mouthed, *Don't move,* then hobbled off through the crowd in her six-inch platforms.

Hildy wasn't going anywhere. She semi-liked it here. The party was noisy enough that she wouldn't have to talk to anyone and she really didn't want to talk to anyone at the moment. She didn't want to think, either, and it was good for that, too.

She leaned against the windowsill and people-watched. This was mostly a torn-jeans-and-ponytail-type crowd but there were a few outliers, wardrobe-wise, even by Xiu's standards. One girl in particular—black bustier, ass-cheek-grazing skirt, fishnet stockings—stood out. It wasn't until a large group of drunken Roman soldiers surged in that Hildy realized the girl was in costume.

Fund-raiser, she remembered. *Drama department.* Hildy suddenly felt slightly ill.

She looked around the room.

They were all rolling in now. There was a guy in green

pantaloons and a frilly Shakespearean collar. Little Red Riding Hood, Rapunzel, and most of the female cast from *Into the Woods* were grinding in a decidedly un-fairy-tale-like way. Xiu was at the bar playing with the mane of a guy with a bare chest and a horse's head. Hildy didn't expect to get her drink anytime soon.

She looked up at the ornate plaster moldings and watched little squares of light from the disco ball flick across the ceiling. She wondered if Bob liked to dance.

She was trying—and failing—to picture him getting down when she noticed a guy in a wide-shouldered suit and fedora coming toward her. *Guys and Dolls,* she thought.

"Hildy!" he said.

Oh god, she thought. *No.* How could she have been so stupid?

"Evan," she said. She managed a small exclamation point of a smile but it came too late to be convincing. She had no makeup on. Her clothes were dirty. She hadn't even brushed her teeth. Why now?

A dancing girl in a college hoodie rammed into Evan from behind. He lunged at Hildy, arms out. Their faces clunked together, his front tooth to her left cheek. They both went, "Ow!" then Evan said, "Thus from my lips, by yours, my sin is purged."

It took her a second to get it. She laughed. "Then have my lips the sin . . . damn. How does it go?"

"Hmm. Something about temptation maybe?" Evan scratched his head like a hammy silent movie star. "Can't remember. God. How long ago did we do *Romeo and Juliet,* anyway?" He shook his head. "Doesn't matter. I'm so glad to see you! C'mere!" He gave her a real hug this time, then held her out at arm's length. "You look great!"

He pushed his fedora off his forehead with an index finger and beamed at her. *Evan Keefe and his megawatt smile!!!!* That's how Max always referred to him, but that was mostly just to protect Hildy. (He'd started calling Evan that after the non-ravaging incident.)

It didn't work. Hildy liked Evan's smile.

"You too. Love the zoot suit."

"I know. I'm mad gangsta." He crossed his arms and raised his fingers in that hip-hop way.

Xiu would have gagged but Hildy didn't care. She laughed. This was exactly what she loved about Evan. His no-holds-barred dorkiness.

"I can't believe it's been so long!" He looked into her eyes like he was searching her soul. It was one of his shticks. She fell for it every time. "All the time we spent together in high school, and now I never see you. What play are you doing this term?"

"Don't know yet. Find out this week."

Evan sat down in Xiu's place on the windowsill. He seemed taller sitting (and, weirdly, too, onstage. Hildy had never thought of him as short). His face was a dizzying mix of grown-up (heavy whiskers and eyebrows) and kid (lashes and sparkly parts). She looked away.

"God, I miss you! Best leading lady *ever*." He'd stopped screaming and taken off his fedora so he could speak right into her ear. "You know how brilliant I think you are? When we did *Grease*, your Sandy was . . . hmm . . . Can I say brilliant again? No, I cannot. That would be boring and Hildy Sangster does not do boring . . . It was, like, innocent and real and . . . and I know the word I'm looking for! Sexy. Innocent and sexy. No wonder Danny fell for her."

He slicked his hair back with his hands like he'd done when he was Danny. Pretended to chew gum. Winked at her.

He didn't seem the least bit embarrassed. Had he totally forgotten what had happened?

Or had she just misread it?

Hildy considered the possibility that, all this time, she'd been torturing herself for nothing. A huge weight lifted.

"Yeah," she said. "And no wonder Sandy fell for Danny." She winked back.

Evan leaned his shoulder into hers, nudging her into the windowsill.

"Ah. Good times. Nothing like the *thee-ah-tah* to arouse passions . . . Speaking of which." He pulled a roll of tickets out of his pocket. "Can I interest you in our fifty/fifty draw? One ticket for three dollars or two for five."

She laughed again. Evan. Always an angle. "Sorry. Xiu's got the purse. I'll buy a couple tickets when she comes back."

"Xiu's here too? Wow. And I saw Max. I mean, how could I miss him? God. It's like a high school drama reunion or something. Mr. Sangster would be so proud . . . Hey. How is he, anyway? I keep meaning to drop by."

A bunch of people whooped, then the music got even louder and the dancing kicked up a notch.

Hildy looked at Evan and considered telling him. She'd told him a lot over the years, although always using words someone else had written.

Which didn't necessarily make them any less true.

"Oh," he said. "Oh no. There something wrong? Did something happen to him?" Evan looked genuinely concerned.

Later, Hildy would be able to pull apart the various thoughts and emotions that had rushed through her head in the seconds that followed, but at the time they weren't clear. There was some jealousy toward Xiu and Max and their newfound sex lives. Wounded pride after the thing with Bob. The revelation that she may have misread things. That liquid feeling she always got looking into Evan's clear brown eyes. She'd probably never really know what the deciding factor had been.

Whatever.

Hildy took a breath, cupped Evan's head in her hands and kissed him right on the mouth.

His lips were soft and scratchy around the edge, but not at all willing.

He held her by the arms and gently pushed her back. "Oh. No. Hildy." He left a large parking space of regret between each word.

She stood up. He stood up. Hildy would have bolted right then, but people were dancing practically on top of them.

"Sorry," he said.

She said, "No, no," as if he'd accidentally stepped on her foot.

Someone went, "Why, Sky Masterson!" and next thing there was a hand on his shoulder and a tall pretty girl squeezing through the crowd toward them. She was dressed in a skin-tight Salvation Army uniform. He put his arm around her and kissed her cheek and then, if that wasn't enough to make his point crystal clear, he said, "Hildy, this is my girlfriend, Julia Ogurundi." He turned to Julia. "I told you about Hildy. She played Sister Sarah in our high school production?"

Julia smiled and twinkled and touched Hildy's arm, then recounted all the fabulous things Evan had said about Hildy and her dad and his "world-class" drama productions. Hildy had to endure talk of her high school triumphs for a good two to three minutes before a space cleared and she could escape.

Xiu saw her leaving and tried to wave her over. Hildy pretended she didn't notice. Max was on the dining room table, half-naked, juggling centurions' helmets, so he didn't see her go.

Hildy walked home alone in the dark.

CHAPTER

6

That night was endless. Hildy finally fell asleep when the sky began to lighten. She lurched awake hours later to the sound of something smashing.

Her heart sped up. Her eyes skittered around the room. She didn't know where she was or what was happening.

A door slammed and then another.

She grabbed her phone, and blinked her vision into focus. 11:19. Sunday. She ignored the multiple texts from Xiu and Max and scrambled downstairs.

There was a broken plate on the kitchen floor with the remains of someone's breakfast sprayed around it.

She heard a car squeal and ran over to the living room window just in time to see her mother's Prius disappear down the street. Her father was standing in the driveway, with his jacket half on and his boots untied. He threw his hat on the snow and started kicking the fender of his car like some gang member teaching an informer a lesson.

Hildy rapped on the window. He turned to look. She raised her hands like *What's going on?* He got in the car as if he hadn't seen her, and screeched off, too.

Hildy stood there staring until her breath had fogged up the window, and her skinny bare arms were covered in goose bumps.

This was really happening.

She got a wad of paper towels and cleaned up the mess on the floor. She didn't want Gabe seeing it. She wondered how much he knew or, more important, if he'd ever forgive her when he found out. She hid the plate in the bottom of the garbage bin and realized that she was humming her grandmother's song again, the one about how there was going to be love and laughter when the war ended.

Not this little war.

She got a yogurt out of the fridge, but only because she knew she'd feel even worse if she didn't eat, and then she went upstairs. She flopped onto her bed. Alec should be informed about what was happening. She'd hesitated telling him until now because she wasn't exactly sure what there was to tell—still wasn't, although less so—and, besides, she never knew how things would go with her big brother. Once he found out, he'd either take it upon himself to save the day or blow things up sky-high. She had to take her chances. She couldn't put it off any longer. She turned on her laptop to Skype him.

Alec wasn't online—no doubt the pubs in Dublin were open by now—but someone else was.

A Facebook alert popped up. It was from "Bob Someone." No profile picture, just a little gray icon.

Hildy's yogurt fell on the floor and splashed over the carpet.

BOB SOMEONE: If u ever want to see ur fish alive again u must answer the following 22 questions

She forgot about Alec, her parents, Gabe, Evan, the sad music of their life. She bit her lip and smiled.

HILDY: How did you find me?

BOB SOMEONE: Told u I'm clever

HILDY: No. Seriously. How?

BOB SOMEONE: Last name starts with S. Mother the head of ER. Father principal at arts high school. Not that hard. Got to <3 Facebook. btw nice jr prom pictures

Hildy's fingers hovered over the keyboard. There was a joke she could make about her fuchsia dress, her overdone updo, her braces.

She slapped her laptop closed. She got a dirty towel out of her hamper and began scrubbing up the yogurt on the carpet.

She was through with guys. It had been less than twelve hours since her last romantic disaster. She was not going to respond.

She heard the ping of another message.

She thought of Evan and his look of horror—or was it pity?—when he'd pushed her away. She was never going to put herself in that position again.

And then another stupid ping.

She threw the towel back in the hamper and opened the laptop.

BOB SOMEONE: Told u pink was ur color

BOB SOMEONE: Am I allowed to say that?

This was just messaging. It wasn't like he was in the room with her. What harm was there to it? It's not like she could throw anything at him from here.

Not even herself.

It would be weirder if she didn't answer.

HILDY: I'm trying not to find this creepy.

BOB SOMEONE: What? that was a compliment

HILDY: I mean you tracking me down like this.

BOB SOMEONE: Now u know how Evan feels

Her heart thumped like it had been dropped off a tall building.
Had Bob been at the party?
Had he seen her?
No. He couldn't have been there. She would have sensed him.
(She was sure of that.)

BOB SOMEONE: That was a joke

It's just improv, she thought.
Relax.
Run with it.

HILDY: WHY did you find me?

BOB SOMEONE: Didn't want to forfit my $40

HILDY: *forfeit

BOB SOMEONE: that's what autocorrect said but didn't look right

HILDY: How do I know the fish is even alive still? You might just be some internet scammer. I want to see the fish before I agree to anything.

BOB SOMEONE: Figured u'd say that

BOB SOMEONE:

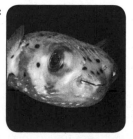

BOB SOMEONE: As u can see hes resting comfortably

HILDY: OMG. I'm actually kind of crying.

BOB SOMEONE: Not just *spillage?

Hildy: Tears of joy

BOB SOMEONE: ur going to be balling ur eyes out when u see what Kong asked me to send u

Hildy: What?

BOB SOMEONE:

Betty,
— Thank you,
I always wanted
to fly.
XOXOX Kong

HILDY: Who's the weirdo in the background?

BOB SOMEONE: The target

HILDY: Was he injured in the attack?

BOB SOMEONE: Shoulda been

HILDY: That sounds almost like *sorry.

BOB SOMEONE: Bad connection can't hear u lines breaking up

HILDY: When do I get my fish?

BOB SOMEONE: When u answer the rest of the questions

HILDY: That's blackmail.

BOB SOMEONE: Better than assault. No animals were harmed in the making of this message

HILDY: How do I know you're not dangerous?

BOB SOMEONE: Wasn't me who thru the fish

HILDY: Not that kind of dangerous. I'm not sure I want to be alone in a room with you again.

BOB SOMEONE: Can't trust urself?

BOB SOMEONE: Hello?

HILDY: Thinking . . .

BOB SOMEONE: About what?

HILDY: What I should do.

BOB SOMEONE: Rescue ur fish. He misses u

HILDY: I have to go.

BOB SOMEONE: Now?!

HILDY: I have to go to brunch.

BOB SOMEONE: Talk later?

HILDY: I don't know.

BOB SOMEONE: I can't guarantee Kong's safety

HILDY: I shouldn't be giving in to a criminal but ok. 1:30

BOB SOMEONE: 👍

CHAPTER

Hildy put on her wireless headphones, cranked up a Taylor Swift video, and started dancing. Sort of because she was happy, but mostly because she was scared and needed to shake it off.

She'd *just* given up guys for good—but first Evan and now this? She felt like a zombie in one of those cheesy black-and-white horror movies Max was always dragging them to. A body completely controlled by otherworldly forces. The only difference was that in Hildy's case her heart was still beating.

Still wildly beating.

She wondered if her mother had felt this way too—terrified but compelled.

Ew. Shake that one off fast.

She kicked the ottoman out of the way and let loose. Hips. Arms. Legs. Attitude. It was going to be all right.

Damn right it was.

Bob wanted her. He was the one who'd gotten in touch with Hildy, not the other way around.

Of course, she'd inadvertently given him lots of clues. Her parents' professions. Her last initial. Both her brothers' names. God. What would Dr. Freud have had to say about *that*? This was way worse than accidently walking off with Prince Charming.

She didn't care. She kicked her leg up as high as it would go and slipped on the rug, landed on her ass. Laughed. Big deal. Happens to everyone.

She got back up on her feet in time to do the *Swan Lake* bit along with Taylor.

Paul. That was the only identifying trait she'd gotten from him. Oh, and an unnamed inner-city school from which he hadn't graduated. Not that that was very helpful. She doubted Bob was the type to show up for picture day.

She slapped her hands over her face, let loose a silent scream.

He knew her real name. He could see it all.

She realized how many photos of her were floating around online. (*She'd* never missed picture day, that's for sure.) She'd kept meaning to fix her privacy settings on Facebook but she never used it anymore so she hadn't bothered. Paul just needed to key in her name to see the hundreds of profile pictures she'd posted of herself singing in high school musicals, winning debate awards, trying out unfortunate new fashions, exposing the true Hildy.

Before contacts.

During braces.

Throughout the whole painfully oblivious nerdiness of her extended adolescence.

He must be laughing his face off.

On the laptop screen, Taylor was still dancing away, undeterred, in that dorky red hoodie and black pleather pants.

So what? Those profile pictures were funny. Everyone had pictures like that. Hildy started dancing again, too. She even crouched down and attempted to twerk. She couldn't figure out how to make her hips work that way but she sure as hell tried.

There was a loud retching noise. Hildy jumped up, then slowly turned around.

Gabe was in the doorway making puking faces. She slipped her headphones onto her neck.

"That was so bad. Like, SO bad." He shuddered. "I'm seriously scarred for life."

"Serves you right. Sneaking up on me like that."

"Sneaking up on you? I've been screaming for, like, hours."

"Hours. Minutes more like."

"Ever since I got back from Owen's. Where is everybody?"

"Oh, you know." She wiped the sweat off her face into the crook of her elbow. "Out."

Gabe picked the half-empty Chobani container off her desk and started scooping yogurt up with his finger. "So who's going to drive me to basketball then? Dad's the one always going nuts about being on time, but I guess it's okay for *him* to be late. He didn't even feed the fish today. So much for being Mr. Responsible."

"Did you try his phone?"

"I'm not an idiot. I tried everyone's phone, even yours. Nobody picked up."

Hildy checked the time on her laptop. Gabe had to be at the gym in half an hour. Who knew when/if her parents would be home? "Oh, right. I forgot. There was something Mom and Dad had to do. You'll have to take the bus. Just let me get dressed and I'll walk you to the stop."

"I'm going to be thirteen in June. I don't need you walking me to the stupid bus stop!" He stormed out and slammed the door. She tried to pretend it was just puberty.

A few minutes later, she heard the front door squeak open and saw Gabe step out. He had his gym bag but no mittens or hat.

She opened the window. "See if the Fitzgibbons can drive you home."

He went, "I know!" without bothering to look at her. She watched him schlep down the street. Things didn't seem like they were going to be all right anymore but she didn't know what she could do about it.

She could hear the tinny sound of Taylor Swift still coming out of her headphones. Her parents were gone. Gabe was gone. Bob was waiting for her. She put her headphones back on and made herself dance.

QUESTION 15

BOB SOMEONE: Hey how was brunch?

HILDY: Fabulous. You?

BOB SOMEONE: I don't do brunch u should no that by now

HILDY: Are you sure you really want to do this?

BOB SOMEONE: do what

HILDY: Answer these questions.

BOB SOMEONE: Yes I need the money. big macs don't buy themselves

HILDY: 22 questions for $40. That's not much.

BOB SOMEONE: Better than 14 for 0$

HILDY: I left my questions in the room.

BOB SOMEONE: I noticed u left in a bit of a rush. I got mine. Want to start?

HILDY: "Want" might not be the right word but go ahead.

BOB SOMEONE: "What is the greatest accomplishment of ur life?"

HILDY: Sorry. I'm going to stop you right there.

I just had a disturbing flashback. I can see what's going to happen. I'm going to do my best to respond thoughtfully to the questions and you're going to give stupid answers.

BOB SOMEONE: I knew this was too good to last & btw stupid doesn't mean wrong

HILDY: Dishonest then. I'm only going to do this if you promise to answer honestly from here on out.

BOB SOMEONE: I have your fish

HILDY: I can get another fish.

BOB SOMEONE: won't be easy. I checked. Jeff isn't just a happy meal expert, he knew a hole bunch about King Kong pufferfish too. he was the one who did the cpr

HILDY: You're doing it again. Honest answers. Yes or no? (And P.S. Whole, in this case, is spelled with a w.)

BOB SOMEONE: Do I only get to pick one? ps am I being marked for speling & puntuation

HILDY: I'm in the middle of a good book. I don't need this. (P.S. No, you aren't, which is lucky for you. You'd fail based on that one sentence alone.) Yes or no?

BOB SOMEONE:

113

HILDY: Thank you. Then I'll go first. My greatest accomplishment is forgiving my mother, at least to the extent that I've managed to forgive her.

BOB SOMEONE: For what? That car accident?

HILDY: No. For something else. Something she did on purpose. At least I presume she did on purpose.

BOB SOMEONE: Didn't you ask her

HILDY: No!

BOB SOMEONE: Not like you. How come

HILDY: There are some things a person's just better not knowing.

BOB SOMEONE: Who is this & what have you done with Betty?!?

HILDY: Right. Like you know me so well.

BOB SOMEONE: I've been studying the FB page of Hildy Sangster aka Dorthy in the wizard of oz, EkoGrrrrrl723, and capt of the unbeaten Citadel Senators debate team 😁 go champs! 😁 & no way ur her. She would want to know

HILDY: Maybe she knew without asking.

BOB SOMEONE: Deep

HILDY: I have to be honest too. Your turn.

HILDY: Strangely long pause. You were just bringing up all this garbage about my true identity as a way to avoid answering the question, weren't you?

HILDY: Should have known.

BOB SOMEONE: My greatest accomplishment is surviving

    HILDY: Meaning?

BOB SOMEONE: Me & Kong are 2 of a kind

    HILDY: You're both slippery and cold-blooded?

    HILDY: Sorry. That was uncalled for.

BOB SOMEONE: But true

    HILDY: I doubt it. Explain the survival thing to me. (And I promise I'll give your answer the respect it deserves.)

BOB SOMEONE: u being sarcastic?

    HILDY: No, I mean it. That was a cheap shot and this is a serious question.

BOB SOMEONE: A lot of pressure

    HILDY: ATQ

BOB SOMEONE: Kong and me both been thrown at a lot of walls but we keep picking ourselves up

    HILDY: That how you broke your nose?

BOB SOMEONE: u could say that

    HILDY: You could get it fixed, you know.

BOB SOMEONE: Who says I want it fixed?

HILDY: Oops. How rude of me.

BOB SOMEONE: I like my nose better now

HILDY: What did it look like before?

BOB SOMEONE: Different

HILDY: Show me.

BOB SOMEONE: No

HILDY: How come?

BOB SOMEONE: Looks have nothing to do with why I like it better

HILDY: Gee. You're not as shallow as you make out.

BOB SOMEONE: u mean as *U make out

HILDY: So why do you like it better now?

BOB SOMEONE: isn't it obvious?

HILDY: No.

BOB SOMEONE: I didn't want to be just another pretty face

HILDY: *sigh

BOB SOMEONE: ok. How about this? Its proof I survived

HILDY: Sort of like the Red Badge of Courage?

BOB SOMEONE: ???

HILDY: Sorry. I forgot you don't read. It's a book.

BOB SOMEONE:

HILDY: Is that what your tattoo's for too?

BOB SOMEONE: ur not making sense

HILDY: Is it proof you survived too?

BOB SOMEONE: No its for something else

HILDY: What?

BOB SOMEONE: Thats not one of the questions

HILDY: Fair

BOB SOMEONE: We're so civilized. Maybe we should have just been penpals

HILDY: Probably safer.

BOB SOMEONE: Kong nodded vigurosly

HILDY: 😄

QUESTION 16

BOB SOMEONE: "What do u value most in a friendship?"

BOB SOMEONE: Take ur time

BOB SOMEONE: Don't worry about me

BOB SOMEONE: I have nothing better to do

HILDY: I want to get this right.

BOB SOMEONE: Wake me when ur ready

HILDY: Perspective. I want my friends to share my perspective so that we find the same things funny and want to do the same things—BUT . . . I also want them to have a different perspective so they can analyze what I'm doing and help me make better decisions.

BOB SOMEONE: Not asking much. U interview people for friend positions? Be part of Team Hildy today!!! Email ur resume to the address below

HILDY: I don't but I probably should. I currently rely on trial and error.

BOB SOMEONE: That what happened to Iris?

HILDY: You have a very good memory.

BOB SOMEONE: No u should upgrade ur Facebook privacy settings

HILDY: You're starting to creep me out again. Are you stalking me?

BOB SOMEONE: A real stalker wouldn't tell

HILDY: Except the truly evil ones who throw you off the scent by pretending to help you.

BOB SOMEONE: I'm smart but not that smart & ps ur name & student # were on that paper u gave me to draw on. U really should be more careful

HILDY: What do you want from a friend?

BOB SOMEONE: Loyalty

HILDY: That all?

BOB SOMEONE: Pretty much altho I never turn down a free drink

    HILDY: That always been the case?

BOB SOMEONE: When I was little I preferred candy

    HILDY: You're doing that thing again. I mean, did you always value loyalty?

BOB SOMEONE: No. I had someone I was really close to back then so I didn't know I needed loyalty

    HILDY: Mysterious.

BOB SOMEONE: but truthful. just following the rules

    HILDY: Good boy

BOB SOMEONE: Can I change my answer?

    HILDY: You'll lose a point but ok.

BOB SOMEONE: Courage

    HILDY: More than loyalty?

BOB SOMEONE: Loyaltys no good if u aren't brave enuf to use it. Gun with no bullets

    HILDY: I sense hidden depths. Or did you see that on a bumper sticker somewhere?

BOB SOMEONE: Don't know why u keep saying there hidden. Once again I find u kind of rude

BOB SOMEONE: Hello?

HILDY: Ok. I admit the nose thing was rude and stupid too.

BOB SOMEONE: Stupid how come

HILDY: Because I actually find the bump kind of attractive.

BOB SOMEONE: Kind of?!?

HILDY: I was rude about the nose but you can't blame me for the hidden depths thing. You're the one who keeps doing the caveman routine.

BOB SOMEONE: not even going to ask what that is

HILDY: You're the one acting like you don't understand words and concepts when you clearly do.

BOB SOMEONE: Says who? Just cuz u came 5th in that national essay comp doesn't mean u know everything

HILDY: Lurking is rude.

BOB SOMEONE: Why did u post it if u don't want people to read it?

HILDY: My friends posted it.

BOB SOMEONE: Ever heard of delete?

HILDY: If I had a fish, I'd throw it at you.

BOB SOMEONE: Don't worry Kong. I won't let the bad lady get u. I think we answered this question.

QUESTION 17

BOB SOMEONE: "What is ur most treasured memory?"

HILDY: I don't like this kind of question.

BOB SOMEONE: Me neither

HILDY: How come?

BOB SOMEONE: Doesn't matter

HILDY: C'mon.

BOB SOMEONE: No

HILDY: Please? 😊

BOB SOMEONE: One more smiley face & I'm out of here. answer the question

HILDY: Then you'll answer it?

BOB SOMEONE: Yes 😊

HILDY: This is hard. A lot of my most treasured memories have been spoiled.

BOB SOMEONE: yeah memories spoil easy. worse than peaches

HILDY: More hidden depths.

BOB SOMEONE: just cut off the bad stuff and keep the rest

HILDY: Deeper and deeper.

BOB SOMEONE: Better than throwing it all out

HILDY: Easier with peaches. You can at least see where the rotten parts are.

BOB SOMEONE: now who's being all deep

HILDY: You were the one who started the peach metaphor. I'm just saying where it's wrong. I think it's more like a drop of poison in the Kool-Aid.

BOB SOMEONE: u have a dark side im not sure I like

HILDY: I just mean it's not as if there's a bruise you can cut out. Say you've been friends with someone for years then you find out they've been spreading nasty rumors about you. You don't think, "Oh, that was just one little blip in our relationship. It won't change all the wonderful times we've had together." That type of betrayal ruins everything.

BOB SOMEONE: u talking about Iris again?

HILDY: No. I just made that particular scenario up to avoid the pain of discussing the real ones.

BOB SOMEONE: ur learning

HILDY: You're an excellent teacher.

BOB SOMEONE: thank u. now answer the question. heres a tip. think peach not poison koolaid

HILDY: I feel as if the right answer would be something like seeing a child born or meeting the Dalai Lama but I don't know. Maybe I've missed out, but the thing that pops into my head—minus the obvious bruises, that is—is just this really normal nothing kind of thing.

BOB SOMEONE: I aint real good with fancy concepts being as I'm only a caveman n all but I don't think ur most treasured memory can be nothing. if its nothing it ain't no memory

HILDY: You know what I mean. My most treasured memory is something normal. Not climbing Everest or winning the Nobel Prize or anything like that.

BOB SOMEONE: Those are just ur hobbies

HILDY: 😄

BOB SOMEONE: So what is it then?

HILDY: It's really boring.

BOB SOMEONE: Thats ok I'm actually playing minecraft while we talk

HILDY: No need for me to be self-conscious then.

BOB SOMEONE: exactly so shoot

HILDY: Ok. This was maybe 8 or 9 years ago. We were at the beach. The sun was going down. Mom and Dad had built a fire. They were in those little short-legged lawn chairs, the ones that kind of look like corgis. They were laughing, probably having daiquiris from a thermos because they did that sometimes and we—the kids I mean—were still in our bathing suits but with hoodies over them now because it was cooling off. We were sandy and sort of burnt after being out all day. We were playing some stupid game with a deflated beach ball and I remember thinking: I'm happy. This is happy. I mean, I'd been happy before but this was the first time I'd ever recognized it. It was sort of like the first time I took a sip of beer and actually kind of understood why people liked it.

BOB SOMEONE: U don't look like the type of girl whod like beer

HILDY: What type of girl do I look like?

BOB SOMEONE: type whod like a green tea smoothie

HILDY: It's very flattering the way you seem to remember every word I said.

BOB SOMEONE: U think thats what Mandela dreamed about all those years in jail? Just 4237 days until my next green tea smoothie

HILDY: You're making fun of me again. And I, being the bigger person, am ignoring you again. What's your most treasured memory?

HILDY: Hello?!?

HILDY: Yoo-hoo!

BOB SOMEONE: Oh so u get time to think but I don't

HILDY: Sorry. I thought you'd run away.

BOB SOMEONE: considering it

BOB SOMEONE: My mother telling me I was hers

HILDY: Her most treasured memory?

BOB SOMEONE: No I mean like really *hers. Nothing could happen to me. I was hers

HILDY: That's sweet. How old were you?

BOB SOMEONE: Old enough to know it wasn't true

HILDY: I thought you said it was your most treasured memory.

BOB SOMEONE: It is. Doesn't matter she was wrong. She meant it. Unlike u I wasn't surprised she was human. I also know how to cut out the bruises

HILDY: We clearly both have mother issues.

BOB SOMEONE: Doesn't everyone? Do u know the poem by that Larkin guy that goes They fuck u up ur Mom & dad

HILDY: I thought you don't read.

BOB SOMEONE: I don't. My mother taught it to me

BOB SOMEONE: Or at least the first line

HILDY: Wow. Your mother and my mother have NOTHING in common.

BOB SOMEONE: Not true. Is ur mother Amy Dwyer-Sangster?

HILDY: Why are you asking? This is like Rumpelstiltskin. You clearly know the answer.

BOB SOMEONE: Trust me. They've got something in common

HILDY: What?

BOB SOMEONE: Kids with mother issues

HILDY: Agreed. What's your mother's name?

BOB SOMEONE: That's not one of the questions

HILDY: Not fair. How come you get to know everything about me and I don't know anything about you?

BOB SOMEONE: u should be more careful about what u post on social media

125

HILDY: I'm not joking.

BOB SOMEONE: Neither am I

QUESTION 18

BOB SOMEONE: "What is your most terrible memory?"

HILDY: Seriously?!

BOB SOMEONE: That's what it says

HILDY: Can we skip it?

BOB SOMEONE: ur the one agreed to answer all the questions honestly

HILDY: Okay, let's not skip it. Let's just answer it later.

BOB SOMEONE: Fine by me

QUESTION 19

BOB SOMEONE: "If you knew that in one year you would die suddenly, would you change anything about the way you are now living? Why?"

HILDY: These are terrible questions!!!!!! Are they all like that from here on out?

BOB SOMEONE: No

HILDY: Phew.

BOB SOMEONE: There worse. They get mushy after this

HILDY: Can we skip this one too?

BOB SOMEONE: No you only get one do-over

    HILDY: How come?

BOB SOMEONE: The umpires decision is final

    HILDY: In other words: your decision.

BOB SOMEONE: Someone needs to keep this thing from turning into a free for all

    HILDY: Why you?

BOB SOMEONE: cuz u weren't doing it. ATQ

    HILDY: Do I have to call you "sir" or "ump" or something?

BOB SOMEONE: No but u can if u like. Just ATQ

    HILDY: Ok. I'd stop thinking so much and just do stuff.

BOB SOMEONE: Thats easy

    HILDY: For you maybe.

BOB SOMEONE: For anyone. Ever heard of drugs & alcohol? Excellent if u ever want to stop thinking

    HILDY: I should have said "overthinking." I still want to have a functioning brain.

BOB SOMEONE: This got something to do with Evan Keefe?

    HILDY: Too late for that.

BOB SOMEONE: 2nd pt of question. why?

    HILDY: Trust me. Evan and I are done.

BOB SOMEONE: Hey don't try that shit on me. that's my shit. why would u want to stop thinking?

    HILDY: Overthinking. There's a difference. Because it keeps me from doing the things I want to do.

BOB SOMEONE: Such as

    HILDY: Telling people stuff.

BOB SOMEONE: like who? u sure didn't hold back with me

HILDY: That's where you're wrong.

BOB SOMEONE: scary thought. Who else u want to tell off?

HILDY: I didn't say tell off. I said tell people stuff.

BOB SOMEONE: Like?

HILDY: I'd tell Xiu to stop wearing dirndl skirts which I know isn't a big thing but they really aren't flattering on her and so many other styles would be. I'd tell Max to use some filters, at least in public, and to turn down the volume a bit. I'd tell Iris she hurt my feelings. Or maybe I wouldn't. As soon as I wrote that I imagined her saying, "Oh yeah? Well, you hurt my feelings too," and I really don't want to wade into that whole argument again especially since I'm probably kind of happier since we got some distance between us. I'd tell my grandmother I hate my name and want to change it.

BOB SOMEONE: To Betty?

HILDY: There's a thought.

BOB SOMEONE: I think ur lying

HILDY: I beg your pardon.

BOB SOMEONE: That's what you'd change if u had 1 year to live? tell your friend to wear a different skirt? & u call me shallow

HILDY: Ok. You're right.

BOB SOMEONE: Say that again

HILDY: You're right. I confess. I wasn't being honest.

BOB SOMEONE: So be honest

    HILDY: I'd tell Dad to grow up. I'd tell Mom how much she disappointed me.

BOB SOMEONE: Wow u want to die with everyone u love mad at u

    HILDY: Good point. Maybe that's not what I want either.

BOB SOMEONE: what DO u want betty? tell dr bob

    HILDY: I'm getting dangerously close to overthinking this too.

BOB SOMEONE: Just put ur hands on the keyboard & type

    HILDY: I'd stop obsessing about all the bad things that could happen if I do something and think about the good things that could happen instead. I want to be the type of person who leaps into things unafraid.

BOB SOMEONE: u go girl! Won't be long before ur having Evans baby

    HILDY: I thought you said he was gay.

BOB SOMEONE: so doesn't mean u can't have his baby. I noticed u never won any prizes in bio. Ever think of getting a tutor?

    HILDY: I'm just going to leave that alone. Your turn. What would you do?

BOB SOMEONE: I'd ask u what your doing Friday night

BOB SOMEONE: You still there?

HILDY: Why?

BOB SOMEONE: We could go out

HILDY: I don't think that's funny.

BOB SOMEONE: Not trying to be

HILDY: How BAD do you want the $40?

BOB SOMEONE: u think thats why I asked

HILDY: Then why?

BOB SOMEONE: Why?!?

HILDY: I seem to remember this is a two-part question so yes, why?

BOB SOMEONE: cuz I have ur fish & want u to take him off my hands. dam things eating me out of house & home

HILDY: Lame answer.

BOB SOMEONE: I called FedEx they don't ship live animals. I have to give him to u myself

HILDY: Even lamer. Real answer please.

BOB SOMEONE: The library is closing

HILDY: So?

BOB SOMEONE: I got to shut down

HILDY: *I've got to shut down. That's your worst answer yet.

BOB SOMEONE: Do u want to go out or not?

HILDY: I don't know

BOB SOMEONE: When will u?

HILDY: I'll tell you tomorrow.

BOB SOMEONE: Message at 7:30?

HILDY: It's a date.

BOB SOMEONE: hold on I didn't say that

HILDY: You drive me crazy.

CHAPTER

Hildy barely slept that night, either. Bob really was driving her crazy. She didn't know which part of her brain to listen to anymore.

She went down to the kitchen at four in the morning to warm herself up some milk. Her mother was sitting at the table, still in her scrubs.

"Oh, sorry, sweetheart. Did I wake you?" Amy closed her laptop. She had a drink beside her. It was the color of apple juice. Hildy was reasonably certain it wasn't juice.

"No. Couldn't sleep."

"Not like you." She folded her hands on the table and gave Hildy a concerned smile. "Anything you want to talk about?"

Hildy considered mentioning the Bob thing—but then noticed the look hovering behind her mother's eyes.

Fear.

Her mother was afraid Hildy was going to ask what was up with Dad and Gabe and the plate and the sudden end to anything resembling a family. Afraid she was going to have to explain.

It kind of freaked Hildy out, that look. She rattled around in the cupboard for the mug with the pigeon on it.

"It's in the dishwasher," her mother said. "So? Problem?"

"Nothing." The fact that her mother knew she was looking for her favorite mug without having to ask made her feel weirdly guilty. "Just on my period." Untrue and a subtle reference to Bob which, despite everything, gave her a happy little tickle in her stomach. Which made her feel even guiltier.

"Hormones." Amy took the elastic out of her ponytail and scratched her hair loose. She highlighted it to be exactly the same color as Hildy's. "They'll probably get better once you start having babies. Until then, a hot bath might help."

Hildy poured some milk and put it in the microwave. "You're working a lot lately."

"The ER's short-staffed. Kiley Nickerson's on maternity leave. Esther Cohen's mother is dying. That just leaves Steve Henderson, Rich Samuels, and me trying to cover all the shifts."

Hildy turned away. She didn't want to let on she suspected anything but still. Hearing her mother mention his name kind of shocked her.

Amy reached for her glass and knocked it over. She jumped up with her laptop in her arms. Hildy grabbed a paper towel and blotted at the mess. It definitely wasn't juice.

"Oh, well, shouldn't have been having a drink at this hour, anyway." Amy pulled a tea towel off the oven handle and started mopping up, too.

"Not like you," Hildy said.

"A lot of things not like me lately." She smiled apologetically, and Hildy almost said, "Anything you want to talk about?" but Amy cut her off at the pass.

"More stress being department head than I'd expected. The paperwork. And politics. Terrible."

They nodded. They both preferred the lie. They had a standing monthly lunch date at the art gallery café next Tuesday. Hildy decided she'd broach the subject then. If necessary. At this hour of the morning and with her own heart so full of Bob, she could almost believe this little thing with her parents would blow over.

She got her milk out of the microwave. She kissed her mother on the forehead and went upstairs for a bath. From the landing, she saw Amy open her laptop and pour herself another drink from a bottle under the table.

CHAPTER

9

The next day, Hildy drove Gabe and a couple of his friends to the pool after school, then went upstairs and hung out in the weight room with Max. She did that a lot. She'd put on some cozy workout wear, then sit on unused equipment and entertain him while he pumped iron. It was the perfect arrangement. She could honestly tell her mother she went to the gym, and Max had a distraction from the monotony.

He wanted to know what had happened with Evan the other night but Hildy just shrugged it off. "It got awkward once his girl-friend showed up."

"Girlfriend?!"

They bickered for a while about whether Evan had the emotional and physical capabilities to maintain a relationship. That seemed like a good sign to Hildy. Clearly, Max hadn't seen what had actually happened. She let him rant on for a while about Evan, then told him about her plans for getting together with Bob.

Max's jaw dropped. "Why, you vixen you!"

The guy on the leg press machine turned and looked. Hildy blew him a kiss, then said to Max, "You think I'm nuts."

"Yeah, but I've been wrong before. I mean, only this week,

I could have sworn you were asexual. And anyway, what difference does it make what I think?" He picked up some barbells and began his repetitions. "You're going to do it. I can see that. And as the parent figure in this relationship, I understand that sooner or later I've got to let my little birdie out of the nest—but can I give you some advice?"

"You're going to do it," she said. "I can see that."

"Don't meet up with him yet. Make him sweat a while. You know what Xiu says: 'Treat 'em mean to keep 'em keen.'"

"Like how mean?"

"How many questions you got left?"

"Seventeen. Eighteen. Something like that."

"String him along for nine or ten more. Make him hunger for you."

"One minute you're worried about me being alone with him. Now, you're saying deny the lion food until right before I throw myself into the den."

"No one likes to ravage on a full stomach. Take it from me."

He got out the big weights, lay on the bench, and made Hildy spot for him. She hated this part because she really wasn't strong enough to help if the barbell fell. She also didn't like the intense look he got on his face when he was lifting something that heavy. She was worried he could blow a blood vessel in his eye and she didn't want to be around to witness it.

"What if he doesn't wait? What if he just wanders away?"

"Do I even have to answer that?" Max let the weight fall back into its cradle. A vein on his neck throbbed rhythmically.

"Yes."

"Hildy. You don't want anyone who 'just wanders away.' This is a potential lover, not an Alzheimer's patient. If you dangle your fruit and he can't be bothered to—"

"Don't say 'dangle my fruit.' That's revolting."

"Okay. If he's not into you enough for a little flirtatious back-and-forth, he doesn't deserve you."

"But—"

"No but."

"He could—"

"Just no. Seriously. What are you? Boneless chicken that's past its best-before date? You don't have to mark yourself down for quick sale."

He wiped his hands on his shorts and gripped the weights again.

"I don't like being so passive."

"You're not being passive. You're actively ignoring him. It's a time-honored strategy."

"You know I'm going to throw this back at you, don't you? Next time, you're offering yourself up to some undeserving slob—"

"I don't do slobs, Hildy. Please."

He grunted and heaved his arms up. Hildy found the whole process disgusting.

Max let the weight bounce back down, then wiped the sweat off his face and armpits.

"You've got nice arms," she said.

"Yeah, I do. And my legs are pretty damn hot, too."

"Remind me not to compliment you again."

"Why?" He motioned for her to follow him over to another machine, then started moving toggles and levers around. "What's the matter with knowing I have nice arms? It's the truth. You should know the truth about you, too, and, more important, you should enjoy it."

"Okay. So what's my truth?"

He settled himself into the footrests. "Nice try, but no way I'm being the gay best friend, listing your good points for you. That's just so clichéd and, frankly, sad."

"Yeah, well, then who's going to? Straight guys haven't exactly been lining up to sing my praises."

"They have. You just haven't been listening. Which is no doubt a good thing."

"Why?"

"Because this is what would happen. They'd butter you up, your ego would soar, then they'd disappear and you'd think 'Oh no! I've been tricked into believing I'm actually a good, worthy, and adorable person when actually I'm not!' Then you'd hurl your little self off the Cliff of False Confidence. And who'd be expected to pick up your broken body and nurse you back to health? Me. No, thank you. If I'm going to be giving anybody a sponge bath, it's the guy in the green T-shirt at six o'clock. Now hand me that towel again."

Hildy picked it up with two fingers and gave it to him.

"Maybe I've been watching too many Disney features, Hildy, but I can't help thinking you need to find the truth within yourself. That's the only way you're going to believe it—and discover the strength to build your own beautiful ice castle in the sky! Don't let me say another thing until I've done seventy-five."

She took a couple of steps back so she wouldn't get sprayed with sweat, then helped him count. She kind of liked his idea about putting off meeting up with Bob for a while. She felt more in control online than in person.

Max finished his routine and wanted to take a sauna, so Hildy left him to it.

She went to the women's changing room and got into her bathing suit. (A cute faux-retro number with a halter top and a hint of a skirt.) She swam a couple of lazy laps until Gabe and his friends were ready to leave.

"What stinks?" Gabe said when they piled into the Volvo. "It's like parmesan cheese dog barf in here or something." While the boys riffed on that idea, Hildy found herself thinking about her father—his car never used to smell—and something Max had gasped out between repetitions:

"Problem with you Sangsters is you expect perfect. I never did. It just wasn't an option. You start liking boys in third grade? You know you're no Cossack's idea of the perfect son. Eighty percent of everything Dad's ever said to me involves either thermal units or ratchets, so he's not winning Father of the Year, either. And mother-daughter time round our place ain't much better. Mom and Katya can't be left alone together for more than five minutes without scratching each other's eyes out. But, weirdly, we're kind of happier than you guys. We're comfortable with the idea that we're screwups. Must be awful just figuring that out now."

She let a minivan pass, then pulled out of the parking lot. Max's little speech kind of bugged her. She found it so lazy. What if Nelson Mandela or Taylor Swift had let themselves think that way? They didn't just cave and let the white guys and/or bullies get their way.

Things could be fixed.

Her family could be fixed.

She looked into the rearview mirror. Gabe was rolling his eyes back, imitating his math teacher going nuts over a wrong answer. "Want to go to Cousin's for smoked meat? Maybe we can bring Dad back some of that German sausage he likes."

CHAPTER

▶────◀

10

There were a couple more notes on the kitchen table when they got home. Amy had been called in to the hospital to deal with a three-car pileup. Greg was at school catching up on some admin stuff. There was apparently plenty of vindaloo left over for supper if they wanted it.

"Just us for dinner again?" Gabe was only twelve and a half but was huge for his age, so Hildy sometimes forgot he was still technically a tween. She was just thinking how upsetting this might be for him when he pumped his fist in the air and went, "All right!"

It cracked her up. It's like what Principal Sangster always said: *Kids are resilient.*

Gabe was supposed to practice clarinet but she let him play some bizarre Korean video game instead while she made omelets. He never complained about omelets, especially if they were heavy on cheese and bacon and light on identifiable vegetable matter.

They ate them in front of the TV.

"Dad's busy a lot these days, huh?" She was poking around, trying to find out how Gabe was doing.

He shrugged. His hair was dark and so curly it stayed wet for hours. *Sponge Sangster*, she thought.

"He's being a jerk." Gabe had never said anything like that before.

"Why's that, you think?"

"How'm I supposed to know? His hemorrhoids acting up again or something. I dunno. He's always on my case."

"He's having a rough time. Cuts to the school budget. Mrs. Atkinson quitting like that. Vandalism. It's a lot to deal with."

"So he's got to ruin everybody else's life."

"Maybe if you just—"

"Maybe if you just shut up."

"Gabe."

He clanged his plate onto the coffee table and loped off. "I've got to feed the fish. Since I'm the only one who cares about them anymore."

"Gabe."

Did he know what was up? Hildy couldn't tell. He'd always been such a happy kid. Weird, but happy. Dad and him, in the shed or at the aquarium, with their various obsessions that no one else quite got.

She put the plates in the dishwasher, put the milk in the fridge, and headed to her room. As she walked down the hall, she saw Gabe sitting cross-legged on the living room floor, staring blankly into the fish tank. It kind of broke her heart.

She made herself do some yoga and tried to concentrate on her breathing. She was in no mood to talk to Bob again. It might be better if she just pretended to forget about their "date."

But then she saw his message come up, and of course she took it. She didn't even hesitate. The heart is a weird thing.

BOB SOMEONE: Hey

HILDY: Hi

BOB SOMEONE: So whats ur answer? u going out with me or what

HILDY: I'm not sure I'm ready to see you yet.

BOB SOMEONE: So we just forfeit the $40

Hildy: Nice spelling. And I said *yet.

BOB SOMEONE: meaning?

Hildy: That we do a few more questions online and I think about it.

BOB SOMEONE: *OVERthink about it

HILDY: Maybe.

BOB SOMEONE:

HILDY: Very funny.

BOB SOMEONE: so when are we going to do the questions?

HILDY: Ready when you are.

BOB SOMEONE: now?

HILDY: Yeah.

BOB SOMEONE: Ok # 20. "what does friendship mean to u?"

HILDY: Laughter. That's important.

HILDY: And a shoulder to cry on.

HILDY: Someone with whom to celebrate the good times.

BOB SOMEONE: With *whom

HILDY: Someone who doesn't bug me about the proper use of prepositional pronouns.

BOB SOMEONE: then I'm out

HILDY: Guess so.

HILDY: Someone who wants what's best for me.

HILDY: Someone to tell me the truth when I need to hear it.

BOB SOMEONE: u ever think of going into the greeting card business?

HILDY: Hey, you asked.

BOB SOMEONE: what happened to *a different perspective?

HILDY: Are you keeping notes? I feel like I'm in a courtroom drama. Anything I say can and will be used against me. Fine. Perspective too. So what does friendship mean to you?

BOB SOMEONE: a beer occasionally. someone I can hit up for money when necessary

HILDY: Ah. The amazing richness of male friendships.

BOB SOMEONE: thats not all. someone to shoot hoops with altho its getting harder & harder to find anyone to play these days. Kong made me stop

HILDY: You and your little imaginary friend.

BOB SOMEONE: best kinda friend. they never complain about the style of skirt Im wearing

HILDY: Haha

HILDY: I just realized something.

BOB SOMEONE: theres no point in doing the rest of the questions & u should just say yes?

> **HILDY:** Wrong. That you have the advantage. You had the questions all week. You could have rehearsed all your answers.

BOB SOMEONE: could have I suppose if I didn't have better things to do

> **HILDY:** Such as?

BOB SOMEONE: anything

> **HILDY:** 😊 How do you know Jeff is even going to pay you? Maybe the questions all had to be answered at the university.

BOB SOMEONE: u see anything that said that?

> **HILDY:** No.

BOB SOMEONE: me neither. he better pay me

> **HILDY:** Otherwise this would just be a waste of time.

BOB SOMEONE: no it wouldn't

> **HILDY:** It wouldn't?

BOB SOMEONE: No u really helped me with my spelling & vocabulary

> **HILDY:** You're incorrigible. (And I wish you'd start putting periods at the end of your sentences.)

BOB SOMEONE: incorrigible! another new word! question 21

> **HILDY:** Not so fast, buster. I'm not satisfied with your answer. Is that really all you want from a friendship? The occasional beer?

BOB SOMEONE: no & money & a pickup game of something from time to time. thats all most guys want. ask around

HILDY: What about someone to talk to?

BOB SOMEONE: what about it

HILDY: Do you guys talk about stuff?

BOB SOMEONE: yeah

HILDY: Like what?

BOB SOMEONE: sports music girls youtube videos

HILDY: Who do you talk to about important things?

BOB SOMEONE: those aren't important?

HILDY: You know what I mean.

BOB SOMEONE: what? love death the meaning of life?

HILDY: Yes. Stuff like that.

BOB SOMEONE: nobody

HILDY: Really?

BOB SOMEONE: ok. U

HILDY: Are you joking?

BOB SOMEONE: sadly no

HILDY: And, worse, you're only talking to me about it because someone is paying you $40.

BOB SOMEONE: sadly yes. NOW can we move on to the next question?

HILDY: Just let me dry my eyes . . .

QUESTION 21

BOB SOMEONE: "what roles do love & affection play in ur life?"

HILDY: Is that a real question? Or are you flirting with me?

BOB SOMEONE: is that how nerds flirt?

> **HILDY:** Yes. Nothing like a psychology study to get the heart all aflutter.

BOB SOMEONE: whatever works. atq

> **HILDY:** Is that you being all manly and forceful?

BOB SOMEONE: u think I'm going to answer that? I'm not stupid. atq

> **HILDY:** "What roles do love and affection play in your life?" What does that even mean? How can I answer something I don't understand?

BOB SOMEONE: just do ur best. extra points for effort

> **HILDY:** I guess an important role. And I think I would have said a good role.

BOB SOMEONE: *would have said but . . .

> **HILDY:** It's not that simple.

BOB SOMEONE: nothing with u is

> **HILDY:** True.

BOB SOMEONE: so go on

> **HILDY:** I grew up in a loving and affectionate family. My friends love me. I know that.

BOB SOMEONE: even Iris?

> **HILDY:** You're obsessed with Iris.

BOB SOMEONE: no just want an honest answer. the truth the whole truth and nothing but the truth. this is a courtroom drama remember

> **HILDY:** Ok. The Whole Truth. Iris might not love me as much as she once did, but Max and Xiu are true-blue.

BOB SOMEONE: there's another *but coming

HILDY: You have very good emotional antennae.

BOB SOMEONE: i love it when u talk dirty—but could u please just finish ur answer

HILDY: . . . But I guess friends and family aren't enough. It's probably natural to want more.

BOB SOMEONE: meaning

HILDY: You know what I mean.

BOB SOMEONE: clearly ur not talking about a pet given the way u treated poor old kong

HILDY: Clearly. OK. Where do YOU stand on the love and affection front?

BOB SOMEONE: Depends what u mean by love & affection. Are we talking physical?

HILDY: If you want.

BOB SOMEONE: Then I'm a big fan

HILDY: Oh, right. I remember your ideal day had a bit of that.

BOB SOMEONE: it did. more than a bit if I'm being honest

HILDY: ARE you being honest?

BOB SOMEONE: trying my best

HILDY: What about the emotional part of love?

BOB SOMEONE: That plays no role in my life

HILDY: That's sad.

BOB SOMEONE: don't cry for me

HILDY: Argentina.

BOB SOMEONE: ???

HILDY: You don't know that song?

BOB SOMEONE: no

HILDY: Sorry. It's a song from this old musical called Evita.

BOB SOMEONE: what roll did u play

HILDY: Who says I played a *role?

BOB SOMEONE: did u

HILDY: Yes.

BOB SOMEONE: what? Evita?

BOB SOMEONE: i knew it

HILDY: Could we just drop the joking around? I shouldn't have started it. You just told me something important and I was disrespectful.

BOB SOMEONE: i don't care. altho i wish u'd quit saying everything about my life is *sad. maybe I think having friends who wear weird skirts is sad. ever think about that?

HILDY: Your mother said you were hers, so you obviously grew up with love.

BOB SOMEONE: i did

HILDY: But you don't have it now.

BOB SOMEONE: correct

BOB SOMEONE: hello?

HILDY: I don't know what to say.

BOB SOMEONE: how about *easy come easy go. Lets leave it at that. Question 22

QUESTION 22

BOB SOMEONE: ur going to go crazy for this one

> **HILDY:** What is it? Let me guess. "Which are your three favorite characters from 19th-century English literature and why?"

BOB SOMEONE: close. "alternate sharing something u consider a positive characteristic of ur partner. share a total of five items"

> **HILDY:** You must be sweating bullets. If you can make it

to five items for me, I'll give you an extra ten bucks.

BOB SOMEONE: that's what I need. my teachers always said i responded well to *incentives. u first

   HILDY: One) You're artistic.

BOB SOMEONE: i handed that one to u on a plate

   HILDY: This isn't a competition. Your turn.

BOB SOMEONE: u talk good

   HILDY: I talk good?!

BOB SOMEONE: i was going to say ur well-spoken but that didn't sound like something i'd say. didn't want u thinking i was getting help

   HILDY: Well-spoken? I'm shocked. I would have thought you considered that one of my faults.

BOB SOMEONE: quality's good. its quantity u sometimes have a problem with

   HILDY: You know, you've improved since we started doing this. Your answers have become much more tactful.

BOB SOMEONE: yeah well nothing like a fish to the side of the head to make a man see the error of his ways

   HILDY: Two) You're funny.

BOB SOMEONE: so r u

BOB SOMEONE: surprisingly

   HILDY: I spoke too soon. It's as if every time you say something nice about me, you feel obliged to start subtly taking it back.

BOB SOMEONE: that was subtle?

   HILDY: No. You're right. It wasn't very subtle.

BOB SOMEONE: sorry about that

HILDY: Well, you can't be expected to be subtle all the time.

BOB SOMEONE: no sorry about not being nice

HILDY: Sorry?! An honest apology? Be still, my beating heart.

BOB SOMEONE: yup *sorry. i wasn't trying to insult u. i meant i didn't think u'd be funny when I first met u. u come across as someone who cant take a joke. the type who get all worked up about something being sexist or racist or *disrespectful

HILDY: I am that type.

BOB SOMEONE: true but u still make me laugh

HILDY: Yeah but I don't always mean to.

BOB SOMEONE: no but even when u mean to

HILDY: Gee. Thanks. I'm blushing.

BOB SOMEONE: which brings me to #3

HILDY: Which is?

BOB SOMEONE: hold on a sec got to put up my fish shield

HILDY: I can tell I'm not going to like this. Spit it out.

BOB SOMEONE: ur sensitive

BOB SOMEONE: I mean that in a good way

BOB SOMEONE: most of the time

HILDY: You just did it again. You're the king of the backhanded compliment.

BOB SOMEONE: wow never been king of anything before. Soooo flattered

HILDY: Doesn't take much.

BOB SOMEONE: yeah well maybe i'm sensitive too

HILDY: Maybe?!? You *definitely are, despite the fact that you try to hide it behind your posturing and your braggadocio.

BOB SOMEONE: bragga-wha? Gonna hafta look that one up

HILDY: Why? So you can try it out on the ladies?

BOB SOMEONE: what do u think I'm doing now?

HILDY: You're so smooth.

BOB SOMEONE: that ur number 3?

HILDY: It wasn't going to be but ok, yes, come to think of it. It is. At the risk of causing your head to explode, you're quite charming. Despite my better judgment— and when I don't feel like clobbering you with a heavy object—I can't help but enjoy it. Clearly, the reason you have "girls with an s" is that you're a ladies man at heart. You could do this professionally.

BOB SOMEONE: wow talk about giving a compliment then taking it back. How to make me sound like a sleazeball

HILDY: A charming sleazeball. There are worse things to be.

BOB SOMEONE: like what?

Hildy: I can't think of anything right now.

BOB SOMEONE: a caveman?

HILDY: Oops. Did I scratch that delicate underbelly of yours again?

BOB SOMEONE: no just want to get things straight. see if I'm coming up or down in the world

HILDY: Up. Although there's definitely been some turbulence along the way. What's your number four?

BOB SOMEONE: its getting harder & harder to come up with something

HILDY: Keep your eye on the prize. Ten bucks if you make it to five, don't forget.

BOB SOMEONE: wow ur either generous or desprate

HILDY: I'm not accepting either of those as answers so don't even try.

BOB SOMEONE: even if there true?

HILDY: Even if they're true. Too jokey. I want a real answer. Remember? We agreed. C'mon. You can do it.

HILDY: You better have just suffered a major medical emergency because that pause was downright insulting.

BOB SOMEONE: u got style

HILDY: Really? Even with my *old man's overcoat?

BOB SOMEONE: yup & ur satchel & the way u wear ur hair & those little dangly earrings. ur not like most girls. ur not plastered in makeup either. i can see ur skin. i like that

BOB SOMEONE: u got nice skin

154

HILDY: It's amazing what you'll say for a couple of bucks. I should have paid you earlier.

BOB SOMEONE: now who's jokey

HILDY: Flattery is embarrassing.

BOB SOMEONE: i'll stop

HILDY: Not yet. You have one more.

BOB SOMEONE: u first u haven't done #4 yet

HILDY: You're masculine.

BOB SOMEONE: did u have to get my pee tested to come up with that one?

HILDY: I don't mean male—although you're that too unless you have something to tell me? I mean you're kind of manly.

BOB SOMEONE: its the broken nose

HILDY: And the way you hold yourself and the way you try not to smile. Your reticence.

BOB SOMEONE: will google that later

HILDY: You do that. You've got a bit of a Marlboro Man thing going.

BOB SOMEONE: ??? The cigarette guy? The cowboy?

HILDY: You're right. Bad example. Especially since I hate smokers.

BOB SOMEONE: i know. saw ur winning poster for cancer society's butt-out campain. btw loved the face paint! u do that urself?

HILDY: I'm going to let that go. What I was trying to say before I was so rudely interrupted is that you're a guy's guy or something. There's nothing feminine about you.

BOB SOMEONE: i like babies

    HILDY: Whoa. That came out of the blue. It's not a *come-on, is it?

BOB SOMEONE: no just saying i'm not *that masculine

    HILDY: You seriously like babies?

BOB SOMEONE: i seriously do. weird i know

    HILDY: Where do you think that came from?

BOB SOMEONE: ur the psychiatrist

    HILDY: That's why I'm asking the questions and you're answering them. Why do you think you like babies?

BOB SOMEONE: I guess cuz it always used to be just mom & me. couple times it looked like she was going to settle down with a guy & i might get a little bro or sis but never happened

    HILDY: So it's like an unfulfilled childhood dream?

BOB SOMEONE: Yeah that & becoming a ninja warrior

    HILDY: What do you like about babies?

BOB SOMEONE: the way they smell. have you ever smelled one?

    HILDY: Plenty. I babysit.

BOB SOMEONE: I mean their heads not their asses

    HILDY: Thank you. I figured that.

BOB SOMEONE: & the way they do that thing with their lips when they're dreaming about the bottle

    HILDY: or the breast.

BOB SOMEONE: get your mind out of the gutter

BOB SOMEONE: just joking. Chill. perfectly natural best thing for baby blah blah blah

> **HILDY:** You chill. I had no intention of lecturing you. I'm more interested in finding out what your next "item" for me is. C'mon. You only have to rack your brain to come up with one more positive thing. Now for the grand finale! Bob's all-time top five picks for Betty . . .

BOB SOMEONE: i did hair i did skin i did eyelashes. gee i got nothing

> **HILDY:** You actually didn't do eyelashes, but they get lumped in with number 4. You have to come up with something different.

BOB SOMEONE: ur persistent

> **HILDY:** Like I'm a *nag?

BOB SOMEONE: yes when u bug me but no the rest of the time. i just mean sticking at stuff. thats usually a good thing especially if u want to be Nelson Mandela 1 day

> **HILDY:** You're persistent too and I don't just mean because you really NEVER, EVER LET A JOKE GO. (Give it a break, would you? Nelly and I are done.) But you stick at stuff too.

BOB SOMEONE: no ones ever accused me of that before

> **HILDY:** May I remind you that you were the one who got in touch with me? That was persistent.

BOB SOMEONE: doesn't matter no copying. ur rule. something else

    HILDY: You're brave.

BOB SOMEONE: how would u know?

    HILDY: The way you barely flinched when I threw Kong at you

BOB SOMEONE: i thought we were supposed to give honest answers

    HILDY: Sorry. Just slipped out. I meant to say "gut feeling." I only met you once. I don't have a lot else to go on.

BOB SOMEONE: ur right i am brave

    HILDY: Really? Or are you just shutting me up?

BOB SOMEONE: really. my mother told me to b so I am

BOB SOMEONE: plus i don't have any choice

    HILDY: How come?

BOB SOMEONE: no one does

BOB SOMEONE: Ok. "How close and warm is ur family? Do u feel ur childhood was happier than most other people's?"

    HILDY: Hmmm. Tough one.

BOB SOMEONE: not for me.

    HILDY: Really?

BOB SOMEONE: Yeah. Part a - not close & warm cuz i don't have a family & part b - yes

    HILDY: *Slack-jawed surprise. Your childhood was happier than most people's?

BOB SOMEONE: u know ur rude right? but yes happier. some of it anyway

    HILDY: Where did you grow up?

BOB SOMEONE: here & there

    HILDY: Literally here?

BOB SOMEONE: off & on

    HILDY: Where's there?

BOB SOMEONE: all over. we traveled a lot

    HILDY: How come?

BOB SOMEONE: A rolling stone gathers no moss

    HILDY: I've never liked that expression. So demeaning. As if people are fungus that will grow on you if you don't keep moving.

BOB SOMEONE: pretty much somes it up. least my mother thought so. shes the one who used to say so

    HILDY: *Sums, not *somes. I'm not even sure that's a word.

BOB SOMEONE: is it spelled aargh or AAAAAAAARGH?

HILDY: 😄 Every so often, I get a glimpse into how annoying I can be. Ignore me.

BOB SOMEONE: doing my best & anyway u honestly don't know anybody youd call fungus?

HILDY: So much for ignoring me.

BOB SOMEONE: well do u?

HILDY: Fungus is a bit harsh. I do know a few single-celled beings and invertebrates.

BOB SOMEONE: rolling stones don't gather those either. could even crush a few on the way past so don't knock em

HILDY: Ooh. Where can I get me one of those?

BOB SOMEONE: it's easy just stop drop & roll. watch ur head

HILDY: That how you broke your nose?

BOB SOMEONE: no & quit asking

HILDY: Did you have friends when you were growing up?

BOB SOMEONE: for a while but then we'd move & have to make new ones. ok when your little but gets harder

HILDY: That's sad.

BOB SOMEONE: would u quit that? ur making me sound pathetic. friends aren't everything. if I had tons of friends I wouldn't have learned to draw or play drums

HILDY: How come you moved so much?

BOB SOMEONE: $

BOB SOMEONE: don't say thats sad again. being poor is

also how come I can draw & play drums. cheap ways to amuse myself. if we had money I never would a learned

HILDY: I had no idea you had such a positive outlook.

BOB SOMEONE: hidden depths. ur turn

HILDY: What was the question again?

BOB SOMEONE: how close and warm is ur family? do u feel ur childhood was happier than most other people's?

HILDY: Part A) Not very. At least at the moment. But it used to be. Or at least I thought it was. Just goes to show how little I knew. Weird—a couple weeks ago I would have given you an entirely different answer.

BOB SOMEONE: what happened a week ago

HILDY: My family imploded.

BOB SOMEONE: what does that mean

HILDY: Implode means to collapse inward.

BOB SOMEONE: I KNOW WHAT IMPLODE MEANS. Im not a moron i do watch tv. u know what i mean. what happened with ur family

HILDY: People stopped talking to each other.

BOB SOMEONE: how come?

HILDY: Something I said.

BOB SOMEONE: what? must have been pretty bad

HILDY: I don't think I can answer that. I don't really know you and I'd be saying something that I've only ever said to two other people in the world and I'm not even sure if it's 100% true, so it would feel like a betrayal. Especially since you know who my parents are now. Can we change the subject? You don't want to make me cry again.

BOB SOMEONE: i hate online crying. nothing worse than a bunch of sad emojis. btw Kong wants to say something to u

HILDY: I'm waiting

BOB SOMEONE: give him a sec. this is painful for him to

BOB SOMEONE:

HILDY: Do King Kong mothers eat their offspring?

BOB SOMEONE: just guessing. best I could do on short notice. u still crying?

HILDY: No.

BOB SOMEONE: then who cares if its true

HILDY: I can see why you're good with the ladies.

BOB SOMEONE: brace urself. "How do u feel about ur relationship with your mother?"

> **HILDY:** Whoever wrote these questions is cruel. If I weren't so *persistent, I'd quit.

BOB SOMEONE: not me. I need the $40

> **HILDY:** I don't believe you. I think you actually enjoy this.

BOB SOMEONE: wrong. trust me

> **HILDY:** I agree this particular question is not a lot of fun. But overall? I think you like this. You don't strike me as the type of person who'd keep doing it just for the money if you hated it.

BOB SOMEONE: busted

> **HILDY:** So why do you do it then?

BOB SOMEONE: i'm a masochist & my whip is broken

BOB SOMEONE: r u giving me the silent treatment?

> **HILDY:** No, I'm just using a technique I learned in journalism class. If you want someone to answer a question, allow the silence to get awkward.

BOB SOMEONE: so u R giving me the silent treatment

BOB SOMEONE: Ok. Fine. i don't actually *like it aka *enjoy it but i don't talk to anybody about stuff like this anymore so i guess i kinda missed it

HILDY: Missed being emotionally tortured?

BOB SOMEONE: weird i know

HILDY: "I don't talk to anybody about stuff like this anymore?" Who did you used to talk with?

BOB SOMEONE: my mother

HILDY: What happened?

BOB SOMEONE: the question is how do u feel about ur relationship with ur mother? i feel like my relationship is over. U?

HILDY: You just redirected me, didn't you?

BOB SOMEONE: Yup & u redirected me

HILDY: So this is payback?

BOB SOMEONE: Could be. tell me about ur relationship with ur mother. i <3 watching u squirm

HILDY: I feel my relationship with my mother is . . . I don't know . . . complicated.

BOB SOMEONE: weasel word. isn't she ur warrior goddess or something

HILDY: Yes—but that's what I mean. Complicated. She is and she isn't. Maybe she's some type of Greek goddess. Weren't they supposed to be immortal but flawed too?

BOB SOMEONE: why r u asking me?

HILDY: You seemed to know so much about Pandora.

BOB SOMEONE: all i know is she didn't have enuf room in her satchel for my problems too

    HILDY: She could get a bigger satchel.

BOB SOMEONE: not that big

    HILDY: What was your relationship like with your mother before it ended?

BOB SOMEONE: complicated

    HILDY: LOL. So it's not a weasel word when you use it.

BOB SOMEONE: correct

    HILDY: What's she like?

BOB SOMEONE: flawed but not immortal

    HILDY: Can you be more specific? Looks? Personality? Hobbies and pastimes?

BOB SOMEONE: tall dark hair beautiful smart funny crazy badtempered painting men

    HILDY: ????

BOB SOMEONE: just answering ur questions. Looks? Personality? Hobbies & pastimes?

    HILDY: Painting men? That's her hobby?

BOB SOMEONE: no. painting comma men

    HILDY: #whypunctuationisimportant

BOB SOMEONE: #whatever. Ur turn. Whats ur mother like?

    HILDY: I wouldn't say she's beautiful. Not in "the usual way," but she has a really nice face and she dresses well. She's smart, very determined, ambitious. She puts her mind to something and she gets it. I was going to add that she's responsible and loyal but I'm not sure about that anymore. I'm kind of not sure about much anymore.

BOB SOMEONE: ur growing up little girl

HILDY: You mean, that's what it's like from here on out?!?

BOB SOMEONE: yup. nobody knows what there doing. expect surprises. sometimes its $40 to answer some dum questions. more often its a fish in the head

HILDY: I'm never going to live that down.

BOB SOMEONE: no u aren't

QUESTION 25

BOB SOMEONE: question 25. not sure what this means. "make three true *we statements each. for instance, We are both in this room feeling . . ."

HILDY: *perplexed.

BOB SOMEONE: true

HILDY: We are both in this room feeling . . .

BOB SOMEONE: wrong we're NOT both in this room

HILDY: Ok. We're both occupying a spot in cyberspace feeling . . .

BOB SOMEONE: exposed

HILDY: Really? Not like you.

BOB SOMEONE: says who?

HILDY: For starters, not a Bob word but also, "exposed"? You sure haven't told me enough to feel exposed.

BOB SOMEONE: more than I've told anyone else

HILDY: Really?

BOB SOMEONE: yup

HILDY: How come?

BOB SOMEONE: i don't trust many people

HILDY: How come?

BOB SOMEONE: ur like a broken record

HILDY: ATQ

BOB SOMEONE: life i guess

HILDY: Can you be more specific?

BOB SOMEONE: people haven't come thru for me in the past. i try to avoid the disappointment these days

HILDY: How?

BOB SOMEONE: the obvious way

HILDY: Which is?

BOB SOMEONE: believe nothing & nobody. i'm going to put that on a tshirt too

HILDY: I'm sure they'll be flying off the shelves.

HILDY: Do you trust me?

BOB SOMEONE: ask me later

HILDY: Thank you.

BOB SOMEONE: no need to be sarcastic

HILDY: I'm not. It's scary to tell someone things. I'm touched you chose me to reveal as much as you have.

BOB SOMEONE: i didn't choose u jeff did

HILDY: You're doing that bait-and-switch thing again. Saying something nice then hitting me with a zinger.

BOB SOMEONE: hate to say this but ur right. Sorry. I find this weirdly embarrassing

HILDY: You? Embarrassed?

HILDY: Are you blushing?

BOB SOMEONE: i don't blush

HILDY: Bet you do.

BOB SOMEONE: this is supposed to be a *we statement. r *u feeling exposed?

HILDY: Yes. But I always am.

BOB SOMEONE: always?

HILDY: Almost.

BOB SOMEONE: so is this more or less than usual?

HILDY: More. And it's getting worse.

BOB SOMEONE: r u blushing?

HILDY: Yes. But duh.

BOB SOMEONE: ur turn. another *we statement

HILDY: We are both feeling exposed

BOB SOMEONE: said that already

HILDY: I didn't finish. "We are both feeling exposed . . . but we like it."

BOB SOMEONE: correct

HILDY: Are you blushing now?

BOB SOMEONE: no

HILDY: Really?

BOB SOMEONE: wouldn't tell u if I was

HILDY: There's that masculine thing again.

BOB SOMEONE: thought u liked it

HILDY: Sometimes

BOB SOMEONE: more or less than usual?

HILDY: Less.

BOB SOMEONE: really?

HILDY: Yes. I like when you're showing your feminine side. I like that you're confiding in me when you wouldn't do that with anyone else.

HILDY: Oops. Why aren't you answering? Did I cross a line?

BOB SOMEONE: no

HILDY: So why didn't you answer?

BOB SOMEONE: didn't feel like it. can we stop?

HILDY: No. We each have one more statement. C'mon. I promise I won't make any more comments impugning your masculinity.

BOB SOMEONE: Gee I've never been impugned before. u shur <3 those fancy words

HILDY: I do—but only when apposite.

BOB SOMEONE: its spelled with an o even I know that

HILDY: No, actually, *apposite means *appropriate. (I was just using it to bug you.)

BOB SOMEONE: congrats! it worked

HILDY: We've strayed from our question. We need another *we statement.

BOB SOMEONE: i went 1st last time

HILDY: No you didn't. I did.

BOB SOMEONE: no i did

HILDY: Did not.

BOB SOMEONE: Ok fine we're both in this spot in cyberspace feeling like the other person is wrong

HILDY: LOL. Very clever.

BOB SOMEONE: ur turn

HILDY: We're both in this spot feeling surprisingly happy.

BOB SOMEONE: no kidding. *surprisingly

HILDY: That's not a bad thing. I like surprises. You're certainly not boring.

BOB SOMEONE: u haven't known me very long. my big surprise might be how boring i am

HILDY: Which is why I think we should stop while we're ahead.

BOB SOMEONE: meaning

HILDY: I think we should end this conversation.

BOB SOMEONE: u wouldn't stop when I wanted to but u want to stop now?!?

HILDY: Yes. I don't want to be boring either. Talk to you tomorrow at the same time.

BOB SOMEONE: betty?

BOB SOMEONE: betty?

BOB SOMEONE: aaaargh

CHAPTER 11

Hildy was late for drama. It was the one thing she was always on time for—her father had been known to cast chronic latecomers as trees and lampposts—but she'd been sucked into a daydream after biology and lost track of time. (Bob's joke about her lousy bio mark. That had been the spark that had led her astray.)

She tiptoed into the room at 4:06. Chairs scraped as everyone turned to see who it was. A few people clapped. Duff Shankel looked up from the scarf he was pretentiously knitting and said, "Why, there you are, Hildy! We were just about to kick in the prop room door."

That was a joke. Evan and Hildy, phone-less, had accidentally locked themselves in the prop room after the closing night of *Grease* the year before. They weren't found for three hours. Despite the fact that Hildy was still wearing Sandy's sex-positive, off-the-shoulder pop-top and despite her making it abundantly clear that he was the one that she wanted (right down to singing the "Ooh! Ooh! Ooh!" part), Evan declined to ravish her.

Bastard.

"Don't worry. We'd knock first." This from Sam Armstrong, who Hildy knew had a record as sad as her own.

"You guys are hilarious. Seriously. A real up-and-coming comedy duo." She gave them each a high five and realized she couldn't care less about Evan. Bob would crack up when he found out they'd passed the time playing Twenty Questions.

"Any chance your dad's in the prop room with someone, too?"

It took her a second to understand what Duff meant.

She looked around the room. No warm-up music on the ancient boom box. No piles of color-coded scripts. No challenging quote neatly chalked on the board.

Her father wasn't there.

"Even funnier, Duff." She kept her voice snappy but her insides had melted. Mr. Sangster was never late for drama club. She realized it wouldn't be long before people figured out what was going on. Everyone would be talking about it. Hildy couldn't even feel indignant. She'd have talked about it, too, if this had been somebody else's train wreck.

She headed to the back of the room where Max and Xiu were sprawled out on beanbag chairs.

"Where is he?" she said, pushing Max over enough that she could sit.

Max had his eyes closed and was trying to master the Braille Rubik's Cube she'd given him for Christmas. "How would I know? I'm a mere spear holder in the thrilling drama of Gregorinko's life."

"Xiu?"

Xiu didn't look up from her phone.

"She's mad at you," Max said, still flipping away. "Not my fault. You should have warned me to keep my mouth shut."

Hildy said, "Mad? About what?" But then the PA system sputtered on and everyone went quiet. Mrs. Walsh, the school secretary, read out the message in her high-pitched granny voice. "Senior drama club members are advised that, due to circumstances beyond

173

his control, Mr. Sangster will not be directing the winter-term production. He apologizes for the late notice. He's actively looking to recruit a new director. Until then, drama club will be on hold."

Everyone turned to Hildy.

"Don't look at me," she said, although she had a pretty good idea what the circumstances were and why he claimed they were beyond his control. Kids started picking up their stuff and leaving.

Max opened his eyes. "What d'you think that's about—or should I ask?"

She spread open her fingers, shook her head. She couldn't say the words. Max hugged her.

Xiu said, "Like I have nothing better to do than hang out in some moldy classroom with the nerd herd all afternoon! You Sangsters are so inconsiderate."

Hildy snapped, "You Sangsters? What did I do?"

Max said, "Going to let you guys fight this one out. Call me when you get to the hair-pulling part." He took his Rubik's Cube and went over to talk to Duff.

Xiu booted it out of the room. Hildy hesitated for a moment then followed.

"What's going on? Tell me."

"Nothing." Xiu kept tip-tapping down the hall in her kitten-heeled boots.

"Liar."

"I am not."

"You are, too."

"I am not lying. I meant 'nothing,' as in that's what you told me. Big long chat with Max about Bob, but me? Totally out of the loop, as if I'm Iris or something. No wonder she dumped you."

Xiu could be mean when she wanted. Hildy didn't need this right now. She grabbed Xiu's arm. Xiu stopped but kept staring straight ahead.

"Okay. Sorry. Look. I didn't mean to hurt your feelings or leave you out. I'm a chicken. That's all it was. I just didn't want you to talk me out of seeing him. That's the truth."

Xiu was wearing a pale pink Jackie Kennedy pillbox hat. When she didn't respond, Hildy gave it a little flick with her finger.

"So. You want to hear what happened or would you prefer to keep sulking?"

Hildy poked her gently in the ear until Xiu batted her hand away, fixed her hat, and said, "I want to walk down to Freak Lunchbox for a chocolate bar. You may accompany me if desired."

Hildy made a face behind Xiu's back, then found herself smiling. Only one part of the peach had gone bad. The rest of Hildy's life could still be sort of normal.

They bundled up and headed outside.

Before Hildy could talk about Bob, she had to listen to Xiu talk about Sweet Baby James. SBJ was apparently kind of moody, but he smelled delicious and was an excellent kisser. Hildy let Xiu go on about him for several blocks, then she launched in on Bob.

"He likes to talk."

"What?" Xiu stopped midcrosswalk. "Did he have a come-to-Jesus moment since he saw you last or something? I understood him to be sullen and uncommunicative."

"I believe the word I used was surly." Hildy laughed.

"Oh, yes . . . in the hotly sexual sense of the word. I think I remember that. But now, suddenly, he's open and giving and oh so emotionally sharing."

Hildy laughed again. "Well. No. Not quite, but he does talk. Or at least message. He actually said he missed talking to someone, that he didn't have the chance to do it anymore."

"Clearly saving himself for the love of a good woman."

"I like to think so."

"Well." Xiu shrugged in that stagey way of hers. "He might not

175

be as bad as I thought. When I first saw SBJ, I never imagined he—"

And she was off again. That was fine. Xiu's boy-talk kept Hildy's mind off her other problems. She used the downtime to figure some stuff out.

They were only on Question 25. Eleven more to go. And they were mushy. That's what he'd said. Another un-Bob-like word. A joke word? A little verbal camouflage to cover his embarrassment? Shyness? Could Bob actually be shy? That made her laugh, too, but in a silent catch-your-breath kind of way.

She'd dreamed all night about mushy questions and him beside her asking them, with that mouth and those hands, and it would have been so easy to say yes to him now.

But no.

No, she wasn't going to do that.

She wasn't ready to see him again. Mr. Sangster—her former drama teacher, not the principal, not her dad, not the strange man inhabiting her house at the moment—used to talk about how, for many actors, it was much easier to perform in front of a large anonymous crowd than communicate one-on-one with another human being. They liked the distance.

She liked the distance.

They got to Freak Lunchbox, and Xiu decided she just wanted gum. She always stopped eating in the first throes of love. Hildy was the one who got the chocolate bar. They found a park bench at the Grand Parade and talked in parallel lines.

"James plays the mandolin, too."

"Bob must have been close to his mother. He mentioned her a lot although he sure didn't give much away. I don't know what happened to her . . . if she took off or he took off or, I don't know . . . Did she die? Is she in jail? I'm almost afraid to ask."

"James did a year of college but felt his music was more important than reading about a bunch of dusty old white guys. He's very much a looking-forward kind of person, despite being known for his reworkings of classic seventies alt rock anthems."

"He practically gushed about her. He called her 'beautiful.' A boy who loves his mother. Don't they say that's a good sign."

"He asked me if I sang. 'Me?' I said. And he was like, 'Don't sound so shocked. You have a beautiful voice. There's a husky quality to it.' I didn't want to tell him it's just my allergies acting up."

"Bob said he felt 'exposed.' *Exposed.* You'd think he'd say there was nothing out there that could touch him."

They went on like that until they started to get cold. It was time to go, anyway. Xiu had a date. Hildy had to get some work done on her English paper, because it, like everything else in her life, had fallen by the wayside.

They were walking up Spring Garden Road when Hildy's phone beeped.

Another Facebook message from Bob.

BOB SOMEONE: ur going to need extra time to prepare for question 26 so here goes. "complete this sentence *i wish i had someone with whom i could share . . ." fill in the blank. Kong said it took him forever to come up with an answer.

I WISH I HAD SOMEONE TO SHARE THIS VAST OCEAN WITH. PLANKTON HAS NO APPEAL WHEN EATEN ALONE.

BOB SOMEONE: ps what time we talking tonite?

HILDY: 7?

BOB SOMEONE: ur on

Just two more hours.

Hildy left Xiu at the bus stop and went straight home. She had her strategy to prepare. She thought she was ready when, precisely at seven, her laptop beeped.

QUESTION 26

BOB SOMEONE: So what's ur answer? i wish i had someone with whom i could share . . .

> **HILDY:** Hard to concentrate on an answer. My mind is blown from you using the word "whom" in a sentence.

BOB SOMEONE: i wish i had someone with whom i could share . . .

> **HILDY:** An order of fries.

BOB SOMEONE: thats something i'd say

> **HILDY:** Irritating, isn't it?

BOB SOMEONE: only when u do it

> **HILDY:** I feel like anything **real* I say you'll just make fun of.

BOB SOMEONE: so ur getting there first?

> **HILDY:** Yup. Classic defense mechanism.

BOB SOMEONE: Ok. promise i won't make fun of u

> **HILDY:** I know my answer to the question: I wish I had someone with whom I could share my real answers.

BOB SOMEONE: u doing it again?

HILDY: No. It's true. That's what I'd like. Someone I can be honest with. So what's your answer?

BOB SOMEONE: sort of the same

HILDY: Sort of the same as?

BOB SOMEONE: ur answer. i wish i had someone with whom i just was

HILDY: Just was what?

BOB SOMEONE: just was period

HILDY: Yes. That's what I meant too.

BOB SOMEONE: where do u think i could find someone like that?

HILDY: Don't know? Do you?

BOB SOMEONE: no

BOB SOMEONE:

179

HILDY: Since we're both looking for the same thing, maybe we should look together.

BOB SOMEONE: isn't that what we're doing?

HILDY: Good point. Next question.

QUESTION 27

BOB SOMEONE: o come on

HILDY: What?

BOB SOMEONE: stupid question. "*if u were going to become a close friend with ur partner, please share what would be important for him or her to know." do we have to even answer this? u already know the important things about me

HILDY: Like what?

BOB SOMEONE: i live alone. don't like talking about the past. like to keep my feelings to myself.

HILDY: I didn't know any of those things!

BOB SOMEONE: well u haven't been listening then

HILDY: Have so. I figured you didn't live with your parents but I didn't know you lived alone. And I got the impression you actually liked talking about your past. Well, maybe not *liked as in <3 <3 <3 but you mentioned how you missed talking about stuff like this. And I think you enjoyed talking about your mother. You said some lovely things about her.

BOB SOMEONE: i answered the question. doesn't mean it was fun

HILDY: I didn't say fun. But bittersweet? Something like that? Discussing intense emotional issues often has aspects of joy and pain.

BOB SOMEONE: wouldnt know. too *manly to notice that emo stuff

HILDY: Liar.

BOB SOMEONE: calling me a liar not cool

HILDY: Sorry.

BOB SOMEONE: normally i'd challenge u to a duel for the insult but i've got the sniffles & anyway i thought u liked that about me. the manly stuff i mean

HILDY: Only sometimes. Didn't I explain that already? It's often kind of irritating.

BOB SOMEONE: careful. as u know I can be a jerk when threatened

HILDY: Another thing I didn't know! (I did, however, know you could be an asshole.)

BOB SOMEONE: LOL something about u swearing cracks me up

HILDY: LMAO

BOB SOMEONE: LOL x2

HILDY: I always feel like such a degenerate when I swear—even in code. I secretly check over my shoulder to make sure my mother, my kindergarten teacher, and/ or god aren't there to catch me.

BOB SOMEONE: what would they do to u if they were?

HILDY: I haven't the faintest idea.

HILDY: Is it sad that I've made it to 18 and never done anything that would require someone to reprimand me?

BOB SOMEONE: i can fix that

HILDY: You're not the first person to offer.

BOB SOMEONE: who? evan?

HILDY: You have no idea how wrong you are.

BOB SOMEONE: so who?

HILDY: Everybody, at one time or another. Well, everybody except Evan. Max, Xiu, Iris, even my brother Alec. (Although with him, it usually entailed me helping sneak his contraband in or out of the house. He never actually wanted me to join in the shenanigans.)

BOB SOMEONE: so why didn't u?

HILDY: Because I'm a card-carrying Good Little Girl. I thought you'd recognize the uniform.

BOB SOMEONE: u? really?!?

HILDY: Hahaha. BTW, do you know how I can erase my history? I don't want my mother finding out I used the *a word . . .

BOB SOMEONE: i do but not going to tell u. time u took a walk on the wild side

HILDY: Using bad words. That's the wild side?

BOB SOMEONE: baby steps baby steps

BOB SOMEONE: in the meantime why don't u answer the question?

HILDY: Question? What question?

BOB SOMEONE: i'm starting to suspect you've been using your feminine whiles to avoid it

HILDY: It's feminine *wiles . . .

BOB SOMEONE: there u go again. u always blame me for sleazing out of questions but ur guilty too

> **HILDY:** *You're . . . (You do that a lot. *Your is the possessive adjective. *You're is the contraction of the words "you are.")

BOB SOMEONE: atq

BOB SOMEONE: spit it out

> **HILDY:** Gimme a sec! Geez. I had to look the question up again. Then I got stuck on the "if we were to become good friends" bit.

BOB SOMEONE: more bullshit excuses

> **HILDY:** No. Seriously. Is that why we're doing this?

BOB SOMEONE: i'm doing this for the money. ur doing it because ur honor bound

> **HILDY:** Oh. Right.

BOB SOMEONE: u got another reason?

> **HILDY:** No. Do you?

BOB SOMEONE: no so atq

> **HILDY:** I'd need you to know that I have an aversion to dogs, that I burn easily, and that I have to be fed regularly or I turn into a crazy person.

BOB SOMEONE: & what else?

HILDY: How do you know there's an *and?

BOB SOMEONE: lurking ur facebook feed

HILDY: All my secrets laid bare on social media. How embarrassing . . .

BOB SOMEONE: yup i know em all

HILDY: So why are you asking then?

BOB SOMEONE: not getting paid to do research. tho i did enjoy watching u go thru puberty. god it took ages. btw still have to wear the headgear?

HILDY: No. I stopped a couple of years ago. The radio signals I was picking up from Pluto were apparently affecting my classmates' hormones. They started doing bizarre things like growing whiskers and kissing in the hall.

BOB SOMEONE: too bad. headgear was a good look for u

HILDY: Someday I will find your real Facebook page and none of this will be so funny.

BOB SOMEONE: good luck with that

HILDY: Which brings me to my *and . . .

BOB SOMEONE: which is?

HILDY: And I'm not as wimpy as you think. I'm actually quite tough.

BOB SOMEONE: never thought ur wimpy. ur a trojan horse. u look harmless enuf but theres a goddam army inside

HILDY: How do you know about the Trojan horse? You pick that up from looking at the pictures too?

BOB SOMEONE: no. saw a cartoon about it & immediately thought of you

HILDY: Hahaha

BOB SOMEONE: truth

HILDY: So what do I need to know about you? Other than the stuff I've already gleaned about you living alone and loving babies. (!!!!!)

BOB SOMEONE: hey! watch it with the !!! someone could lose an eye

HILDY: Ever thought of putting a little baby smell behind your ears? Best. Perfume. Ever.

BOB SOMEONE: better than Axe?

HILDY: Even better than Old Spice and the guy in the towel that comes with it.

BOB SOMEONE: do all girls think that way?

HILDY: Why not get yourself a bottle and find out?

BOB SOMEONE: don't need to

HILDY: You have a very healthy self-regard.

BOB SOMEONE: that a problem?

HILDY: Did I say it was a problem?

BOB SOMEONE: something about ur tone

HILDY: My *typing tone? I had no idea you were sooooo sensitive. "You have a very healthy self-regard 😊" That better?

BOB SOMEONE: yes

HILDY: Ok. I know you live alone, like babies, and have a deep psychological dependency on emoticons.

Anything else?

BOB SOMEONE: i need time to myself. i hate cooked carrots and pajamas. i like my stuff in its proper place

HILDY: Including your *girls?

BOB SOMEONE: ur always trying to make me sound like a pig. no not my girls

HILDY: How do you like your girls?

BOB SOMEONE: natural

HILDY: As in au naturel?

BOB SOMEONE: french?

HILDY: Yes. It means *naked

BOB SOMEONE: ??!?!?!?!?!

HILDY: Oops. Was that inappropriate?

BOB SOMEONE: may no! i like ze naked french girls

HILDY: But that's not what you meant by natural?

BOB SOMEONE: no tho come to think of it . . .

HILDY: What did you mean then?

BOB SOMEONE: i like girls when there just being themselves. as in natural but with there clothes on. not big on phony girls

HILDY: Why does this make me feel uncomfortable?

BOB SOMEONE: cuz u remember what u were like in rm 417?

HILDY: Maybe.

BOB SOMEONE: i liked u better when u ran OUT OF rm 417

HILDY: I bet you did. You couldn't wait to get rid of me.

BOB SOMEONE: no it wasn't that. it was cuz u were

finally acting normally

> **HILDY:** Throwing something at a person is normal for you?

BOB SOMEONE: yeah. that time it was anyway. u threw Kong at me cuz that's what u felt like doing. not cuz it fit some stupid image u have of urself

> **HILDY:** Wrong. I threw Kong at you because I couldn't help it.

BOB SOMEONE: that's what i mean. Natural. u should do more things u can't help. won't kill u & might put that girl in rm 417 out of her misery

> **HILDY:** You actually like the type of person who throws things at you?

BOB SOMEONE: what can i say? guys always fall for there mothers

> **HILDY:** Did she abuse you?

BOB SOMEONE: NO. oh my god u are such a southender. like throwing stuff is abuse. u guys have got to man up

BOB SOMEONE: & ps so maybe she did throw things at me time to time but least she enjoyed it more than u did

> **HILDY:** You make that sound like a good thing.

BOB SOMEONE: got to enjoy life. thats all there is

> **HILDY:** Do you enjoy life?

BOB SOMEONE: parts of it

HILDY: Which parts?

BOB SOMEONE: the parts I told u about. drawing drumming sleeping

HILDY: Girls?

BOB SOMEONE: your obsessed with my sex life

HILDY: *You're

BOB SOMEONE: nice redirect & would u pls quit it with the spelling shit

HILDY: No. Can't help it. Won't kill you.

BOB SOMEONE: ha

HILDY: Which parts *don't you enjoy?

BOB SOMEONE: to many to mention

HILDY: Just your top five then.

BOB SOMEONE: assholes slush EDM soggy lettuce

HILDY: That's four

BOB SOMEONE: Can't count?

HILDY: "Soggy" is part of "lettuce."

BOB SOMEONE: Oh right

HILDY: So? Proceed.

BOB SOMEONE: # 5: people who say there going to do something and don't. sorry. make that # 1. i really truly hate that

HILDY: No one likes that.

BOB SOMEONE: altho lots of people love assholes, soggy lettuce, and EDM?

HILDY: Only partially right. I like EDM (in reasonable doses) but am not fond of a**holes or soggy lettuce.

BOB SOMEONE: don't u mean so**y lettuce? i find ur language offensive

> **HILDY:** More or less offensive than EDM?

BOB SOMEONE: less but just barely. ok ur turn. what parts of life do u enjoy?

> **HILDY:** Too numerous to mention.

BOB SOMEONE: don't believe u but whatever. give me yr top 5

> **HILDY:** Reading. Writing. Lattes. Sheepskin slippers, especially when slightly warmed by the fire. Getting my hair braided.

BOB SOMEONE: what don't u enjoy?

> **HILDY:** What you said minus the EDM.

BOB SOMEONE: how many times do i have to tell u no copying. come up with something else

> **HILDY:** Eggplant. Exercising. Plucking my eyebrows, although I suffer through it anyway in order to avoid looking like I have a large caterpillar crawling across my forehead.

BOB SOMEONE: instead of two smaller ones

> **HILDY:** Haha

BOB SOMEONE: what else don't u like

> **HILDY:** Biology. You were right about that. I have no mind for sciences although before you say anything it has nothing to do with my being female (I don't want to turn this into a Barbie-can't-do-math type thing) and I DO know gay men can father babies.

189

BOB SOMEONE: but I taught u that

    HILDY: Doesn't matter how I know it, I know it.

BOB SOMEONE: cmon 1 more . . .

    HILDY: My parents fighting. I hate that. I'm going to be a skeleton soon if they don't stop. Even when they don't raise their voices—which they don't do, of course, given who they are and what images they have to protect—it doesn't matter. Just the buzz of them arguing in another room makes my throat close. You know when you stay underwater for a long time and your throat burns? That's what it feels like all the time when I'm at home now. Like I've gone too long without taking a breath.

BOB SOMEONE: my parents never fought #BestThingAboutNotHavingADad

    HILDY: do you always look on the bright side of life?

BOB SOMEONE: try

    HILDY: My parents didnt used to fight, but now it's like they're on some bad drug that makes them do crazy things. Marital meth or something.

BOB SOMEONE: i got some survival tips for u

    HILDY: Where'd you pick those up? Didn't you just say your parents never fought?

BOB SOMEONE: yeah but my mother fought with everyone else so i picked up some pointers. tried the pillow over ur head?

    HILDY: Yes.

BOB SOMEONE: the long shower

    HILDY: Yes. It dries out my skin.

BOB SOMEONE: going for a run

    HILDY: No. I told you. I don't like to exercise.

BOB SOMEONE: more or less than hearing ur parents fight?

    HILDY: More, but I'm really lazy so it doesn't matter. I end up listening to them fight AND feeling guilty about not running. Your suggestions aren't helping.

BOB SOMEONE: sorry doing my best

    HILDY: Not your fault. Nothing helps. Even if I don't actually hear them fighting out loud, I hear them in my head.

BOB SOMEONE: been there done that. sucks big time

    HILDY: Actually I'm wrong. Something does help.

BOB SOMEONE: what?

    HILDY: I don't think about them when I'm talking to you.

BOB SOMEONE: kind of like hitting urself in the head to distract urself from an itch

    HILDY: Kind of, I guess.

BOB SOMEONE: u can hit urself in the head with me anytime u want

    HILDY: That is the weirdest thing anyone has ever said to me.

BOB SOMEONE: i like to think u mean that in a good way

    HILDY: I like to think the same thing about what you said.

BOB SOMEONE: u think right

    HILDY: Ditto.

BOB SOMEONE: we kind of moved away from the question

    HILDY: We've been doing that a lot lately. I forget what it even was.

BOB SOMEONE: something about friendship

    HILDY: Did we answer it?

BOB SOMEONE: must have

    HILDY: Is that your official ruling, ump?

BOB SOMEONE: hearing u say ump is almost as funny as hearing u swear

    HILDY: I'm not as stuck-up as you think I am. I know what an ump is.

BOB SOMEONE: cuz u played one in the school musical?

    HILDY: LOL. Busted, as you say. I have a question for you.

BOB SOMEONE: Proceed, as u say

HILDY: Nice use of a comma.

BOB SOMEONE: whats the question

HILDY: Want to get together?

BOB SOMEONE: When?

HILDY: Answer the question first.

BOB SOMEONE: yes when?

HILDY: Tomorrow?

BOB SOMEONE: ok where?

HILDY: I don't know. Somewhere we could talk and get something fattening. (Upside of parents fighting: I'm down on my calorie count. Room to splurge.)

BOB SOMEONE: upside of that coat: nobody can tell.

HILDY: #WhyIBoughtIt.

BOB SOMEONE: Theres a new place at the corner of north and agricola or bloomfield or whatever. looks like it would have fattening stuff. maybe even coffee in bowls

HILDY: Near the bridge? With black trim and a yellow door?

BOB SOMEONE: yeah. don't know what its called

HILDY: Me neither, but that would work. I've been wanting to try it. What time?

BOB SOMEONE: how about 7? i may have to be somewhere at 8:30

HILDY: *may have to be. How mysterious . . .

BOB SOMEONE: im a man of mystery

HILDY: You are indeed. What's your number in case I'm late?

BOB SOMEONE: i forgot to add lateness to my list of things i hate so don't be late

HILDY: I won't. Promise. But just in case, can I have your number?

BOB SOMEONE: so u can give me some lame excuse? sorry running late my hamster choked on a raisin then my grandmother died be there in a sec. no way

HILDY: I promise. No lame excuses. Just give me your phone number to be on the safe side.

BOB SOMEONE: sorry can't. don't have a phone

HILDY: Seriously?

BOB SOMEONE: yes

HILDY: How come?

BOB SOMEONE: don't want the govt listening in on my conversations

HILDY: You're joking.

BOB SOMEONE: i am

HILDY: So what's your number then?

BOB SOMEONE: joking about the govt. wasn't joking about the phone

HILDY: You really don't have one? Why?

BOB SOMEONE: don't want the govt listening in . . .

HILDY: Aargh. You're stonewalling.

BOB SOMEONE: must be soooooooooo irritating!! how u going to get that big old trojan horse thru when the

194

gates won't even open? c u at the no name café at 7

HILDY: You know I'm just going to ask you then . . .

BOB SOMEONE: good luck with that. in the meantime heres ur homework. question 28 "*tell ur partner what u like about them. be very honest this time saying things that u might not say to someone u've just met"

HILDY: A lot of these questions are sort of the same.

BOB SOMEONE: this ones different. I have to be very honest this time.

HILDY: You must *really like that part.

BOB SOMEONE: i love a challenge

HILDY: So do I.

BOB SOMEONE: good. heres ur 1st one. don't be late

CHAPTER

12

"Would you like to tell the class what you find so amusing, Ms. Sangster?" Mr. Goora tapped on her desk with his textbook.

Hildy came to with a start. *Damn.* She must be doing it again. She hadn't been able to control her face all day.

"My guess is you're not thinking about polynomials," he said.

"Close!" Xiu put on her best Mae West voice. "At least you got the *Paul* part right."

Kids started whistling and cheering and making semi-crude comments about Hildy's fantasy life.

Mr. Goora said, "Enough. Enough," and shut everybody up, but of course it wasn't enough for Hildy. She was obsessed with the boy.

Bobsessed. She hunched over her equations so Mr. G couldn't see her smile again.

She still hadn't come up with an answer for tonight.

Tell your partner what you like about them;
be very honest
say things that you might not say to someone you've just met.

The mere question made her laugh and blush and go all funny in the stomach. Not even her father "forgetting" to pick Gabe up from his regular Wednesday morning swim meet could ruin it for her. Upset her a bit. Throw her off for a while. But not ruin it.

The bell rang. Hildy packed up her stuff and headed to the common room for the monthly after-school meeting of the Citadel Classic Film Society. Xiu tried to drag her out for a smoothie instead but Hildy felt she should go. She'd missed last month's movie, and Duff got huffy when members didn't show up regularly.

Xiu rolled her eyes. "Why bother? You're just going to sit in the dark and think about Bob."

Hildy shrugged her off, waved good-bye, and found herself a seat at the back of the room. Today's feature was *Citizen Kane*.

Hildy sat in the dark and thought about Bob.

She needed to come up with an answer. She ruled out the obvious stuff: his arms, his eyes, the way he'd looked down and made those micro lip movements before he said anything serious.

She ruled out things she'd mentioned before, too—artistic, masculine, reticent, funny. That would just make her look lazy. She wanted to make it clear that she wasn't tossing the answer off. That this was meaningful to her. (But not too meaningful. Not my-whole-happiness-depends-on-this meaningful. Just normal, well-adjusted meaningful. It was a hard target to hit.)

She pictured Bob. She tried to think of something new to say. Before she knew it, the closing credits were rolling. Still no answer.

She checked the time. Quarter past five already. She grabbed her satchel and slipped out before Duff turned up the lights. Fifteen minutes to walk home. Fifteen to freshen up. Five to the bus stop. Maybe twenty to the café. She had loads of time.

Time to work out her answer.

On the way home, she realized what she was going to tell Bob. What she *had* to tell Bob. The "very honest" part to the question pretty much ruled everything else out.

She laughed, put her hands over her mouth, looked behind her. Even on a deserted street with nothing moving except the occasional sparkly whirlwind of snow, she was embarrassed.

Thrilled and embarrassed. She unwound one loop of the gray cashmere scarf her mother had given her for Christmas and let the cold air hit her skin.

Hildy practically ran the rest of the way. She was going to put on that moss-green silk shirt with the mother-of-pearl buttons she'd miraculously found at the consignment store. (It made her look like she had a waist, which she didn't, no matter how thin she got. She was built more or less like a Popsicle.) She considered stealing a little of her mother's J'adore, too, but Bob hadn't said anything about perfume, other than the Eau-de-Baby-Head kind, and she wasn't sure if he lumped it into the makeup category. She decided against it. Perfume always made her sneeze, and it was hardly foolproof, anyway. The gallons she'd doused herself in sure hadn't worked on Evan.

Ha!

Evan Keefe.

She kicked a small block of ice and watched it tinkle off down the street. That big, fat FAIL on her romantic report card was almost laughable now.

The snow on their front yard had turned mauve in the afternoon shadows. Her mother's Prius was gone but her father's Volvo was in the driveway. For the first time in almost two weeks, that didn't seem like a cause for alarm. She realized her parents and their problems had barely crossed her mind all day.

She wiped her boots on the back porch and stepped into the kitchen. The house was quiet and no one had turned any lights on yet. That struck her as a bit odd. Dinner preparations had usually started by now. Not that it mattered. She wouldn't be home again until nine.

What did Bob have to do at eight thirty?

Correction: What did Bob *maybe* have to do at eight thirty?

Hildy slipped off her boots, threw her coat over a kitchen chair, and checked her reflection in the mirror by the door. Her cheeks were bright pink sponges and there were tiny dots of snow in her hair. Was he afraid of getting stuck with her?

Xiu had done some online dating before spotting Sweet Baby James and had always built an escape hatch into her plans.

Was this an escape hatch? *Gee, Betty, sorry. Really love to stay, but gotta run. Maybe see you around some time.*

Was he just building in a polite excuse?

She bit her lip and let out a little laugh. One thing she knew: Bob was not polite.

She headed out of the kitchen. At some just-barely conscious level she must have figured—lights out, car in driveway—that her dad had gone for a run. But then she crossed the living room on her way to the stairs and a noise made her jump.

Her father laughed. A wheezy, joyless laugh.

"Dad! You scared me. What are you doing?"

He was leaning against the aquarium holding a small metal sieve by the handle. A fish flipped and flopped in it. Water dripped onto the floor.

"Trying to catch these goddamn fish." Her father never swore.

"Wouldn't it be easier with the lights on?"

Some fumbling, and a lamp turned on.

"What are you taking the fish out for, anyway?"

"Guy buying it doesn't want them."

"Buying what?"

"The aquarium."

Hildy's throat began to burn. "You're selling the aquarium? Does Gabe know?"

"Does he?! Ha!"

"What does that mean?" Hildy looked around the room as if Gabe might be there. She noticed the bottle of rye on the coffee table. She noticed her father's expression, his hair, the tins of fish food scattered on the floor, the fish.

There were actual live fish floundering around on the floor.

"You're drunk?"

The answer was clearly yes, but no. Not possible. A glass of wine? Of course. Sunset daiquiris on the beach? Almost a Greg 'n' Amy tradition. But drunk? Never.

He didn't answer.

"What's going on?"

"I told you." Her father dumped another fish onto the floor and started swishing around in the tank for more. "I put an ad on Craigslist for this goddamn fish hatchery, and I'm getting it the fuck out of my life."

"Dad!"

"Oh, excuse *you*, Miss Perfect."

Hildy picked the fish up off the carpet with her bare hands and threw it back in the aquarium.

"Hey! What the hell do you—" He was actually swaying slightly on his feet.

"Dad. Where's Gabe?"

"Not my problem!" He said it all singsongy, the way Max would have said it if he'd been trying to bug Xiu.

"Please. Don't do this to Gabe. He's going to be really upset. And—"

"*Go*ing to be? Ha! He *is*. You should have seen the look on his face." Prolonged snicker, eyes closed. "And the things he said. Well, I never!"

He started fishing around in the tank again. Hildy grabbed the scoop from his hands and threw it across the room. He laughed at that, too.

"Where is he?" She grabbed his shirt and shook him. "Where is Gabe?"

"All right. Let me tell you where Gabe is." Wiping her hands away. Trying to pull himself together now. "Do you know that Gabriel was named after an angel?"

"Dad."

"And not just any angel. We're talking, like, head honcho angel. The guy who told Mary—pure, *'innocent'* Mary—that she was going to have a baby. The widdle baby Jesus. Can you believe that?" He leaned forward, his jaw dangling.

"You're not answering my question."

"I know. I just thought you'd appreciate the irony."

He shrugged and turned his attention back to the aquarium. He tried to grab a fish with his hands and missed. "Slippery little so-n-sos."

Hildy wanted to hit him. She wanted to tell him to shut up. Grow up. Turn back into the person she'd thought he was.

"Hey! I know!" He stuck his finger in the air. "I'll pump the water out! Hildy. Grab my siphon and a bucket. There's a good girl."

He circled his hand at her like *c'mon, c'mon.*

She looked down at her feet, took a breath. "Where is Gabe?"

"Why do you keep asking me that?" He slapped his forehead. "I can't be worried about every goddamn little bastard who takes it into his head to run away. What do you think this is? A youth hostel? I—"

Hildy hit him hard across the face. He staggered a few sloppy steps back, slipped on a fish, fell to the floor, and laughed.

She put one hand on her chest and the other across her mouth. Her teeth were chattering. She looked at him for a moment, unbelieving. Her father. Spazzing around on the carpet like some sewered high school kid on prom night.

She didn't help him up.

She grabbed her coat and her phone and the keys to the Volvo, then she went out to find Gabe.

CHAPTER

13

Xiu didn't pick up her phone. No doubt she was out somewhere with SBJ and couldn't hear it ring over the snap, crackle, and pop of all that passion.

Max answered his, but Hildy could tell by the tone of his voice he was with someone, too. "Come get me," he said, anyway. "Give me ten and I'll be at the Sportsplex, south door."

He was waiting there for her, sweaty but ready, when she arrived six minutes later.

"Drive. Please," she said. He shrugged like *you're asking for it* and took her place. He was a terrible driver. He hunched over the wheel, knuckles white, foot randomly moving between brake and accelerator like he was playing honky-tonk on an old piano, but it was her only option. Hildy in her current state would be no better. Plus she had calls to make.

She tried Gabe's cell phone but it went straight to message.

"Hey, Monkey, it's me." She tried to keep the panic out of her voice. "You hungry? Max and I thought we'd go out for some linguine at Il Cantino. I'm paying. Call me. Kisses!"

She sent a text, more or less the same, then went to call him again.

"Enough. Chill. Give the boy a second," Max said. "Or are you actually *trying* to freak him out? He'll call if he gets it. You know that. The kid can't resist pasta."

"Asshole." Hildy put her head in her hands. Max wasn't offended, for himself or Gabe. He knew she meant her father.

"Craigslist." He shook his head. "I mean, whoa. Hissy fit. You don't think Gregoire has finally snapped, do you? Always said it was going to happen one day. God, I wish I still had that bet on with Winton."

She looked up from her phone and glared at him.

"Sorry . . . Sorry . . . Timing's a bit off tonight."

She shook her head, meaning something closer to *drop it* than *you're forgiven*. He carried on.

"Okay, not snapped—but still. *Such* a diva move. What was he thinking? Your father cannot sell the aquarium out from under Gabe's feet and toss his precious goldfish all over your mother's precious Persian carpet and actually think the marriage— by which I mean family—would survive, no matter how shit-faced he is."

They were now taking their third painfully slow spin around the neighborhood. People may have been getting suspicious about what they were up to, but at least at this speed Max wasn't in danger of hurting anyone.

"And speaking of which—footnote! Principal Sangster *drunk*? Not to ramp up the stress level or anything, Hildy, but Gregorinko von Stalin *willfully* losing control? The man who rules everything he touches with an iron fist? Sloppy drunk is so not his style. This is definitely a desperate call for help of some kind."

"Oh my god, Max. You *are* ramping up the stress level! Why did you even come? You really think I need to have all my worst fears confirmed when my family is falling apart and my little brother has gone missing and the temperature has just plunged below freezing? This isn't a timing issue. This is a complete and absolute lack of judgment on your part."

"Oops." He slapped himself in the side of the head. "It's out of my system now. Promise. Idiot." He leaned over and cranked the heat up. He briefly swerved into the other lane but managed to right the car when a bus barreling straight at them honked.

"Look. About Gabe. You don't have to worry. It'll be nice and warm in here when we find him. And we will. You keep calling people. I'll keep driving."

He reached out and patted her leg. She put his hand back on the wheel, then tried calling Gabe's friend Owen.

When he didn't answer, she called his mother's landline and found out Owen was at Tae Kwon Do. Mrs. Kutchner didn't know where Gabe was but she gave Hildy the names and numbers of some other kids who might. Hildy called. They didn't know.

Max drove them to H2Eau. It was closed. Hildy thought the boot prints in the snow near the fish store window looked like Gabe's, but Max wouldn't even entertain the idea. "Or mine. Or that homeless guy's over there. Or any of the hundreds of big-footed males who tromp by here every day. You're working your-self up into a snot, Hil."

"Well, what am I supposed to do?! Dad is drunk, acting—as you so kindly pointed out—like some fascist dictator psychopath, tor-turing animals and ruining Gabe's favorite thing in the world, and the poor little kid is out in the cold somewhere, distraught, con-fused, hopeless—"

"Stop right there. Reality check. *Drunk*—I'll take your word for it. *Fascist dictator*—we've done almost four years together at Gulag High. This is news? *Psychopath*—I never said that, so don't go putting words in my mouth. As for Gabe, 'poor little kid' he is not. Brick shithouses quake at the sight of him. He's a beast. So he may be cold, but he's hardly going to die."

Hearing the word *die* was too much. Hildy started to leak tears. (She'd been doing so well until now.)

Max slammed on the brakes and turned and looked at her. "Hildegarde. You're overreacting. This is not *Revenge of the Baby Snatchers*. Gabe's a big, strong guy and he's no doubt upset—I mean, who wouldn't be with a dickwad like your dad—but we're going to find him and he's going to be okay."

"Find him? Where? We've looked everywhere."

The car behind screeched out in front of them, the driver slowing down just long enough to give Max the finger on his way past. Max did his best beauty queen wave, then got back to business.

"No, we haven't. Leave it to me. I'm going to channel my inner twelve-year-old boy and search out every place he could possibly be. Trust me. He's not far."

"How can you be so sure?"

He looked at her like *please*. "Because you Sangsters move like slugs. That's why. Large, if adorable, slugs. We've just got to find Gabe's slime trail and follow it."

Hildy laughed for the first time that night and wiped her face on her sleeve. Max was right. Their parents might Fitbit their way through life—always running, skiing, biking, swimming—but Gabe was practically as physically lazy as Hildy. In Ireland, Alec had actually found someone to deliver beer to his door.

Max really got to work now. They checked out a nearby school that had a nook behind the portable classrooms where kids went to smoke, the park with the climbing gym that looked like a lighthouse, several McDonald's, a really grotty donut shop that made the best maple nut crullers ever. (The key, Max claimed, were was the mouse poo sprinkles.) They drove around and through and back and over and over Gabe's known world.

No sign of him.

Of anybody.

It had gotten that cold out.

Meanwhile, Hildy called the hospital. The lady on the switchboard said her mother was attending to patients and thus, they figured, not with Gabe. Hildy didn't leave her name or try her mother's cell phone. No use alarming her unnecessarily. This—the aquarium, the drinking, Gabe's taking off—would be the final straw. Hildy knew that and was determined to avoid it.

Max kept up a constant, "He's fiiiiiiiine, Hildy. He's probably just at . . ."—*wherever*—before heading off on another fruitless search. His optimism got old. Hildy eventually told him to shut up. He managed to do so until the Volvo's pinging became insistent and he said, "I don't mind driving you around but I draw the line at pushing the car. We're stopping for gas."

First station they saw, he pulled in over the curb and more or less up to the pumps. He took out the credit card her dad kept in the glove compartment and started filling the tank.

Hildy sat in the passenger seat, staring straight ahead, trying to conjure up last names and addresses of other kids Gabe might hang out with. She couldn't think of anyone. She pictured him huddled over a manhole cover, cold, wet, whimpering, shivering—just another "runaway." Just another sad statistic.

Then she saw him.

Like actual *him*. Gabe. Coming out of the service station convenience store with a family-sized bag of cheese puffs and a large slushy. She screamed, scrambled to open the door, and ran toward him. He opened his eyes wide and froze. A big dumb cartoon bear, caught in the act.

She threw her arms around him, knocking neon-lime liquid all over her coat and his jacket and the grubby gray snow. His face was cold. His nose was running. He smelled slightly of BO. (She needed to talk to him about washing more.)

He was so much taller than her now. She'd forgotten that. The more they'd looked for him in the real world, the smaller he'd become in her head.

"Hey! What the . . . Quit it, would you?" he said, but he didn't actually push her off, which he could have done if he'd really wanted to. She knew he was glad to see her, too.

"Gabe, where have you been?" Tears were streaming down Hildy's face, and her breath, when she finally managed to catch it, had a honking quality.

"God! The library. What's the big deal? I'm not, like, two."

"You're, like, a knucklehead is what you are." Max cuffed him upside the head. "Now apologize, you brute! You've upset your sister."

"Cha. What doesn't upset her?"

"Good point." Max tapped his index finger on his cheek. "Sorry, Hildy. Kid's right."

"Yeah. So, chill, would you? It's not even eight o'clock."

Hildy was laughing now, too, although the tears kept coming. The boys ignored them. (They were used to her.)

"Why did you run away?" she said and slipped her arm in Gabe's.

"I didn't run away." He slipped his arm back out.

"Dad said you did."

"You listen to him? I ran *out*, not away. You don't expect me to stay in the house with him, do you? Did you hear what he did? Jerk. He sold the aquarium! He didn't even ask me. It's just, like, bang. Gone. Screw you, Gabe."

He took a big noisy slurp from the remains of the slushy. Hildy realized it was to hide a sob.

"By the sound of that, you could use another one," Max said. "Green or blue? Both taste the same. It's honestly just about what color you want your caca to be tomorrow morning. Your choice."

Gabe held up the cup he had. Max nodded and went inside.

Hildy bounced her forehead off Gabe's chest. She was sort of saying she loved him while trying not to get too soppy about it. He really didn't need her crying anymore, but it was so hard to stop once she'd started.

"Dad's a prick," Gabe said.

"He is," she said.

"And I don't know why. What's the matter with him? I don't know how a guy could just wake up one day and decide he hates fish and his favorite hobby and, like, I don't know, me or something. People don't do that. Normal people."

"He doesn't hate you," Hildy said. She wanted to believe it.

"Well, he sure acts like—" Gabe tried to cover up another sob with another slurp. It was agony for Hildy, standing there with her head on his chest while he made desperate sucking sounds into an empty plastic cup and they both tried to act as if they were perfectly okay with the situation.

Max finally arrived with three 72-ouncers and a large shopping bag full of junk to share.

"Gregorinko's going to be some sort of pissed when he gets his credit card statement this month," he said as they got in the car. "Thank goodness convenience stores are such rip-offs."

"A little passive-aggressive, but whatever," Hildy said, and tore open a bag of dark chocolate almond clusters. Max knew what she liked, she thought. He knew how to take her mind off her problems.

Then, hot on the heels of that, another thought.

"Oh my god!" she screamed. "Oh my god, oh my god, oh my god!"

"What now?" Gabe said, mouth full, comfy in the backseat of the warm car, and suddenly bored.

Max guessed immediately. "Bob?"

Hildy whimpered.

"Relax. Use your words."

She hit her head repeatedly against her palm.

"This family's nuts," Gabe said.

"I forgot about Bob. I was supposed to meet Bob at seven!"

Max started up the car. "Where?"

"That new café. Near the bridge."

Max burnt out of the parking lot, heading north.

"Hey. No way. Stop!" Gabe grabbed their headrests and pulled himself up between them. "If I'm late for curfew, you're the one in trouble. I mean it. I'm not losing my allowance over this."

Hildy told him to put his seat belt on and directed Max to the café. It's was 7:43. What were the chances he was still there?

"Call him," Max said. "Tell him to wait." But Bob didn't have a cell phone, and she didn't know the name of the place, and the whole situation was, of course, hopeless but that didn't matter. She made Max take an illegal turn, cut someone off, and run yellow lights all the way there.

She had to. Number one on Bob's list of things he hated: people who let him down.

CHAPTER

14

Max rode the curb outside while Hildy banged on the door of the café. It was locked. A waitress, clearing a table, looked up and shook her head.

Hildy banged some more and mouthed, *Pleeease*. The waitress mouthed back, *Sorry*. Hildy banged harder.

The waitress sighed and opened the door.

"Look, our machines are all off. We've dumped out the coffee. Nothing I can do. We're closed."

Hildy peered around her. The place was empty. Completely devoid of Bob.

"I know. I don't want coffee. I was supposed to meet someone here. Just wondering if you knew where he went."

The waitress screwed up her mouth and put her hand on her hip. She'd had a long shift. She wanted to go home.

"What did he look like?"

"He, um—" Hildy spread her hands out to her side, then slapped them palms down on her chest, then looked up at the light above the door.

She had no idea. This guy who'd occupied all her thoughts for days, who'd exposed himself to her—he'd disappeared. She didn't have one word to describe him.

"Tall?" the waitress said, maybe in embarrassment for her, maybe just wanting to hurry her along.

Hildy remembered. "Almost six feet . . . Light brown hair . . ."

"Little—um—thing with his nose?" The waitress waved her hand uncertainly in front of her face.

"Yes. Yes. That's him. He was here?"

"Yup. You the girlfriend he was waiting for?"

Hildy nodded. The waitress whistled. "You're in trouble."

"Where'd he go? You know?"

"No idea. Owner might. She was talking to him." She leaned over her shoulder and called, "Colleen. Got a sec?" She waved Hildy in, then went back to cleaning up.

A middle-aged woman with frazzled burgundy hair and an eyebrow ring came out of the kitchen, wiping her hands on her apron.

"That guy waiting. You know where he went?" The waitress scrunched up the brown paper covering a table.

"Paul?"

"You know him?" Hildy said.

"Apparently I do," the owner said. "He recognized me. Said his mother was Molly, um, Bergman . . . no, sorry, Durgan. Didn't know who he was until then."

"Molly," Hildy repeated. The mother he'd talked about. Bob's.

"Yeah. We worked together at The Uptown Grill, must be fifteen years ago now. Paul—I used to call him Paulie. Molly and Paulie. Cute kid."

"Cute grown-up," the waitress said, and shook out her hand like *hot.*

"Don't know where he went, do you?" Hildy felt hope springing eternal. "He's mad at me. Hates it when I'm late. Won't answer his phone." She had no idea why she felt the need to embellish the story.

"Sorry. We chatted for a bit, then things got busy and I had to go. He was sitting over there." Colleen threw her chin toward the window. "Didn't have a chance to ask about his mother. By the time I finished up, he was gone."

Hildy noticed some things crumpled up on the table. She knew immediately what they were.

"Oh," she said in the most casual voice she could find. "The cards on the table? He must have left them for me. Mind if I take them?"

"Better you than the landfill." Colleen gave her head a little shake and her curls swayed like underwater plant life. "Funny seeing him sitting there drawing. That's what he used to do when he was little, too. Always plunked at some table in the back, working away on something, his tongue out to one side. Waiting for his mother to get off work, quit flirting, whatever."

She gave a sad little laugh. "Hard life for a kid." Another shake of the head. "Molly. Molly Durgan of all people."

Colleen and the waitress got back to closing up the café. Hildy went to collect the cards with the questions. That's when she noticed the brown paper covering the tabletop was filled with drawings. Kong was prominent, and so was the hand Bob liked to draw, and Bambi's dad, and a bowl of cappuccino with a heart etched in the crema and, also, several times, a girl with large lips, small eyes, and, occasionally, huge orthodontic headgear.

"Mind if I take this, too?" Hildy said. She'd beg for it if they said no. She'd honestly get down on her knees and beg.

"All yours," Colleen said. "But if it turns out to be worth something one day, we're splitting the profit."

Hildy laughed, rolled up the brown paper, and headed to the car, giddy with happiness.

Gabe and Max were pretty happy, too. They'd cranked up

the music and decorated the inside of Greg's Volvo with a fringe of bright orange cheese puffs and red gummy worms. It was like stepping into a little Mexican cantina on a cold winter's night.

CHAPTER 15

Hildy felt as if the gods were smiling down on her. Gods with an *s*. It must have taken more than one to fix the mess they'd been in. (Maybe that was why Bob needed girls with an *s*. To fix those messes he'd alluded to.)

She got Max to go in the front door of their house and create a racket while she snuck Gabe in the back. Gabe was old enough to do it himself, as he pointed out in an angry whisper, but Hildy needed to be the smoke screen. Dead fish and his drunk father were not what she wanted Gabe seeing at the moment. She distracted him all the way up the stairs.

It turned out the situation in the living room was not as bad as she'd feared. Alcohol has its virtues. Greg was still in the spot she'd left him, pretty much comatose. The rest of the fish had survived. The man from Craiglist had either stood Greg up or Greg hadn't heard the doorbell. In either case, the aquarium was still there.

For the time being.

And that was fine.

Max was strong enough and—in this case at least—discreet enough to get Greg upstairs and into bed before her mother got home. By the time he came back down, Hildy had cleaned up the floor and put all the fish paraphernalia back in its proper spot. She gave Max the dregs of the bottle of rye and a full quart of scotch as thanks.

"You don't need to do this," he said, flapping one hand at her while pocketing the bottles with the other. "Tonight was weirdly fun. I mean, a high-speed chase. A missing kid. A race against time. I felt like a younger, better-looking version of Liam Neeson. I haven't had this much excitement since—"

"TMI," she said.

"What? You don't even know what I was going to say."

"Am I wrong?" She kissed him good-bye and pushed him out the door.

Gabe would notice fish were missing when he woke up. Amy would smell booze when she got home. Greg could very well get up the next day and start this all over again—but that was the next day.

Hildy didn't care. For now, it was all about Bob. She opened her laptop and messaged him. She could explain everything. He'd understand.

An alert came up. No "Bob Someone" existed anymore.

Okay. He was mad. She got that. She'd just have to find another way.

And she could, she realized.

He wasn't Bob Someone. She knew who he was now.

She could make this right.

CHAPTER

16

Hildy thought it was going to be easy. She could find Bob.

"But do you really want to?" Xiu was still groggy from an epic date with SBJ. Hildy's call had woken her up. "Still not convinced he's the guy for you."

Hildy looked out her bedroom window. Her mother's car was gone. Her father was going to lose it when he saw the inside of his. She answered sweetly, "Yes, I do, and that's your problem not mine."

"Fine then. If you're that hot for him, go for it."

Hildy clamped the phone between her ear and shoulder so her hands were free to get dressed. "I might be dense, but I really don't get why you think Bob and me would be such a disaster?"

"There's your answer in a nutshell. 'Bob and me.' Just a few hours with him and already your grammar's suffering."

Given their recent conversations, that was actually kind of funny.

"Bob and I. Excuse me. I'm tired. And that's beside the point. I still don't understand your big objection. You haven't even met him." Hildy put on leggings, then jeans, and thick wool socks, too.

"I've met him through your eyes and what you're showing me is a guy totally at odds with who you are."

"So? Opposites attract."

"Sure. But I can't help feeling like I'm watching my beloved vegan friend about to chow down on a big bloody slab of prime rib. I feel obliged to warn her that it might be hard on her system."

Hildy put Xiu on speaker so she could get her top part dressed. "Look, do you know a Paul Durgan or don't you? That's all I called about."

"Paul what?" Xiu gave a gravelly unbrushed-teeth type of cough.

"Durgan. D-U-R—"

"No, I don't. At least not at this time in the morning. Maybe after I've had my tea."

She tried to direct the conversation back to her date with SBJ but Hildy said, "Later," and hung up. She had work to do.

She started online. She found a few Paul Durgans, but unless he'd drastically changed his hair, age, or race, not the one she was looking for. She checked an old phone book for a Molly Durgan, an M. Durgan, a Paul or P. Durgan. The closest she came was an E. M. Durgan on Oxford Street. Her heart thumped. She'd found him. She just knew it.

She considered phoning but that seemed lame. He might just hang up.

He'd have every right to hang up.

She decided to walk over instead. Pull the full rom-com thing. Show up at his door with three Egg McMuffins, a Dunkin' Donuts coffee, a sincere apology, and some joke about being the girl he needed to round out his perfect day. (Question 4, if he missed the reference.)

She fixed herself up, then got ready to go. She peeked in Gabe's room. He was still asleep. Her dad usually took him to the market Saturday morning but she guessed that wasn't part of the routine anymore.

The door to her parents' room was ajar. The bed was unmade. No one was there or downstairs, either, and that was a relief. She bundled up and left. She stopped at the strip mall for her supplies, then headed over to 2012 Oxford Street.

She was surprised when she saw it: a big old Victorian house with shrubs out front neatly bundled in burlap and a late-model Mercedes in the driveway.

This was either the wrong place or Bob had been lying to her.

She stared at the house for a couple of seconds before mentally shrugging and walking up the front path. No stopping her now. She rang the bell. She could hear a TV click off, then footsteps. The door opened. An older lady with glasses around her neck and stiff curls smiled and said, "Yes?"

Hildy apologized for disturbing her and asked if Paul Durgan lived there. She felt obliged to lie and say she'd lost his phone number and needed to find him.

"Before his breakfast gets cold?" The old lady laughed. "Sorry, dear. Paul, you say? Not any Durgan I know of by that name." She waved Hildy in. "Let me call my sister-in-law. She's the family historian. She might know."

In the next hour, Hildy learned Mrs. Durgan and Nana had been friends at nursing school and, when her sister-in-law finally returned her call, that there was no known Paul or Molly in that branch of the family.

As she was walking Hildy to the door, Mrs. Durgan said, "So what's the real reason you're bringing that boy breakfast?"

And because she'd been friends with Nana, Hildy told her.

Mrs. Durgan listened with a nurse's smile on her face, kind and sympathetic, but no nonsense, too.

When she was done talking, Hildy grimaced. "I feel sort of

ridiculous. Sorry I bothered you."

"Not at all!" Mrs. Durgan gave Hildy's arm a squeeze. "When you're eighty-two and a widow, human contact of any kind is welcome. And it's a wonderful story, anyway. Now can I tell you one?"

"Sure."

"When I was a little older than you, I was going with a boy named Don. Charming? Oh. And handsome? I went weak in the knees just looking at him. But he treated me terribly. Always standing me up or cutting me off or putting me down. And finally I'd had enough. I told him we were through. 'Don't bother calling.' I remember saying that to him, then flouncing out and feeling like a million bucks. Next day, I packed my bags, got on a train, and headed off to a new life in a new city. We were about twenty minutes out of the station when all hell broke loose. Sirens going, brakes squealing, people shouting. Word got down to our car that, at the railway bridge, some damn fool had jumped onto the moving train and crawled along the roof to the caboose. Two minutes later, who comes running in but Don, with the conductor in hot pursuit. The poor boy just managed to get down on one knee and ask me to marry him before he was dragged off for a night in the cooler."

"So . . . did you marry him?"

"Yes—but not before I straightened him out. I wasn't about to say 'I do' until I was damn sure *he* knew what he had to do to make this marriage work."

"And did he?"

Mrs. Durgan laughed. "Mostly. I had to beat that streak of arrogance out of him first. Men back then didn't know their place. And, Lord knows, I wasn't perfect, either, so we had our ups and downs. But at the worst of times, when I'd almost had enough of his boneheadedness, I thought of him lovestruck enough to jump onto that train and, you know, that saw us through forty-six years together."

"So, in other words, I wasn't that crazy buying my bag of Egg

McMuffins and hunting Paul down."

"No! You go, girl. Isn't that what they say these days?"

Mrs. Durgan gave her a little hug good-bye. "But no jumping on moving trains, please. That was just asinine. But that, of course, was my Don. No matter who you get, you gotta take a little bad with the good."

When Hildy got back home, Gabe was up and ransacking the kitchen for something to eat. She zapped the three Egg McMuffins and handed them to him.

"What's with this?" he said, stuffing his mouth. "I thought you hate McDonald's."

"I do, but I'm not the one eating." She was sitting at the kitchen table, texting various friends to find out if they knew anyone named Paul Durgan.

"Never let me eat them before."

Hildy shrugged. "You've got cheese on your—" She almost said mustache. She realized Gabe had fine dark hair growing on his upper lip. She just motioned to his face instead.

He wiped it off and ate it. She didn't say anything. Her phone buzzed a couple of times. Both texts said *Never heard of him.*

Gabe said, "I'm sorry I messed things up for you, Hildy."

"What? How?"

"With that guy. Your date. What's-his-name."

"You didn't." Hildy got up to make herself some coffee. She'd thrown the Dunkin' Donuts stuff out. She didn't know how Bob could drink it. "He'll be back."

"Right. How could he ever resist you?"

She pushed his head with the palm of her hand. "Nice."

"I sort of mean it," he said.

Hildy went, "Ahhhh . . ." and gave him a hug. "You need a shower, Gabe. Every day. You need to shower."

He pulled his T-shirt up to his nose and sniffed. Even he

winced. He took the last half of the last Egg McMuffin and headed off to the bathroom.

Six more texts came in.

No.

No.

Sorry.

Can't help you.

No.

I used to work with a guy called Paul Durgan.

Emmeline Mitchell. Flute-playing, poetry-writing Emmeline Mitchell. The very last person Hildy would have thought knew Bob.

Where?

Walmart. I had a part-time job there a couple of summers ago.

I wonder if it's the same one. The guy I'm looking for is a drummer and has a tattoo on his face.

Sounds like him. Didn't know he was a drummer but he has a tattoo and I know he was in a band. Asked me to switch shifts couple times so he could play.

Know how to reach him?

Got his email but not sure if still good. Pau.durg@sympatico. net. Say hi to him for me. He's a really nice guy. Not at all what you think he's like at first.

I know. Thx!

The coffee was ready but Hildy wasn't sure she should have any. Her heart was having trouble staying in her chest as it was.

She went to her room and wrote him an email.

Paul (Do you mind if I call you that?)

Emmeline Mitchell gave me your contact info. She told me exactly what I suspected: that you're a really nice guy. I desperately need to talk to you. Any chance we could get together? We could even meet at Dunkin'

Donuts if you like. I'm around all afternoon. You just say
the time and I'll be there.

Hildy

She got an answer almost immediately. Short and to the point.

Ok. Hows 2? Dunkin Donuts next to the Riverview
Walmart?

Great. See you then!

Hildy was there at ten to two. The last thing she wanted to do was be late. She found a table midway back that gave her a good view of both doors.

By five after two, she was beginning to panic. Lots of people breezing in and out to get their large coffees and dozen donuts, but no Bob.

Maybe he wasn't such a nice guy. Maybe he'd done this to her on purpose. See how she liked being stood up.

By quarter after, she was picking up her satchel to go when she heard someone say her name. She looked up. There was a tall, skinny guy with a shaved head, large ear gauges, and a full-face tattoo.

"I thought that must be you." He sat down at the chair beside her and gave her a big smile.

It was an honest mistake. This Paul Durgan was in a band—Decomposing Remains—and had a small but dedicated group of fans. He'd just figured she must be a new one. He was flattered she'd gotten in touch.

Hildy was too startled to bluff her way out of it. What the hell. She told him the truth.

Like Emmeline said, Paul turned out to be a really good guy.

He bought a blueberry muffin for her and a cruller for himself, and she told him everything. "Nothing to be ashamed of," he said when she'd finished. "It's all about love."

"What is?"

"This." He motioned around the room. Hildy looked but all she saw were two old guys sitting alone at separate tables and, near the recycling bin, an aging goth couple fighting over who's turn it was to buy the laundry softener.

"Love," Paul said again. "Here. There. Wherever. For real. That's all that matters. See this? Beside the skeleton?" He leaned forward and pointed to his forehead. "Can you read it?"

It was a bit difficult to make out. Most of his skin was tattooed a kind of dark green and there was a pentagon and an enraged lion entwined around the word, too.

"Jocelyn?" Hildy guessed.

"Jodilyn. She was my girlfriend for six years. I loved her more than anything on earth."

"Loved? What happened?"

He leaned back in his chair and shrugged. "The usual. I got a little too 'intimate' with one of my fans. She hooked up with my best friend. End of story."

"And now you have her name tattooed on your forehead for the rest of your life. That doesn't sound like a good thing to me."

He shook his head and laughed. "That's what I thought, too, but then I met Kit. The girl I'm going out with now. I laid eyes on her and wow. It was like lightning. Love at first sight. Next morning I booked an appointment at the tattoo parlor. I was going to have 'Jodilyn' turned into a serpent but Kit wouldn't let me. She likes a man of passion, she said. Better to have loved and lost than never to have loved at all. That's her philosophy."

He put his hand on his chest. Each finger sported a large skull-shaped ring and several tattoos. "Take it from me. Love's like anything else. You're going to screw up a few times before you get it right. Just make sure you screw up big. Not worth it otherwise."

"Yeah, well. I've done that already."

"Great. So go out and screw it up again. You won't regret it. Or actually, you might. But not as much as if you didn't try."

They talked for over an hour about love and life, then he drove her home. Hildy's dad must have had a mini heart attack when he looked up from shoveling the walkway and saw a big bald tat-tooed guy hug her good-bye, but, of course, he was in no position to comment.

CHAPTER
17

Hildy felt encouraged at first by her meeting with this Paul Durgan. He was right. She'd regret it if she didn't try. She started pestering distant friends and random acquaintances to see if anyone knew the other Paul Durgan, but no luck.

Several days passed. Life carried on. Her father was sheepish and uncommunicative, but there was no more talk of selling the aquarium. Gabe was still thrilled about sneaking in after curfew and was quietly enjoying his victory in the stench of his room. It was year-end at the hospital so Amy was busy with reports or, at least, that was her story. They'd all retreated to their corners. They'd become one of those sad families where everyone ate dinner alone in their respective rooms in front of their respective laptops, but at least they weren't fighting.

The Bob thing was different. He knew how to reach her, but he hadn't.

He was mad.

He hated her now.

Maybe she'd already loved him and lost him and never even had the chance to enjoy it.

Every day that passed made it a little worse. The door between them had been just barely ajar. How long before it clicked shut? How long before he locked it behind him?

She took down the Barcelona poster she'd had on her wall since the junior high class trip and taped up the brown paper from the café. She studied the drawings like an Egyptologist studied hieroglyphs. The short-lived Bob and Betty Dynasty, chronicled in pictograms. She thought she'd figured out the symbols for fear and happiness and anger and maybe even physical attraction, but she couldn't decipher an address.

She thought about Bob constantly—when she was trying to study, when she was trying to eat, each time she saw one of those missing cat posters stapled to a telephone pole. Her thoughts of him had moved from the pain of longing to just plain pain. His pain, as much as hers. She'd let him down. She'd hurt him. She kept hearing Colleen say, "Hard life for a kid." Colleen had the face of a woman who'd seen her share of bad things and yet that's what made her sad.

And now Hildy was the one letting him down.

She was in the library trying not to think about stuff like that when Xiu messaged her about getting some lunch. The last thing Hildy wanted to do was join her in the cafeteria, but she no doubt needed food and Xiu could be a sounding board or, at least, someone to split a beet salad with.

Hildy managed to nod and wave her way through the noon hour crowd, only to realize Sweet Baby James had dropped by the school and was joining them, too. She mentally groaned when she saw the two of them curled up together at a table near the back. She was in no mood to meet anyone. Her hair was greasy and she had a cold sore starting. She looked like a bad mugshot of a white-collar criminal.

Xiu bounced up and kissed her on either cheek. "James. This is she! The fabulous Hildy Sangster."

He smiled out of one side of his mouth. Hildy couldn't tell if he was shy or cool or just a jerk who liked to look it. Handsome though. No doubt about that. Xiu coiled herself into the seat beside him. He rested his hand on her thigh.

This was going to be agony. Xiu looked gorgeous, glowing. Her happiness was actually causing Hildy a kind of physical pain. A massage therapist with his thumb driving deep into a knotted muscle, acting as if it was going to help. That's what it felt like.

"Hildy is a wonderful singer."

No. Please. Not this. Hildy gave a downward smile and shook her head. "I'm not. Really. I'm, like, high school musical passable. That's about all."

SBJ gave one of those noncommittal gestures somewhere between a shrug and a nod. They both just wanted it to stop.

"Don't believe a word, sweetie. She's *very* musical. That's why I've been dying to get the two of you together. So much in common." Xiu adjusted the collar of his wrinkled, unadjustable plaid shirt. "And I don't just mean your mutual love for me."

A little nose laugh from SBJ. Not even that from Hildy.

"Oh, hey!" Xiu, all lit up, looked right at Hildy. "Maybe James will know."

Know what? This couldn't be good. The thought of having to dredge up something like enthusiasm for one of Xiu's brilliant ideas made Hildy feel like dissolving.

"Do you know a Paul Durgan?" Since meeting SBJ, Xiu's voice had gotten permanently husky. It made everything she said sound slightly dirty.

"Durgan?" SBJ shook his head.

"Phooey. Thought you might. He plays the drums."

"Don't mean Paul *Bergin*, do you? *B*-E-R-G-I-N?"

They both turned toward Hildy.

"Um. Maybe?" She remembered Colleen at the café stumbling

to recall Molly's last name.

"He played with us a few times. About my height. Little tattoo under his eye."

Hildy sat up straight. "Yes. Teardrop."

He got out his phone and scrolled through some pictures. "That him?"

It was taken at some gig. SBJ was in front on guitar, leaning into the microphone. Bob was behind—head back, drum sticks raised.

"Yes."

Xiu clapped the tips of her fingers together. Hildy tried not to explode.

"Know how I can reach him?"

"Sorry. Don't think he has a phone. My buddy George always arranged it." SBJ went through his contacts. "I'll give him a call. See if he knows."

Xiu turned to Hildy and mouthed, "He's soooo nice!" then bit her lip and scrunched up her eyes.

Hildy sat on the edge of her seat, hands folded in her lap, heart drumming. Bob drumming. Maybe she'd found Bob. SBJ made various one- and two-word replies, then said thanks and hung up.

"He doesn't know the address but says it's a white house with a purple door two up from the corner of Young and Cork. Paul's place is in the back. Kind of tucked behind the Dumpster. Door to the basement. George used to put a note through his mail slot when we needed him. He'd usually turn up. Good drummer. I'm surprised he's still in town. Thought he was leaving."

"Why? Where?"

SBJ shrugged. "Just said he wanted to get out of town. Got the feeling he doesn't hang around long. Bit of a loner. My impression at least. Not big on socializing."

There was so much Hildy wanted to ask SBJ about. Bob's mother. His friends. Girls with an *s*. But Xiu said, "What are you waiting for? Go! Go!"

Hildy grabbed her satchel and ran.

"Make good choices!" Xiu called out after her, then went back to nuzzling SBJ's neck.

CHAPTER

18

Hildy didn't know that area of town very well, but it wasn't hard to find the house. Two doors down from the corner, just like SBJ said. Entrance to the basement apartment tucked in behind the Dumpster out back.

She'd washed her hair and applied some subtle makeup and put on those little earrings Bob seemed to like, but she was relieved just the same when she knocked and no one answered.

No one opened the door and looked at her with blank eyes.

No one told her to get the hell out.

No one laughed at her.

It felt like a kind of Russian roulette. Pulling the trigger and realizing life would go on. She'd have another chance.

She peered into the window beside the door. The apartment was tiny. Only the light above the stove was on. It lit up a single saucepan and cast a thin bluish line around the edge of a neatly made bed. The glimmer on the table, she realized after a few seconds, was a fish bowl. Kong, at least, was still okay.

She leaned against the Dumpster and looked around the backyard. It was dark out but the security light in the parking lot next door flooded across the property line. There was a dingy crust on the snow, only broken where some dog had peed and some owner had followed. The remains of a bike was still chained to the fence. The Dumpster must have stunk in the summer.

This is where he lived. Paul Bergin. She tried not to find it sad. (He hated it when she did that.)

She didn't want him to catch her here. She thought of Xiu calling SBJ "sweetie" and wrapping herself around him.

She took the envelope out of her satchel, wrote *Paul Bergin/ Bob Someone* on the front, and put it through his mail slot, quickly, before she changed her mind.

CHAPTER
19

Dear Bob,

This, if you can't tell, is a picture of me imploring you to read the following letter. (Despite all the expensive lessons, I'm still a terrible drawer—but I'm desperate.)

I know you don't want to hear any excuses as to why I missed our meeting, so I won't even try. Instead, I'll just answer a few of the remaining questions in an attempt to win back your faith in me. (You did have a little faith in me once upon a time, didn't you?)

So here goes.

QUESTION 29: Share with your partner an embarrassing moment in your life.

Oh, boy. So many to choose from. But I thought you might like this one. A few days ago I was supposed to meet a guy in a café at the corner of North and Agricola. (You might know it. It's called the Groundskeeper.) By the time I'd got there, they'd already closed and he was gone, but I lied my way in by implying I was the guy's girlfriend. Based on that piece of misinformation, the owner let me take the papers he'd left behind. You might not find that particularly embarrassing, but that's because you're not a Good Little Girl who has a psychic posse of authority figures (her mother, various teachers, a former Brownie leader, and major deities of most global religions) following her around in her head. They were all bitterly disappointed in me for lying (except, of course, Eros, but you know those Greek gods. Incorrigible . . .).

I embarrassed myself further by basically stalking the guy I'd missed. I harassed people for any information about him. I bullied my way into an old lady's home. At a strip mall Dunkin' Donuts, I shared "intimate" details of my feelings for the guy with the thirty-four-year-old lead singer of the deathrock band Decomposing Remains just because he had a strikingly similar name.

I was worried I was becoming that staple of horror fiction: the delusional girl stalking the uninterested guy. But not *that* worried. It didn't stop me. I carried on until an acquaintance mentioned he knew a drummer—a very good drummer—named Paul "Bergin with a *B*" and gave me his address. This led me to the embarrassing thing I'm doing now. Laying myself bare. Exposing myself. But you—the guy, of course, in question—must be used to that by now.

QUESTION 30 (A DREADED TWO—PARTER): A) When did you last cry in front of another person? B) By yourself?

A) It was just before the incident relayed above. The reason I was late for my meeting with this very important person was because my younger brother had gone missing after an argument with my father. It was freezing out and I was afraid he'd run away. That's why I cried in front of another person. (Several, in fact. But, hey. Par for the course.)

B) I cried by myself because I woke up that night in a panic thinking my brother was still missing. Then I remembered we'd found him and he was fine and that got me started again. (I cry for both good and bad reasons—and also, occasionally, reasons in between.) I cried some more when I realized he wouldn't be fine forever and, for the first time in my life, I wouldn't be able to do anything about it.

On a positive note, I didn't cry about missing the meeting. It made me very sad but not as sad as my brother's situation. I finally had some perspective on my life. And I think you know how much I appreciate perspective.

QUESTION 31: Tell your partner something that you like about them already.

I feel like we've already answered this question. (Sensitive, funny, very good-looking, etc., etc.) That's why I'm going to tell you instead what I hope SOMEDAY I find I like about you, and it is this: your forgiving nature. I hope that you'll realize there were extenuating circumstances holding me up. That you'll understand I'm not just another person bent on disappointing you. And that you'll give me another chance.

If only so I can see how you answered these questions.

And get Kong back, too, of course.

QUESTION 32: What, if anything, is too serious to be joked about?

If you asked Max, he'd say "zip" (or maybe *nada*—he's kind of in a Spanish phase at the moment). His irreverence is one of the many reasons I love him. If you asked me, I'd say "a lot," most of which (see below) won't surprise you.

-Race relations
-The role of women and the variously abled in society
-Mental illness
-Guaranteed government funding of high school arts programs
-Endangered species (including snakes even though I can't help thinking the world would be better off without them)
-Female circumcision
-Good grammar
-The right to a safe workplace
-The mess my family is in
-Anything by/about Jane Austen, Emily Brontë, or Taylor Swift
-The size of my lips

On the other hand, you can joke all you want about my pretensions, my misconceptions, and my sad, sad delusions about someday becoming a short, white, female Nelson Mandela. In fact, I wish you would. I like it when you make me laugh at myself.

QUESTION 33: (If you're still reading by this point which, frankly, would be an absolute miracle and so not like you. Or at least the you I know. Or think I know.) A) If you were to die this evening with no opportunity to communicate with anyone, what would you most regret not having told someone? B) Why haven't you told them yet?

A) I'd be sorry I hadn't told you the answer to Question 28. (I bet you thought I'd forgotten about that.) I spent the whole night before we were supposed to meet trying to come up with a "very honest" answer that I could actually say to you without the application of drugs and/or alcohol. I came up with one (although I might need a little nip of something to spit it out).

B) "Why haven't you told them yet?" Because I have to tell you to your face. That's the only way I can and/or should do it. I've got to think of myself, too. Because, honestly, if you don't want to see me, you probably don't deserve to know the answer, in which case it'll be my secret which I will take to the death.

So, now, a question for you: Do you want to see me?
If you do, you know how to reach me.
Hopefully yours, I remain,

Betty

PS Would it be appropriate to add xoxo? If not, please ignore.

CHAPTER
20

Days passed. Hildy shut down her brain. That was the only way she managed to get to class, get her paper done, get some sleep, exhale. Max bought her dark-chocolate-and-sea-salt caramels and made her eat. Xiu sat patiently on her bed and covered Hildy's head in tiny braids. "He's an asshole," she said. "So uncool just leaving you hanging like that after you opened your heart and everything." Although she couldn't resist adding, "But SBJ says he's an excellent drummer and kind of funny, when he actually talks, that is."

Hildy switched with another girl so she could do her poetry presentation after spring break instead of before. She took three extra buses to get to her dentist appointment so she wouldn't pass the stop near his house. She did her best to control her anxiety whenever she saw a tattoo, a doodle, a question mark, a fish. She was in survival mode.

She went to class every day but only to get away from home. Even empty, the house buzzed with unhappiness, as if misery were some bad fluorescent bulb but the only light they had. Her parents talked like marionettes in front of her, droned like agitated bees behind closed doors. And Gabe? He'd become a teenager. Sullen, angry, with not even enough energy to actively hate anything out loud.

She'd never have bothered going home if it weren't for him. No one made meals anymore or checked his homework or his clarinet practice or his personal hygiene. She couldn't bug him about that stuff—he was no longer open to advice—but she could at least feed him. Give him some semblance of normalcy.

It was a Monday. Six days after she'd left the note at Bob's. Four days after she'd given up hope. Three days since she'd fit into her old size two jeans. She was at a café, far enough from school that no one she knew would ever go there and fair-trade enough that Paul wouldn't, either. She had her laptop open in front of her. She was three paragraphs into her *Brideshead Revisited* paper, and had been for hours. There was a thin wrinkled film on her coffee. She looked out the window. It was almost five and snowing hard. The place was emptying out. Even committed caffeine addicts were packing up. Word was the buses might stop running and nobody wanted to get marooned out here in the middle of nowhere.

Other than Hildy. She wouldn't have minded.

But there was Gabe to consider. He'd eat a few packages of raw ramen and sleep in his clothes if she didn't get back and at least pretend there was a point to all this.

She packed up her stuff and headed out into the storm. She'd forgotten to wear a hat that day. Her ears were freezing. Within blocks, snow had infiltrated her braid, burnt her forehead, and given her the bushy white eyebrows of an Antarctic explorer.

She stopped at the Kwik-Way and got three frozen dinners. One for her. Two for Gabe. She put them in her purse. (She'd stopped thinking of it as a satchel, even though it held more of the world's woes than ever.) She trudged the rest of the way home, squinting against the snow. Both cars were in the driveway when she got there, so people were in the house, but it was unlikely anyone had bothered to get the mail. That's just what it was like these days.

Their grandmother had given Gabe a subscription to *Tropical Fish Hobbyist*. Hildy wiped the snow off the mailbox and checked to see if it had arrived. Gabe pretended he didn't care about fish or Nana or anyone acting like he still mattered, but he did.

No magazine. Just a few bills for her parents. Multiple flyers despite the NO FLYERS sticker. And a letter.

Addressed to her.

Hildy immediately recognized the handwriting. It was neat and boxy like the font in a cartoon strip.

No stamp.

He must have dropped the letter off here himself.

Bob had been here. He'd come looking for her.

She raced around to the back of the house and barreled in the door.

Her father was sitting at the kitchen table. Her mother was standing, arms crossed, by the bulletin board. They both said some sort of hi/hello thing but Hildy barely responded. She dumped the Kwik-Way bag on the counter and ran up to her room in her boots.

She slammed the door. Threw off her coat. Tore open the envelope. There were four sheets of paper inside.

No one needs four sheets of paper to say they never want to see you again.

Her heart revved to life.

Her eyebrows melted.

She had to sit down before she could read it.

QUESTION 29 "Share with your partner an embarrassing moment in your life."

Seriously? You have to ask?

QUESTION 30 "A) When did you last cry in front of another person?"

I was 6. I lost Pookie. The big boys at school made fun of me. I never cried in front of another person again.

(p.s. My life changed when Pookie disappeared. I realized you can't count on anyone, even yellow puppies with pink hearts & dog tags that say "Boy's Best Friend." From then on I've always had stuffed toys with an *s*.)

"B) By yourself?"

The day I got your letter. I saw it on the floor of my apartment, bent down to pick it up & cracked my head on the corner of my dresser. Bawled my eyes out. You should have seen the bruise.

QUESTION 31 "Tell your partner something that you like about them already."

Can I tell you more than one?

The answer is yes cause I'm the ump & I get to decide.

Things I like about Betty

1. You embarrassed yourself trying to find me. I picture you all fushia & flustered & I'm weirdly flattered by that. Even more flattered than by what you said in the letter.

2. You cried over your little brother but knew better than to cry over me. I like smart girls (& naked girls & maybe French girls altho I'll have to reserve judgment until I actually meet one).

3. You like it when I make you laugh at yourself. (I like laughing girls, too.)

4. You're making me wait to find out the answer to Question 28. It would make me nervous if you were suddenly too nice to me.

QUESTION 32 "What, if anything, is too serious to be joked about?"

The size of your lips

That's about it

QUESTION 33 "If you were to die this evening with no opportunity to communicate with anyone, what would you most regret not having told someone?"

That I'll be @ The Groundskeeper 7 tonight

("Why haven't you told them yet?"

I just did)

CHAPTER

21

Seven.

Oh my god.

Seven tonight.

Hildy looked at her phone. Jumped off her bed.

6:22. Dirty hair. Dirty clothes. Unbrushed teeth. Unrehearsed answers. A howling snowstorm. Thirty-eight minutes to get to the North End.

She'd never make it.

She shook her hands in front of her. She hopped up and down. She did several tight turns of her room. And then she thought: *Stop.*

Get a grip.

She Googled the Groundskeeper's number and hit dial. She checked her armpits while it rang. Found an almost-clean shirt while it rang. Rebraided her hair while it rang. Gave up.

Suppertime. They must all be too busy to answer.

She washed her face in her bathroom, brushed her teeth. Slapped some concealer under her eyes. Threw a bit of mascara on. Found those earrings he liked.

She took a breath and turned to the mirror, thinking it was

going to be terrible. But then she smiled at the idea of him writing that letter and her eyes disappeared in all those lashes and she thought, *I'm okay. I'm good.*

Happy.

She'd make it. She'd just have to.

She put on her coat, grabbed her satchel, then, at the last minute, threw in the cards with the remaining questions, too. They might need them. Whenever they'd had a problem—dead air, wrong turn, misunderstandings—the questions had helped.

There was a knock at her door.

Gabe.

She forgot to tell him she'd brought dinner.

It wouldn't kill him to microwave it himself. He was going to have to start taking a little more responsibility, at least for tonight.

She opened the door. Her mother and father were standing there, several safe inches apart. Blank, unsmiling. Parental humanoids.

"Sweetheart," her mother said, and Hildy knew it was going to be bad. "Your father and I need to talk to you."

Hildy knew what they were going to say. She looked back and forth between them. Their heads were tilted, their eyes sad and wrinkled.

Bob didn't have a cell phone.

She couldn't reach the café.

This was her last chance.

They'd had years. They'd done this. Not her.

"I've got to go."

"This is important, I'm afraid." Her father's principal voice.

"I've got to go." She pushed her way past them.

"Go where?" they said in unison as they turned and watched her race down the stairs.

"Out."

"In this storm?" Her mother leaned over the railing. "Out?!"

"I'm taking the Volvo."

"No, you are not. Not in this weather. Police are saying stay off the roads. Greg. For god's sake. Say something."

He did, but Hildy didn't hear it. She was already out the door.

CHAPTER

22

She considered taking the car anyway. What were they going to do? Arrest her? But the plow had just come by and snowed it in. She'd never dig out in time.

She wrapped her scarf hijab-like around her head and neck and ran toward Robie Street. A cab. A bus. Hitchhike. There had to be some way to make it.

She turned the corner and saw the fuzzy glow of a bus lumbering through the snowfall. She raced toward it, arms flapping overhead, satchel slapping at her back.

The bus drove past. She swore and kept running after it. At the intersection, it stopped and the driver leaned out the door. "C'mon, girl! I see you." The light turned green, but he waited for her.

She got on, thanked him, out of breath. The two other people on the bus clapped and cheered for her.

"Where the heck you going on a night like this?" he said while she rooted around for her fare.

"North and Agricola."

He shook his head. "Wrong bus. You want the number nine.

Not sure when she'll be coming."

"How far do you go?"

"Chebucto."

"I'll get off there. Walk the rest."

The bus driver clicked his tongue and winked. "Scott of the Antarctic. That's the spirit."

She didn't sit. She held the pole by the door and checked the time. Twelve minutes. Bob would give her a little leeway in this weather. He'd have to.

What was the matter with the guy, not having a cell phone in this day and age?

What was the matter with the guy?

She couldn't think of anything.

She was so happy.

She wasn't going to let her parents and their execution order ruin that.

"Far as I go, girly." The bus driver shook his head and opened the door for her. "Be careful now. Some awful slippery out there."

She ran anyway. She slipped. Got up. Ran harder. Slipped again. Three blocks north, four east, and she'd be there. She blotted her nose on her mitten and kept running through knee-deep snow and waist-high drifts until she was just across the street from the Groundskeeper.

Bob was standing out front under the streetlamp. He looked like he was in a snow globe, white flakes flickering in the light overhead. He had a hat pulled down low over his ears but he was in the same jacket he'd worn before. He couldn't be warm enough with no scarf and no mitts. His arms were crossed and his hands tucked under his armpits. He didn't see her.

"Bob!" she shouted.

He didn't answer.

"Bob!" She waved her arms. He didn't look up.

She was halfway across the street before she'd tried again. This time, he raised his head, turned toward her, and smiled, if only briefly.

She scrambled over the drift the plow had left at the corner.

"Bob. You waited."

"Paul," he said. "You can call me Paul now. Not like I can hide anymore. You know where I live."

"Paul. Right." She laughed. Of course. He was Paul. "I thought I was going to miss you. I just got your letter. I stayed late at school today. Gabe needed to eat. I stopped at the Kwik-Way. The car was—"

"You've got mascara . . ." he said.

"Oh." Her hand went up to her face and she realized what he meant—what she must look like—and she started rooting in her satchel, hoping for a Kleenex, an old napkin, a scrap of paper.

"Here," he said. He took a slightly damp tissue out of his pocket and wiped under her eye.

She jumped. He'd touched her.

"Relax," he said. "You're good. I got it."

She nodded.

"They're closed."

She didn't understand.

"The café. Note on the door. Weather I guess."

"Oh. Right."

"Looks like everything's closing. Least around here."

She should respond—she knew that—but she had nothing to say. She looked up and down the street, just buying time until her brain kicked back in gear.

She was an actor.

The show must go on, etc.

Deep breath.

"Any idea where we could go?" she said.

He scratched his fingers up and down his neck. They were red and wet. He must be freezing.

"The only place I can think of is a bit of a hike but the owner lives upstairs so I've never seen it close. Wanna try it?"

"How much of a hike?" It wasn't going to make any difference to her but this was like improv. Always respond. Keep the scene going.

"Good half hour in this weather."

"Sure." She shrugged as if that was nothing to an outdoorsy girl such as herself.

"Okay. This way then." He jerked his head to the left.

They started walking. He kept his hands under his armpits.

"Want one of my mitts?"

"I'm fine."

"Quit being so manly."

"I thought you liked manly."

"Not 'manly' as in stupid."

He laughed.

"Here. I mean it. Take it." She handed him her left mitt.

"Wow. Sheepskin. You southenders sure know how to live."

"Or at least shop." She put her bare hand in her pocket.

He laughed again. "Well, next time you're at the mall, you should maybe pick up some waterproof mascara."

She groaned. "How bad this time?"

"Depends how you feel about heavy metal groupies."

She slapped her hand across her eyes. He took it away and got out his Kleenex again. "There. That's pretty much all of it." Then he went, "Hey! Stop!" and she realized he'd seen something.

A cab. Heading their way. They both started jumping and waving their arms, then he grabbed her hand and they ran down the street after the car until it slowed and fishtailed gently into the curb half a block ahead of them.

"Yes!" He aimed a huge smile at her, as if they'd done this together. As if they'd made magic happen. A cab in a snowstorm, stopping just for them.

They piled in.

The car was hot and smelled of pine freshener and cigarettes of years gone by. The cabbie was an old guy with too-long white hair and a bright orange hunting vest. He was listening to country music.

"Where to, folks?"

"Cousin's Diner," Paul said, sliding along the backseat. The cabbie nodded and pulled out onto the street.

"Cousin's?" Hildy looked at Paul and laughed. "I love Cousin's."

"I can't believe you know Cousin's."

"And here you thought you knew everything about me . . . I'm full of surprises."

"Yeah, well, so am I."

"Oh, yeah. Like what?"

"Close your eyes and I'll show you."

"'Scuse me." Judging from his voice, the cabbie smoked a couple of packs a day. "This might be the right time to direct your attention to my list of passenger rules, taped to the back of the seats. Take a moment to read them before considering your next move. Number three in particular."

Hildy and Paul both made *we're-in-trouble* faces, then read the rules.

1. NO DRINKING OR INGESTION OF ILLEGAL SUBSTANCES.
2. NO SWEARING.
3. NO PUBLIC DISPLAYS OF AFFECTION.
4. NO SUDDEN LOUD NOISES. THESE CAN DISTRACT THE DRIVER.
5. PERSONS VOMITING AND/OR URINATING IN THE CAB WILL BE ASKED TO LEAVE THE CAR. A $75 CLEANING FEE TO REMOVE BODILY FLUIDS WILL BE LEVIED.

Thank you for your consideration,
Lloyd Meisener, Independent Operator

"Understood?" Lloyd looked at them in the rearview mirror.

"We're good," Paul said. "Unless my friend has other plans. Betty?"

She laughed, hoped he couldn't see her blushing in this light. "No. Fine by me too."

"Thanks for your cooperation, folks. Wouldn't have instituted the rules if I hadn't seen a need. Carry on."

Hildy looked at Paul. "You were saying? Surprises?"

"Oh, yeah. Close your eyes."

"I feel much better about this, knowing you're not going to be taking advantage of me."

"Honor bound not to. Ready?"

She nodded. He rummaged around inside his jacket, then handed her something. She screamed. Lloyd cleared his throat. "Number four. No sudden noises."

"Sorry," Hildy said, and looked down at her hand. Paul had handed her a cold, wet bag. Of Kong. Still alive. Still swimming. She laughed.

"He missed you."

"I bet he did." Hildy held the bag up to catch the light from a passing car. Kong did a few turns. His markings glowed neon. "Looks like you took good care of him."

"We took good care of each other. He's an excellent room-mate. He agrees with everything I say."

"Don't you wish you could find a girl like that?"

"Not really."

Hildy looked out the window. A song about breaking hearts and broken dreams was playing on the radio. Lloyd was humming along. Melting snow trickled down her forehead. She thought she would burst.

"Here she be," Lloyd said, and pulled up in front of Cousin's. The lights in the diner were on and the windows fogged up from the heat. "Eight seventy-five, folks. Cash or credit."

Hildy got out her wallet to pay, but Paul had already handed him a ten.

"No. No," she said. "You need the money."

"I got a job," he said, and jerked his head like *let's get out.* "That's where I was going the other night."

"As in 'maybe' at eight thirty?"

He waved at Lloyd and closed the door behind her.

"Yeah, exactly. Turned out to be 'for sure' at eight thirty."

"What kind of work starts at eight thirty?"

"Drawing. Someone hired me to do drawings at a party."

"That's a thing?"

They stepped into Cousin's. The place was noisy and smelled like sausage and wet clothes. No lineup tonight but almost every booth was full. Brown melting snow pooled on the checkerboard floor.

"Yeah. Some fancy fund-raiser. People all dressed up. I sat around doing these fast sketches of everybody. Some guy auctioned them off at the end of the night."

"Wow. Drawing for a living. That's what you wanted to do."

The guy at the counter waved at Paul and pointed them to a booth near the back.

"Hardly a living, but thirty-five bucks an hour, and she wants me back. Doing a convention next weekend. Bunch of plastic surgeons in town."

"That's fantastic!" Hildy resisted the urge to say something about his nose. That joke was dead. And anyway, she liked his nose.

"Don't get too excited. It's a start. Know what you want?"

They checked the menu written on the paper placemats. Hildy realized she was starving.

"Full all-day breakfast. Eggs over easy, ham, home fries, hold the beans," she said.

"No beans? I would have taken you for a 'beans, no home fries' type of person. No offense."

She pulled off her mitt, unwrapped her scarf, and laughed. "Why would I be offended? I didn't even know there was such a thing as a no-home-fries type of person."

"You know. People who won't order them themselves but then eat yours. Drives me crazy."

"You're safe with me but you sure wouldn't like Xiu." *But he'd just have to get over that*, she thought. They wouldn't be here without her.

They took off their coats, even Hildy.

Paul said, "Wow. There's a real person under there."

"Or close enough. What did you expect?"

He pulled back his chin and shrugged. "That's the thing with you. Never know what you're going to spring on me."

"Oh, like you're Mr. Predictable. Loving the smell of baby heads and everything."

The waiter came by with another table's orders balanced on his arms.

"Hey, Paul. What can I get you?"

They both ordered the same thing, only Bob got the beans, too. The waiter nodded and headed off.

"You come here much?" Hildy said.

"Whoa. Lame pickup line. That the best you can do?"

"I already picked you up. I don't need one. It's just the waiter called you Paul. I figured he must know you."

"My mother used to work here."

"She got around."

"She did indeed." He looked away. She hadn't meant it to sound the way it no doubt sounded but it seemed weird to apologize.

The neon OPEN sign buzzed in the window by their booth.

Part of the P was missing.

"I brought the questions." She made her voice sound perky. "Thought we could do them tonight. We only have three to go."

He turned back to her. He didn't look upset. "Five."

"No, we're on thirty-four."

"Yeah but we didn't do eighteen or twenty-eight."

"That's why you're the ump, I guess."

The waiter brought coffee without asking and a little rack full of jam and peanut butter packages. "Orders will be up in a minute."

Hildy got out the cards. The snow had collected around the zipper of her satchel and was melting now. The cards were damp and limp. "Which first?" she said. "Eighteen is . . . Oh, god. I forgot about this. *What is your most terrible memory?*"

She thought of that day in the kitchen. One month and a thousand years ago. The look on her mother's face when Hildy'd pointed out the pop-up on her screen. The silence after she'd said it. Her father suddenly turning toward the stove and not turning back. Gabe bewildered. Totally innocent. A bystander, caught in the crossfire.

"Do we have to do that one first?" she said.

"Sooner or later ya got to face the music."

"But on an empty stomach?"

"What's number twenty-eight then?"

"*Tell your partner what you like about them; be very honest, etc.*"

He lifted his eyebrows, rocked his head back and forth. "Might need a little warm up for that one, too."

"Thirty-four is pretty inoffensive. Sounds like something you'd hear on a game show. *Your house, containing everything you own, catches fire. After saving your loved ones and pets, you have time to safely make a final dash to save any one item. What would it be? Why?*"

Hildy had to lift the card halfway through the question so the waiter could deliver their meals.

"Sure. That one." Paul waited until she took her first bite before he dug in. He had surprisingly nice table manners. Napkin on his lap and everything. She remembered he'd grown up in restaurants. She knew so little about him.

QUESTION 34

HILDY: So. Me first I guess. What would I take out of my burning house? Really only one answer: The Italian shoes my mother brought back for me from a conference in Milan last year.

PAUL: Very funny.

HILDY: Seriously . . . Sorry, mouth full . . . No, I mean it. First thing I thought of.

PAUL: That's bad. Or sad. Or maybe both.

HILDY: I know, but just trying to be honest here.

PAUL: Are not.

HILDY: I am. I mean, a lot of what I'd normally risk my life to save is already looked after. We've stored our photos in the cloud. Mom and Dad have a safety deposit box where they keep Grampa's medals and the family papers and whatever. The question specifically ruled out loved ones and pets. What else do I care about? What else do I even *have*? Clothes? My laptop?

PAUL: Tweezers?

HILDY: You never forget an-y-thing.

PAUL: That's why it's important you give me a good answer. Whatever you say is forever. So. Really? Italian shoes? That's what you'd take?

HILDY: So much pressure.

HILDY: Hmm.

PAUL: You can't do worse than your last answer so just say it.

HILDY: Okay. The diary I kept as a little kid. My friends all had them. Pink plushy vinyl with the little lock. You know the ones.

PAUL: You needed to lock it? Jesus. What skeevy things were you up to at six years old?

HILDY: Nothing. I'm sure it's boring-boring-boring—just *My Little Pony* cartoon updates and what I did at recess, that type of thing—but I'd still hate to lose it. It's—I don't know—a record of something that doesn't exist anymore.

PAUL: Yeah, well, everyone grows up.

HILDY: No. Not just childhood. I guess I'm talking about, I don't know, happiness. My family was happy back then. I remember my parents actually saying how "blessed" we all were to have such a happy family. All the silly diary stuff feels like happiness to me . . . What about you?

PAUL: Me?

HILDY: What would you save? . . . No. Don't tell me. Your drawings.

PAUL: First thing I'd throw in the fire.

HILDY: Really? Why?

PAUL: Dime a dozen. I can make more whenever I want.

HILDY: Or whether you want to or not. I've never seen anyone draw with egg yolk before. Is that Lloyd's cab?

PAUL: Yeah. Sorry. It's like a twitch.

HILDY: Or a way to avoid answering the question.

PAUL: Yeah. That too.

HILDY: So what would you take?

PAUL: A cassette.

HILDY: A cassette?

PAUL: Yeah. I've got a videocassette of my parents meeting for the first time.

HILDY: You have? Really? Wow. Where'd that come from?

PAUL: One of those weird things. Got it in the mail a couple of months ago from some lady who'd been friends with my mother before I was born. She tracked me down somehow. Figured I'd like to have it.

HILDY: That's amazing. What's it like?

PAUL: Pretty grainy. You know technology back then. I had to have it put on a USB stick so I could watch it. The lady said she taped it in a place called the Pirate's Den. Scuzzy old bar used to be down by the waterfront. It was open mic night and my mother got up to sing and that's when the lady took it.

HILDY: You didn't tell me your mother was a singer.

PAUL: She wasn't. You should hear her. Worst voice ever, but she made up for it in, like, enthusiasm. She sang "Proud Mary." You know that song?

HILDY: Course I know it.

PAUL: Anyway, the MC introduces her and she gets up and just starts dancing and belting it out like she's Tina Turner or something. She'd probably had a few, but she's having fun and she's beautiful, and then this guy jumps up onstage and starts singing and dancing with her and the bar goes crazy. The guy can sing. With him there, they actually sound kind of good. Then the song ends and they kiss and the MC comes back on again and says "Molly Bergin, folks! And a surprise performance by Deep Blue's Steve Hardiman!" And then the video kind of wobbles because the lady put the camera down on the table and you see Mom come back, or at least half of her, and Steve, too, and there's a bit of "You were great" stuff and Mom introduces Steve to Caroline—that's her friend's name—but she calls him Scott and he says no it's Steve and she laughs and says "You look like a Scott" and asks him where he's from. And then you hear Caroline go "Oops" and you realize she must have just noticed the camera was still running and she turns it off and that's that.

HILDY: Steve's your dad.

PAUL: Yup.

HILDY: I'm guessing they didn't get married.

PAUL: Didn't even live together.

HILDY: Did you know him when you were growing up?

PAUL: Not that I remembered.

HILDY: Did you know who he was?

PAUL: Oh, yeah. I knew his name. I knew he was a musician. Knew he was an asshole. A married asshole.

HILDY: Your mother said that?

PAUL: Many times. Every time I brought him up. She'd kept a poster for his band. When I was little, I used to get it out from under her bed and stare at him with his gelled hair and shades and think, *My dad's a rock star!* I wanted to see him so bad, but Mom always told me he was on the road.

HILDY: She just didn't want you to meet him?

PAUL: Yeah. But he probably was on the road most of the time, too. Only way he could survive was to do the circuit. He was just in some crap cover band. I figured that out later.

HILDY: How long were they together? Your parents.

PAUL: Ha! Good question. I thought it was some big love affair gone wrong, then I got the tape. I probably watched it five times before I checked the date stamp and did the math. My guess is they knew each other for one whole night. Maybe two or three. Nine months later I came along. Caroline's note said something about "Typical Molly. Always so lucky. Gets up to do karaoke and a professional singer just happens to be in town that night." So he wasn't even from here. They apparently won three hundred dollars as best act and blew it on Courvoisier.

HILDY: Ever think of looking him up?

PAUL: Sure. He saw me when I was a baby so he knows I exist. Soon as I was old enough to spell his name, I Googled him. Deep Blue's got a two-line wiki entry. I could probably find him if I wanted. Probably will someday but don't particularly want to now. Just a sperm donor to me. Not a big deal.

HILDY: And yet that's what you'd save. The cassette.

PAUL: Yup. Don't have any Italian shoes.

QUESTION 35

HILDY: The next one's a bad one.

PAUL: Hit me with it.

HILDY: All right. *Of all the people in your family, whose death would you find most disturbing? Why?*

HILDY: We don't have to answer it.

258

PAUL: Come this far. Can't stop now.

HILDY: You want me to go first then?

PAUL: Why don't you.

HILDY: It's easy for me. Gabe. I mean, my parents aren't perfect, but I'd be devastated if anything happened to them. Or to Alec— even though we don't have a lot in common and he pretty much ignores me most of the time. Mom always says relationships evolve and we'll appreciate each other when we're older and that's probably true, but Gabe—I mean, Gabe. I'm only six years older but he was like my baby! My doll. I've spent my whole life looking after him. If anything happened to him, I'd just die. . . . So, um, the other night? When I missed you? That's why. He'd disappeared and I was so worried about him. Which is, of course, ridiculous. Gabe's big and strong. Way bigger than me. But I guess that's what it's like to be a mother. You never stop worrying. I'd still carry him if I could.

PAUL: That's weirdly sweet.

HILDY: Weirdly neurotic.

PAUL: Yeah. Kind of.

HILDY: You didn't have to agree with me.

PAUL: Sorry.

HILDY: So. You.

PAUL: Yeah?

HILDY: I mean, the question.

HILDY: If you want to answer it, that is.

PAUL: Whose death would I find most disturbing? That's easy for me, too. Nobody's.

HILDY: Nobody's?

PAUL: Yeah. Because nobody's left. Not really.

HILDY: Oh.

PAUL: I want to answer number eighteen now.

QUESTION 18

HILDY: Okay. Sure. Eighteen? Um . . . Let me just find it.

PAUL: You don't have to look it up. It's *What is your worst memory?*

HILDY: Oh.

PAUL: My worst memory happened July third, two years ago. I can actually be more specific if you want.

HILDY: If you want.

PAUL: 9:36 p.m.

HILDY: You sure you want to do this?

PAUL: Too late. Let's get this over with.

HILDY: You don't have to.

PAUL: Yeah. I do.

PAUL: Okay.

PAUL: Anyway.

PAUL: I was with my mother. We were driving back from the country. There was a drum set this guy was selling that I wanted to look at. Sad thing is, in the end, we didn't even get it. We drove all that way in the pissing rain to look at a piece of crap. Anyway, on the way back, we started fighting. Like, screaming at each other. Mom told me she'd met some guy online and he was "the one," so we were going to pack up and move again. I was near the end of high school. I had a really good art teacher, a bunch of guys I played in a band with. I said no way, and she said it wasn't my decision and I was being selfish and I was just a kid, what did I know, and this was her one true chance at happiness. She was ranting like that when she took a corner. Too fast. In the rain. Looking at me, not the road. We flipped, slammed into a telephone pole, flipped back. When I came to, there was blood everywhere and Mom kind of murmuring my name. She'd already called 9-1-1. My nose was bleeding like crazy and so was her face, but she kept going, "I'm okay, I'm okay. Head wounds bleed a lot. I'm just cold." That's what bothers me now. I should have known things were worse than she was making out. I mean, it wasn't cold. It was raining and everything, but it was July. I wanted to go flag someone down but she said, "No. Stay with me. Ambulance will be here soon," all cheery and everything. Then she said, "Why don't you sing me something?" Which was ridiculous. I never sang to her. I never sang to anyone but she asked, so what could I do? The only song I could think of was "My Bonnie Lies over the Ocean," so that's what I sang. And she said, "I always loved that song," which was a crock of shit, but she joined in on the "Bring back, bring back my Bonnie to me" part. Then she said, "I'm tired. All the excitement I guess." Like it was a joke. And I said, "They'll be here soon, Mom. You're going to be okay." And she said, "I know I am. You be a good boy." And I went, "I will," like I was a little kid or something. And she laughed and said, "No. Screw that, Paulie. You give 'em hell. Be brave enough to give 'em hell." And that made me laugh, sort of, and she moved her hand and put it on my leg, with her fingers kind of turned up, and I was looking at it because I guess I was too scared to look at her face and, just like that, I saw the life go out of it. I looked up and her eyes were half closed and her mouth was sort of open and I knew she was dead. I jumped out of the car and waved my arms and screamed and I could hear the siren and see the lights. Twelve minutes it took them to come. That's what happened to my mother. And my nose.

HILDY: I'm—

PAUL: You don't have to say anything.

HILDY: I'm really sorry.

PAUL: That's okay.

HILDY: The hand. That's why you draw the hand.

PAUL: Yeah. I thought maybe if I kept drawing it, I wouldn't be, like, haunted by it anymore. You know, sort of what they do to treat phobias? Make a person stay in a room full of spiders until they stop being scared of them. That's what I was trying to do.

HILDY: Does it work?

PAUL: Maybe with spiders, but not for me.

PAUL: No, that's not true. I'm not freaked out by it anymore. I mean, it's her living hand I draw, not her dead one. It makes me feel like she's still here. Kind of like it was with her clothes. I could smell her on them ages after the accident. I could almost pretend she'd just stepped out somewhere and she'd be back soon. But I had to move in with my uncle Hugh for a while after she died and he'd just got divorced and was living in this sad little one-bedroom and there was no place for anything, so I gave all her stuff away. I also didn't want to look like a creep, smelling my dead mother's clothes and everything. But now I'm sort of sorry

I've got nothing left of hers, except what I draw.

HILDY: Do you still see your uncle?

PAUL: Not much. He's a good guy and everything but probably even more screwed up than I am. And with even less money. Good for a laugh, but not the most responsible person in the world. Kind of like Mom. Must run in the family.

HILDY: Families . . . I'm starting to think they're all complicated.

PAUL: Your mother signed the death certificate.

HILDY: My mother. She was the doctor?

PAUL: Yeah. I know. I was surprised, too, when I realized that. I recognized the name. And the eyes, I guess. She's a nice lady. She's like you. She wanted to fix my nose, too, but I wouldn't let her.

PAUL: That was a joke.

HILDY: I'm sorry. I'm really sorry she couldn't do some—

PAUL: No. No one could. Mom was long gone by the time we got to the hospital. Your mother just happened to be the person there to sign the certificate. A coincidence. No one's fault.

PAUL: Not even mine.

HILDY: You thought it was?

HILDY: Is that why . . .

HILDY: I mean, the tattoo . . .

PAUL: Yeah. Kind of pathetic. Type of thing you do when you're seventeen and think the world revolves around you.

HILDY: But *your* world does. Same as my world revolves around me. You lost someone you love. You have every right to a teardrop tattoo.

PAUL: "Every death of a loved one comes with a complimentary tattoo. This week only."

HILDY: Sorry.

PAUL: No. Sorry. That was an asshole thing to say. I know what you mean. I just don't need stranger's eyes filling up with tears because my mother died. *Thank you for your sympathy but would you mind moving out of my way.* That's kind of what I feel like now.

PAUL: Didn't mean to sound so harsh.

HILDY: That's okay.

PAUL: Just the way it is. I think about her every day but people don't need to know that.

PAUL: Other than you. I'm glad you know. I'm glad I told you. And I'm *really* glad you didn't cry.

HILDY: Well, I . . .

PAUL: Although, on the other hand, I'm kind of shocked. I mean, what kind of heartless monster doesn't cry after finding out someone's mother was killed in a tragic accident?

PAUL: Oh my god. And now she's laughing. A new low.

HILDY: I'm not laughing.

PAUL: Actually you are.

HILDY: I'm not laughing because it's funny. I'm laughing because *you're* funny.

PAUL: Oh, I'm funny. The victim.

HILDY: And I'm funny. I mean, listen. Wait till you hear my worst memory.

PAUL: I can hardly wait.

HILDY: You're going to crack up when you find out what memory I thought was just . . . so . . . terrible. After what you've been through, it's—

PAUL: Before I met you, I didn't even know what a preamble was. Now I live in fear of them. Just spit it out, would you?

PAUL: And stop laughing. This is supposed to be a terrible memory. I'm going to be pissed if it wasn't at least semi-traumatizing.

HILDY: It was. For me, anyway. But it's all about perspective, right?

PAUL: Just say it.

HILDY: Okay . . . This happened, like, a month ago. My grandmother's birthday was coming up, and I thought I'd make her something. I'd seen this crafty thing on Pinterest about how you can decoupage photos onto driftwood. I know. Corny. But that's the type of thing Nana would like for the cottage. Anyway, I'd gotten Mom to email me some family photos. We were all in the kitchen. It was a Sunday. Dad was cooking. Mom had just gotten off her shift and was doing the crossword. I had my laptop and was moving the pictures into iPhoto and I noticed something. You know how iPhoto will see a face and a thing will pop up saying, "Is this so-and-so"?

PAUL: Facial recognition. I'm not totally out of it.

HILDY: Well, it kept doing that with Mom and me. "Is this Hildy?" No, it's Amy. Or vice versa. We were all laughing because Mom's almost fifty. Then I noticed it was happening with Gabe, too, but instead of saying, "Is this Greg?" or "Is this Alec?" it said, "Is this Rich Samuels?"

PAUL: Who's he?

HILDY: One of the ER docs Mom works with.

PAUL: Why would he be tagged in your family photos?

HILDY: There'd been a hospital party at our house a while back. Mom asked me to take some pictures and I'd tagged people for her. She always claims she doesn't know how to do any of that stuff.

PAUL: She can sew someone's leg back on but can't tag photos.

HILDY: Yeah. Too "technical" for her. Anyway. Every picture of Gabe I looked at that day came up tagged the same way. I was like, "Wow, iPhoto is right. Ever notice how much Rich and Gabe look alike?" Then suddenly it was as if all the air got sucked out of the room. Dad went, "Let me see," this really scary look on his face. Mom said, "I think I'll go for a run." Then Gabe went, "I'm starving." Typical normal Gabe comment. No big deal, but Dad went nuts. Started yelling at him about stuffing his face 24/7 like he was some type of animal, and Gabe looked at me like what the heck, and I knew right then. Like knew. It was weird. I'd never even suspected before. I mean, people had always joked. It was like the four of us all belonged to the same little chess set and then there was this big GI Joe named Gabe we were trying to pass off as a missing piece. Mom had some story about her great-grandfather being a tall, dark, curly headed guy, and fine. Sure. Made sense. Or maybe made just enough sense. But now I think Dad must have suspected before . . .

PAUL: How come?

HILDY: I don't know. I think of Dad and Gabe in the, like, good old days and I can't help feeling as if Dad was trying too hard. They'd always done everything together. Same interests. Same books. And the tropical fish, of course. It's as if Dad wanted so bad to believe Gabe was his that he did everything he could to make it seem true. Then facial recognition came along and it was as bad as getting the DNA results. He couldn't pretend anymore. As soon as I blurted out the Dr. Samuels thing, they were done. Over. Dad stopped having anything to do with Gabe right then and there.

PAUL: So you bought Kong to make Gabe feel better.

HILDY: You'd think—but actually that was just Step One in my brilliant plan to "save the day."

PAUL: Explain.

HILDY: Oh god. That makes it sound like you're expecting something rational.

PAUL: I'm way past that point. Just go for it.

HILDY: It's stupid but this is what I was thinking. Dad and Gabe had always talked about getting a King Kong but they're expensive and since the deal was that Dad paid for the equipment and Gabe paid for the fish, it never happened. So I went out and bought one. I thought they'd be so excited by it that maybe ... I don't know ... they'd forget, or at least Dad would forget or manage to see past it or realize—news flash—that family is more than just flesh and blood but ... Look, I know it was a dumb idea but I couldn't think of anything else to do. It all just seemed so beyond my control ... What?

PAUL: Oh my god. Kong.

HILDY: Yeah?

PAUL: Do you have him?

HILDY: No. You have him.

PAUL: I gave him to you. Remember?

HILDY: I don't know why I'm laughing. This isn't funny, either.

PAUL: I can't believe after all that we went and left Kong in the cab. Should we go try and find him?

HILDY: Now? Where? We'd never find him. Forget about it. The cabbie just got a really, really good tip. A one-hundred-and-twenty-two-dollar fish on an eight-dollar fare.

PAUL: One hundred and twenty-two dollars!?! Tell me you're kidding.

HILDY: No.

PAUL: I'm having trouble breathing.

HILDY: I know. I know. Don't remind me.

PAUL: For a sardine.

HILDY: King Kong puffer fish, please, aka the key to my family's happiness. What a joke.

PAUL: Don't be so hard on yourself. It might have worked. Maybe once your Dad has a chance to get over the shock, he'll be able to accept things and move on.

HILDY: "Move out" more like it.

PAUL: Meaning?

HILDY: My parents are over, too.

PAUL: How do you know?

HILDY: Long story.

PAUL: I got nowhere to go.

HILDY: Wow. The new you. Actually *asking* for a long story.

PAUL: Begging.

HILDY: Okay. You know that night I was supposed to meet you at the Groundskeeper? There was this big drama happening at home. Dad tried to sell the aquarium on Craigslist. He was drunk out of his mind and literally throwing fish onto the floor. That's why Gabe took off and that's why I was late to meet you. I went looking for him. I was in a total panic for a while but then it looked like everything was going to work out. I found Gabe. The guy who was going to buy the aquarium didn't show up. Dad dropped the idea of selling it. Most of the fish lived. So part of me was thinking people just had to get it out of their systems and everything would go back to normal—but it's apparently not that easy. You can't just, like, do a juice cleanse and purge all your toxic feelings about having raised someone else's kid.

PAUL: Lots of kids have stepparents who love them.

HILDY: This is different. Nobody tricks you into having stepkids. Dad got tricked and now he's pissed and he's done.

PAUL: You sure?

HILDY: Yeah. Right before I left tonight, Mom and Dad came to my door and did the old, "There's something we have to talk to you about." You should have seen the look on their faces. They can't stand each other. I just hate to think what it's going to do to Gabe. Especially if he thinks it's his fault.

HILDY: I just realized my worst memory might still be waiting for me when I get home tonight.

PAUL: Mine too. But that's never going to change.

HILDY: Sorry.

PAUL: For what?

HILDY: I can't believe I even said that. Here you told me all about your mother dying and I'm still making a big deal about this. So much for perspective. At least my family's still alive.

PAUL: It's not a competition.

HILDY: I know but—

PAUL: Listen. When I was in the hospital that night, there was some woman in the ER next to me all burned to shit. And her two kids died in the fire and she'd lost everything she owned, too. I just lost my mother. Everybody loses their mother sooner or later. Imagine how much it sucks to lose your kids. So count your lucky stars. You got off easy. Your time will come.

PAUL: I cannot believe you're laughing.

PAUL: Laughing? Seriously?

PAUL: You're sick, you know that?

HILDY: You're laughing, too.

PAUL: Now I am—but only because you made me. What are *you* laughing at?

HILDY: You. And your pathetic attempt to cheer me up. "Your time will come." Talk about fail. Boy, you know how to heap on the misery.

PAUL: All her Italian shoes went up in the blaze, too.

HILDY: Stop. People are looking. I'm clearly exhausted or something. Oh, god. I even cry when I laugh. Do I have more mascara under my eyes?

PAUL: Don't move . . . There. Why do you even wear mascara? You don't need mascara.

HILDY: Guys are so naive. Believe me. I need mascara.

PAUL: I need more coffee. You?

HILDY: No. It's probably the caffeine that's doing this to me.

PAUL: I like it. Jerry! Two refills when you got a sec?

HILDY: You'll regret it. Want to do the next question?

PAUL: Bring 'er on.

HILDY: This is the last one.

PAUL: No. We still haven't done number twenty-eight. Let's do that first. Thanks, Jerry.

HILDY: None for me, thanks.

PAUL: Sure?

HILDY: Yeah. Caffeine isn't what I need to do twenty-eight. I need alcohol.

PAUL: Shall I call him back? Jerry's probably got a bottle under the counter . . .

HILDY: No. I've got to face my challenges head-on.

PAUL: Okay. Let's hear it then.

QUESTION 28

HILDY: "Tell your partner what you like about them; be very honest this time saying things that you might not say to someone you've just met."

PAUL: Why would you need alcohol to answer that? You've just blurted out all your family scandals.

HILDY: That's different.

PAUL: How?

HILDY: I don't know. You reject me because you don't like what my parents are up to, that's one thing. You reject me after I tell you how much I like you, well, that's personal. That's like, the essence of me you're rejecting.

PAUL: Your very essence?

HILDY: Quit making fun of me.

PAUL: I'm not. You've got nothing to be afraid of. Let's hear your answer.

HILDY: You have to answer, too, you know.

PAUL: I know how this works. Want me to go first?

HILDY: No. I don't want you doing that thing again when your answer's so good anything I say will look stupid.

PAUL: When did I do that?

HILDY: The terrible memory question.

HILDY: Oh my god. Oh my god. Oh my god.

PAUL: You are unbelievable. Talk about competitive.

HILDY: I can't believe I said that.

PAUL: Yay! The dead mother wins again! Hooray for me!

HILDY: I am so sorry. Thank you for having the decency to laugh about it.

PAUL: What're you talking about? It's not decency. I'm laughing because it's funny. And if I was allowed to answer the question first and not ruin it for you, that's one of the things I'd say. You're kind of hilarious. At the core. I'm not talking one-liners. I'm talking your essence. It's one big frigging hysterically funny mess.

HILDY: That actually doesn't sound like a good thing. Is that your answer?

PAUL: No. You first. Things you like about me are dot dot dot . . .

HILDY: Okay. As you've no doubt gathered, I'm not the most experienced girl in the world, so it was easy to sway me with the obvious stuff but—

PAUL: What obvious stuff?

HILDY: Doesn't matter. We don't have to go into that.

PAUL: Sorry. Hand me the card. No. The question . . . See? Right here? "Tell your partner what you like about them. Be very honest . . ." That's not picking and choosing. Start with the obvious stuff.

HILDY: I can't believe you.

PAUL: Honor bound . . .

HILDY: Most of it I've already told you.

HILDY: Not that you needed to be told, of course.

PAUL: ATQ.

HILDY: You're an excellent drawer. You're smart. Funny. Good-looking. In fact, to be very honest, incredibly good-looking. Sometimes you're so good-looking that it's almost hard to look at you. When I think about you, I try not to imagine your face because it's so distracting.

PAUL: That's a good thing?

HILDY: No. Not strictly speaking, especially when you—as in, "I"—have papers due or need to remember to turn off the bath before water spills all over the floor.

PAUL: But it's okay as long as you don't think of my face?

HILDY: Pretty much.

PAUL: What do you think of instead?

HILDY: Quit it.

PAUL: See? This is what I mean about the essence of you being hysterical. You should see the color of your neck right now.

HILDY: Would you please shut up.

HILDY: Thank you. What I was going to say is those obvious things are the outside of you. And I admit that's what I was attracted to.

PAUL: Was?

HILDY: Sigh.

PAUL: "Be very honest."

HILDY: I am. But . . . well, it's like what I'm seeing—the outside, I mean—is just the bouncer at the door. You know, the guy with the swagger and the muscles and the wink. The one who keeps everyone away. What I really like about you is that other person. The one the bouncer's trying to keep me from seeing.

PAUL: This is confusing.

HILDY: It's a metaphor.

PAUL: Not what I was hoping for.

HILDY: I'm saying your outward personality is this big brash guy but who I really like is—

PAUL: The little dweeby sniveling guy inside.

HILDY: Yeah. He's more my type. Brad may be out charming the ladies but—

PAUL: Who's Brad?

HILDY: The bouncer.

PAUL: He has a name?

HILDY: I just gave him one.

PAUL: Shouldn't he be Bob?

HILDY: Yeah, I guess he should. But that will make the little sniveling guy Paul. You okay with that?

PAUL: I'm man enough to take it.

HILDY: Anyway, Paul's the one I like. The sensitive one. The one who tells the truth, draws the pictures, gives me a second chance.

PAUL: That's nice.

HILDY: There he is again.

PAUL: Can't get rid of him. Lord knows I've tried.

HILDY: But here's the thing. I'm not finished. I think that sniveling guy inside likes me, too.

PAUL: Oh, yeah?

HILDY: Yeah. While Bob was out throwing his muscle around and pushing back the crowds, I saw Paul, banging at the window, going, "Hildy, come get me! Save me!"

PAUL: Paul's voice is that high?

HILDY: He was afraid I'd leave.

PAUL: He needed his damsel in shining armor to rescue him?

HILDY: Yeah. More or less.

PAUL: Not very manly.

HILDY: In the traditional sense, no.

PAUL: But you still liked him?

HILDY: Like him. Yes.

PAUL: That was a good answer. If weird.

HILDY: Thank you.

HILDY: Okay. Your turn. You have to start with the obvious stuff, too. And, enough with the hot mess business. Just stick to the flat-out compliments. Girls love those.

HILDY: What is taking you so long?

HILDY: And why are you looking at me like that?

PAUL: Just savoring the moment.

HILDY: Well, don't.

PAUL: I like that about you. You seem insecure at first but you're actually weirdly confident.

HILDY: Sorry. Can we just stop there for a moment? None of your so-called compliments should include the word "weirdly" or any variations thereof. Kind of dulls the effect.

PAUL: See? That's what I'm talking about. You're smart, funny, sensitive, yada-yada-yada.

HILDY: No yada-yada-yada, either.

PAUL: Didn't think I'd get away with that. You're—what's the word I'm looking for? When you see things? When you understand what's really happening even though things might not seem that way? Not perspective . . .

HILDY: Perceptive.

PAUL: Yes. And you also have a good vocabulary. And you're hot. And you're good to talk to. You listen.

HILDY: Whoa. Stop. Go back. Hot? Me.

PAUL: Yeah. You.

HILDY: What about me's so hot?

PAUL: Specifically?

HILDY: Yeah. I might need this information later.

PAUL: The hair. The lips. Those skinny little fingers of yours. The general package. Evan Keefe was brain-dead. Or something-dead.

PAUL: And the way you blush.

HILDY: No one has ever said anything like that to me before except maybe Max, but he's my best friend and he's gay so, like, you know.

PAUL: Maybe you're so hot they were afraid to say it.

HILDY: Now you're just playing with me.

PAUL: I like that about you, too. You get all bent out of shape and all indignant and everything but then you laugh at yourself.

HILDY: Better than crying. Which I do, too.

PAUL: Which I don't like quite as much.

HILDY: Stick to the good stuff.

PAUL: You're pure.

HILDY: Oh, god.

PAUL: What?

HILDY: It's like I've got VIRGIN stamped on my forehead or something.

PAUL: HOT VIRGIN. In flashing lights.

HILDY: That's worse. Sounds like a cable TV show you'd stumble on at three in the morning.

PAUL: Not what I meant by pure. I meant . . .

HILDY: Yes?

PAUL: I don't know. Pure. Like it says. Not cut with bad stuff.

PAUL: It's a compliment.

HILDY: I get that. I just don't quite understand it.

PAUL: Neither do I exactly. You're kind of the same as your hair or your skin or your eyelashes without mascara. You're just the way you're supposed to be. Despite everything.

PAUL: Sorry. Scratch the "despite everything" bit. You're pure.

HILDY: Thank you.

PAUL: That's what I mean right there.

QUESTION 36

HILDY: This is the last question.

PAUL: Then what happens?

HILDY: I don't know. Collect our forty bucks, then it's up to us I guess.

PAUL: Forty bucks. That's like a third of the cost of your fish. A lot of work for not much payoff.

HILDY: No one promised a payoff. As I recall, Jeff said they were just trying to see if they could "facilitate" a relationship.

PAUL: What?

HILDY: "Facilitate a relationship." They didn't promise we'd fall in love or even in like for that matter.

PAUL: What are you talking about?

HILDY: The point of the study.

PAUL: That's what this is about? No one told me that.

HILDY: Why were you doing it then?

PAUL: For the forty bucks.

HILDY: Oh my god. What a pair. You didn't care why and I didn't care how much . . . You okay?

PAUL: I'm just kind of stunned. It's like mind control or something.

HILDY: You mean if you saw me on the street you wouldn't have naturally thought how hot and pure I was.

PAUL: No, I would but . . .

HILDY: So what are you complaining about then? . . . I'm asking the final question.

PAUL: This calls for a drumroll.

HILDY: Thank you. Okay. Here goes: *Share a personal problem and ask your partner's advice on how he or she might handle it. Also, ask your partner to reflect back to you how you seem to be feeling about the problem you have chosen.* No idea what that second part means. But I've got a personal problem to share.

PAUL: Go ahead.

HILDY: And I know it's probably not as big as your problem.

PAUL: Not a competition, remember?

HILDY: Right.

HILDY: I don't know how I'm going to face my parents. I mean, like, respect them again. My mother cheated on my father and let him raise someone else's kid. My father raised the kid and loved him but wasn't man enough to get beyond the fact Gabe's not his. I don't admire them anymore and I don't know what to do about it.

PAUL: I'm probably the wrong person to be asking about parent problems.

HILDY: You're the only person I've got at the moment. Give it a try.

PAUL: Look. My mother couldn't keep a job. Couldn't keep a man, or a friend, either. Didn't do anything with her talents. She was pretty hopeless. But I loved her—and I respected her, too, at least most of the time. She screwed up but she kept trying and failing and trying again. I'm not sure you can expect anything more from people than that. And, shit, I mean, your parents—yeah, they messed up this time, but look at all the other stuff they did. The

281

house, the careers, the family. And Gabe—that person you'd die for? They made him, too, whether it was your dad's sperm or not.

HILDY: Please try to avoid saying "your dad's sperm" from now on.

PAUL: Sorry. Anyway, what I mean is your dad raised him. He made him who he is. And imagine how pissed off you'd be in his shoes. This kid he's crazy about isn't even his. Give the guy a break. He needs some time to get over it.

HILDY: What about my mother? She started this.

PAUL: So? Maybe she got drunk one night and did something crazy. People do. Or maybe your dad was an asshole. Or Rich What's-his-name was her own true love but she decided to stay with your father for the good of the family. You have no idea. She deserves a break, too. She brought those shoes back from Milan for you, don't forget.

HILDY: Easier said than done.

PAUL: Get used to it.

HILDY: I need ice cream.

PAUL: In this weather?

HILDY: It makes depressing news easier to take.

PAUL: Menu says vanilla or chocolate.

HILDY: Jerry! A bowl of chocolate ice cream, please.

PAUL: A woman who knows what she wants. I also like that.

HILDY: What's your personal problem you need help with?

PAUL: It's small. I mean, at least compared to yours.

HILDY: Yay! Looks like I'm finally going to win a round.

PAUL: Small but vicious.

HILDY: You're just going to make something up to keep me from scoring.

PAUL: No. This is real.

HILDY: Okay. Let's hear it.

PAUL: This is harder than I thought it was going to be.

HILDY: You're making me nervous.

PAUL: Here comes Jerry.

HILDY: Oh, ice cream. And two spoons! Perfect. Thanks very much. Here . . . Help yourself.

PAUL: Ice cream is not going to help me.

HILDY: Then just say it. Get it out.

PAUL: I need you to help figure me out what my next move should be.

HILDY: With what?

PAUL: With you.

HILDY: Me?

PAUL: You.

PAUL: You've posed kind of a problem for me.

HILDY: Which is?

PAUL: I don't usually know girls this well before the, um, next step.

HILDY: What next step?

PAUL: Well, for starters, I guess, the kiss.

HILDY: That's a bad thing?

PAUL: Yeah.

HILDY: How come?

PAUL: It can get messy.

HILDY: Messy? You're not a drooler, are you?

PAUL: Ha. Ha.

HILDY: Sorry. Stupid joke. I don't know why I said it.

PAUL: You're nervous.

HILDY: Yeah.

PAUL: Me too.

HILDY: What do you mean by messy?

PAUL: I don't know. Messy in the head or the heart or whatever. I can usually just walk away. But I can't this time.

PAUL: And I don't like that.

HILDY: So what are you going to do?

PAUL: Classic rock-and-a-hard-place situation. I can leave and be miserable or stay and it may be something worse. You tell me.

PAUL: It's your fault. You shouldn't have thrown that fish at me.

PAUL: You're not eating your ice cream.

PAUL: It's going to melt.

HILDY: I think you should stay.

PAUL: And then what?

HILDY: How am I supposed to know?

PAUL: That's all you're saying?

HILDY: Yes.

PAUL: Not like you.

HILDY: I know. But what else can I say? I thought you were brave. So be brave.

HILDY: And I'll try to be, too.

PAUL: Okay. Well, that's settled. So are we done then?

HILDY: No. One more thing. We're supposed to stare into each other's eyes for four minutes without speaking.

PAUL: You're joking.

HILDY: That's what it says here. *Participants should . . .* Hey! What happened?

PAUL: Power's out. The storm, I guess . . .

HILDY: Oh my god. It's so dark.

PAUL: Perfect. Won't be so awkward staring into each other's eyes.

JERRY: Well, that's it, folks. Hotel-motel time! You don't have to go home, but you can't stay here. If you wouldn't mind leaving a rough tally of your bill on the table, we'll settle things some other time. Bundle up, people. It's ugly out there.

CHAPTER
23

Before he'd bought his cab, Lloyd Meisener was an old navy guy. He'd been back and forth across the North Atlantic many times in ships not much better than tin cans. It killed him now the way a little snow had people running scared.

Oh well. Better for him. He always made a bundle on stormy nights.

He was busy, so he didn't notice something had been left in his car until after nine. He was taking a nurse to the hospital for the late shift and she found the fish on the backseat. It took him a while to figure out whose it was and where he'd dropped them off. It was almost ten by the time he made it back to Cousin's.

He didn't think he'd find them. The whole North End was pitched into darkness. The radio was saying a plow driver had lost control and taken down a power pole. Lloyd kept going anyway. If he didn't find the young couple, he'd no doubt manage to pick up another fare.

He turned onto Hammond Drive. He couldn't remember the last time he'd seen the lights out at Cousin's. He wouldn't even have slowed down had his headlights not caught two people standing in front of the diner. He was pretty sure it was the boy and girl he was looking for. (He prided himself on his memory. He'd had enough ride-'n'-dash patrons that he always kept good mental notes on his passengers.) He was about to pull up to the curb and honk, but something stopped him. They were standing so still. The boy's arms were slipped into the girl's sleeves, like he was cupping her elbows in his hands. They were looking into each other's eyes.

Lloyd chose to wait it out. He had his in-car rules—number three was no PDA—but that didn't mean he was a prude. He was all for young love. A big fan. He'd been young once himself. He kept a picture of Donna clipped to his sun visor. It was taken in 1974. A stranger might not recognize her on the street today but, as far as he was concerned, that was still the girl Lloyd climbed into bed with every night.

He decided he'd let them have their kiss, then wait a respectable amount of time, and toot his horn. The last thing he wanted was to be stuck with some damn fish and he wasn't the type to flush it down the toilet. He'd heard too many horror stories about what was growing in the harbor.

He waited.

Get a move on, son, he thought. In his day, he'd be halfway to second base by this point. But the boy just kept looking at the girl, mesmerized, until finally they both smiled. Laughed really. Then the boy took his arms out of her sleeves and wrapped one around her neck and the other around her waist and pulled her close and they kissed.

Lloyd smiled and looked away. Love. It did the heart good.

He sat there averting his eyes and listening to Country 101 FM for half an hour, then he laid on the horn.

ACKNOWLEDGMENTS

▶————————◀

The very first thing I should acknowledge goes without saying: I clearly have no background in psychology.

Zero.

None.

Not a single undergraduate-level course, or at least not a single one I managed to stay awake through.

As a result, I'm missing the mental equipment necessary to process the results of Arthur Aron's 1997 study, "The Experimental Generation of Interpersonal Closeness." I do, however, know a good story idea when I see one. So many, many thanks, first, to Dr. Aron and his team for inspiring this work of fiction—and just as many apologies for everything I got wrong therein.

Thanks as well to guinea pig extraordinaire, Jean H. H. Richardson. Her appetite for expensive boots and cheap *bière* caused her to become a regular probe-for-hire subject at McGill University. Occasionally she'd tell me about the experiments, or at least about the cute guys conducting them—and another idea was born. (That's not enough to qualify for a cut of royalties, but nice try, anyway.)

Adrienne Szpyrka is a fabulous editor. So good, in fact, that, as a token of my appreciation, I'd like to propose *szpyrka* as a verb meaning "to gently and adroitly encourage a person to write a funnier, clearer, and more moving story." I mean this purely as a homage to Adrienne's amazing editing skills. It has absolutely nothing to do with the fact that *szpyrka* would be the best Scrabble word ever.

Thanks, too, to the magnificent Fiona Kenshole. It's not an exaggeration to say my life has changed for the better since she became my agent. What a difference having her enthusiasm, experience, and doggedness on my side. She's made writing fun again, sold my book around the world, and given me some handy haircare tips, too. What more could I want in an agent?

My posse of girlfriends cannot go unmentioned, either. Neighborhood pals, high school friends, bridge partners, bookclub buddies, workmates: year in, year out, they turn up for bad wine, limp appetizers, and yet another book. They laugh at my jokes, cheer me on, and deluge their kids, relatives, and acquaintances with "the latest Vicki Grant." I owe them, big-time. Grease babies all around this Christmas, girls!

And last but not least my funny, smart, beautiful, kind, irreplaceable family. They know my answer to Question 9 without even asking—and they know, too, that merely thinking about it has caused my face to be covered in, not just "spillage," but an absolute torrent of real tears.

A
Q&A
with Vicki Grant

What was the initial inspiration for your book?

A few years ago, I read a "Modern Love" column in *The New York Times* about an actual study from the 1990s called "The Experimental Generation of Interpersonal Closeness." That's a long, boring title for a fascinating idea: Is there a way to artificially create intimacy? I immediately thought, *There's my next book!*

It seemed so brilliant. Imagine being able to replace all the headache, heartache, frustration, and even boredom of looking for love with a nice, neat thirty-six-question interview. I figured lots of people would jump at the chance, especially if they were already bruised from having fallen hard before. I used the actual questions as the framework for the novel but did my best to make sure there was nothing nice and neat about the interview.

Do you believe an experiment like this could actually work?
Do you think it could make strangers fall in love?

I don't know about actually "making" anyone fall in love, but the study certainly does an excellent job of replicating the process (or at least parts of it!) in a concentrated way. Dr. Arthur Aron and his team, who devised the original experiment, came up with deceptively simple questions to mimic the stages people go through on the way to becoming lovers. The questions cover everything from seemingly innocent chitchat through flirtation and heartfelt talk of dreams and disappointments to potentially shameful revelations. And that range is important. The hearts-and-flowers part is fun, but love isn't real until you've found someone who can handle your ugly stuff too.

Another clever aspect of the study is that so many of the questions come out of left field. "When did you last sing to someone?" *Seriously?* You have only thirty-six questions to ask a stranger and *that's* the one you'd choose?

I didn't understand the rational at first. Then I saw what Dr. Aron was up to. Ask us a pat question and most of us have a pat answer. We know what our favorite color is or our favorite hobby or whether we prefer cats or dogs. Wonky questions like this one, though, throw us off guard, actually make us *think*. Whether we like it or not, we end up exposing more of our true selves than a straight-forward "Are you a romantic?" would. Anyone could say "yes" but prove it. When *exactly* did you last sing to someone? You can see why Paul wouldn't like them.

You use a variety of formats in the book, from classic third-person narration to straight dialogue and texts. How did you decide on this approach?

I had initially planned for the novel to be just Hildy and Paul's unadorned dialogue as they answer Dr. Aron's original questions. That was fun but restrictive. To fill in the picture for the reader, I would have had to have them saying things to each other they'd never normally say, so I broadened my approach. I wanted to show what Hildy was struggling with at home—and in her head—so I interspersed chapters of Hildy in her "natural habitat" with chapters of her in the artificial environment of the lab. I hoped her friends and family would help fill in aspects of her character she was reluctant to reveal to Paul.

I also needed more leeway than straight dialogue allowed because the book is a mystery of sorts. Both characters have secrets that are revealed when they have to answer, "What is your most terrible memory?" That's Question 18 in Dr. Aron's study that, unfortunately, is only halfway through the interview—a little early for the central mystery to be solved.

So I came up with ways to separate Hildy and Paul. They fight. Things are thrown. Hildy storms off midway through the study. They track each other down through social media, tiptoe back together through texting, then resume answering the questions. A classic case of form following function!

The questions that form the framework of 36 Questions That Changed My Mind About You are used verbatim from the original psychological study. Is there anything else you've taken directly from real life?

Yes, for sure. Some things I stole consciously. For instance, I set the story in a geographical area I'm familiar with, simply because it's easier to keep track of my characters in a place I know. (That said, I'm not above moving major thoroughfares to make the story work.) Likewise, the restaurants and coffee shops Hildy and Paul go to are cribbed heavily from the ones I frequent.

Real life, though, also creeped into the book while I wasn't looking. I was surprised to realize how much of Hildy's life was like my own at that age. I hadn't planned that. In fact, I didn't even recognize what I was doing until the book came out. Hildy definitely isn't me, but my parents separated when I was a teenager—for entirely different reasons, I assure you—and, like her, I remember feeling, I guess, *untethered*. It was as if someone had been hanging on to me then let go and suddenly I was careening off on my own and I didn't know how to steer or even which way I was supposed to be heading.

Hildy's relationship with her younger brother mimicked my own too. Little blondish older sister with a mother complex. Big dark-haired younger brother with personal hygiene issues. Been there, done that. If anything, I was even more protective than Hildy. My little brother literally came on dates with me. Someone had to look after him and

I didn't think anyone else would. Like Hildy, I felt somehow responsible and/or to blame for everyone and everything.

And then of course there's Paul. "Any resemblance to actual persons, living or dead, is purely coincidental." That's the standard copyright disclaimer and I'm sticking to it, although a flip through my high school yearbook might suggest I'm not telling the entire truth. (No one will be able to prove it though, because I was too shy to ever even have talked to the boy who may or may not have morphed into Paul.)

What kinds of stories do you feel most drawn to?

I've just had a recent revelation about this actually. Every book needs something terrible happening to the main character. That's why we have bullies and vampires and mental illness and debilitating disease. All excellent dilemmas around which to build a plot—but those aren't the kind of stories that appeal to me.

For whatever reason, I often write about young people dealing with the fallout of what I call "adults behaving badly." Most of the grownups we gossip about—the drunks, the adulterers, the losers, the felons, the makers of sex-tapes— have kids at home coping with the consequences of their parents' bad choices. Those situations are as common as divorce and as rare as mass murder. In many cases, the young people feel responsible for what happened. And that's where I get interested.

The kids and teens I write about are often having to come to terms with the fact that one of the people they love most in the world has done something wrong or shameful or even cruel. They have to keep trying to build their own lives and become the person they want to be, all while processing the earth-shattering revelation that their parents are human after all. It's a difficult struggle but one that we all, to a greater or lesser extent, have to get through.

Hildy and Paul often laugh and joke even when they're talking about the most painful parts of their lives. Is this resilience or avoidance?

Both. And something else too: totally normal. People *do* laugh when terrible things happen. Some of the funniest people I know have been through the worst traumas. And I mean *real* trauma. Murder, incest, total family breakdown, that kind of stuff. Those people had a choice. They could let the trauma define their life or they could move on. Humor is not just a way to make catastrophe bearable; it's a way to rob it of its power. Laughing at disaster gives you the upper hand. Plus, it's way more fun than crying about it. . . .

ABOUT THE AUTHOR

Vicki Grant is an award-winning author and screenwriter. She lives in Nova Scotia, which is every bit as beautiful as it sounds. She loves to read, travel, pester her children, and walk the length of a certain white sand beach. She has small tear ducts so people often think she's crying when she's really not. Visit her at www. vickigrant.com.